When Savannah and her best friend Charlotte decide to flip a foreclosed property in nearby Columbia, they talk Savannah's sister Darcy into putting up the money for the renovations, and go to work.

But no sooner have they ripped up the carpet and torn out the kitchen cabinets, than the previous owner shows up and invokes his statutory right of redemption. After four years in prison for a crime he says he didn't commit, he's back in town to clear his name, and he wants his house back. And according to Savannah's legal-eagle brother Dix, there's nothing anyone can do to stop him.

Until someone drops him in his tracks, with a murder weapon that has Charlotte's fingerprints all over it.

Savannah's husband Rafe has his hands full at the local PD, so the murder investigation falls on another detective, one who doesn't share Savannah's conviction that Charlotte wouldn't hurt a fly. But when Savannah decides to do some investigating of her own, it soon becomes clear that there's more to this flipping fiasco than meets the eye…

OTHER BOOKS IN THIS SERIES

A Cutthroat Business

Hot Property

Contract Pending

Close to Home

A Done Deal

Change of Heart

Kickout Clause

Past Due

Dirty Deeds

Unfinished Business

Adverse Possession

Uncertain Terms

Scared Money

Bad Debt

Home Stretch

Wrongful Termination

Conflict of Interest

RIGHT OF REDEMPTION

Savannah Martin Mystery #18

Jenna Bennett

RIGHT OF REDEMPTION

Savannah Martin Mystery #18

Interior design and formatting: B. Gallagher

Cover design: Dar Albert, Wicked Smart Designs

Magpie Ink

ROTTEN

Tyler H. Jolley

C.J. Xavier

Rotten

Cover Art and Design by Brandon Dorman

Interior by Melissa Williams Design

Published in the United States by Tyler H. Jolley

ISBN: 978-1-958734-04-9 (print)
　　　 978-1-958734-05-6 (ebook)

ROTTEN

Tyler H. Jolley

C.J. Xavier

JOLLEY CHRONICLES

For my good friend Frank

Chapter 1

I had never seen a dead body before. Not like that. Up close and personal and not already crammed in a coffin at a funeral.

But that guy was dead. Not sleeping, mind you. Not unconscious.

He was a corpse with decaying flesh sliding off his rotten skull.

"Are you going to answer me or not?" a voice shouted from somewhere up the stone staircase. It belonged to my best friend, Jaylen Monroe. Jaylen had been waiting for me to give the all-clear, so he and the others could come down and join me—that was the deal.

"I'm good," I answered, steeling my nerves. "I'm at the bottom."

"Then why are you screaming like that?" Jaylen called out.

Panic filled me. Not from the corpse, but from my date and friends above hearing me scream. I hoped my high-pitched scream didn't bubble over so my date would notice. I had taken great care to never break that rule throughout my life, and I had been mostly successful until tonight. In all fairness, I had never expected to see a dead body. I couldn't believe I'd gotten myself into this. And over a lousy game of truth or dare, no less. I should have known Jaylen would dare me to do something *he* thought would impress my date.

"I didn't scream," I said. "I just slipped on something."

"Calvin, stop acting like a jerk!" Shelby Gibb's voice quivered with amazing volume. "If you're not back up here in five minutes, we're all leaving."

I smirked and rolled my eyes. Yeah right. How could she leave? I had the keys to my mom's Suburban, and I was her ride. I was all their rides, unless they wanted to start hoofing it several miles back into town.

"Seriously, this isn't funny." Shelby sounded like an obnoxious eight-year-old. I imagined her polishing her nose ring and checking to see if it still sparkled in the moonlight. That girl drove me nuts. I didn't see what Isaac saw in her. Why'd we bring them along?

"Do you want us to come down or what?" Jaylen's voice seemed closer now. He wasn't all the way down, probably still at the top of the staircase, but at least he had poked his head through the opening. "Shelby and Isaac are already heading for the gate."

"Fine!" I fired back. "They're going to miss out."

They never wanted to come in the first place. Shelby had called the whole trip to the mausoleum a bad idea. Maybe it wasn't the *best* idea, but we didn't have a ton of options in Jewkes, and there wasn't any movie worth watching at the Plex. I had hoped the creepiness of Hudson Cemetery would impress my friends, but I could sense I was striking out big time.

"Come on, man. Now Moira and Reyna are considering leaving as well. What do you want me to do?" Jaylen asked.

"Two minutes," I said. "Give me two minutes and then come down. I'm just looking at something."

To be honest, I wouldn't have minded if Jaylen had joined me. He would have appreciated this. The rest of my friends, on the other hand, would have pissed their pants. I hadn't told any of them about the body yet, because I wanted to experience everything for myself before anyone else joined in and things got muddled on who had discovered it first. Childish and immature maybe, but I didn't care. It wasn't every day you got to see a dead body.

Kneeling down, I pointed my flashlight toward the rotting remains of the man crushed beneath the rubble from what had to have been a roof collapse. The rocks had him pinned from the waist down, as well as most of his left side next to the wall. His right arm, rail thin and caked in dark, dried blood, rested atop more rubble. Fractured ribs poked out from his chest like gnarly barracuda teeth. The man's eyes were closed, sunken behind dark gray lids, and his face had shriveled like a putrid fish left on a dock in the summer's heat.

I could hear my heartbeat pounding in my temples.

"This can't be him," I whispered to myself. "Could it?" I instantly knew it couldn't be true the moment I uttered the words.

Everyone in Jewkes, Louisiana, knew about the Crenshaw Mausoleum. It was once open to the public as somewhat of a tourist attraction. Smack dab in the center of the mausoleum was an empty casket. No name markers. No dates. No one knew who it belonged to, but people would come from all over the state to see inside the empty stone coffin.

That was until twenty years ago, when Parry Hathspin,

a sixth-grader on a field trip with Griffin Elementary, fell through a crack in the floor and died. It turned out there was a whole other room beneath the mausoleum no one had ever known about. Of course, people didn't like it when someone died, especially a kid, and the mausoleum was deemed unsafe, and it was sealed up for good. But that kid was long gone, and dead people didn't age, which made it impossible for the corpse in the corner to be Parry Hathspin.

As I began brushing the dirt from my knees, I noticed something move out of the corner of my eye. I honed the flashlight in on the spot where I saw movement, and my breath caught in my throat.

The dead man's fingers were twitching.

Unable to blink, I watched as the corpse squirmed beneath the heavy load of rocks, mouth opening, struggling to breathe. His eyes flitted open. They were a dark yellow in color, but bloodshot, with obsidian pupils too large to be normal. I took a step backward toward the entrance, and his eyes widened, searching the room. After a few seconds of looking, he found what he was looking for.

Me.

We locked eyes, staring at each other for what had to be a solid minute, until he broke the silence with a raised hand, beckoning me to his side, finger joints popping with each motion. I shuddered. Icy chills ran up my back and into my ears. I sucked in a deep breath, but my breathing didn't slow.

"No way!" It was all I could think to say. My mouth had gone numb, and my brain had turned into a useless slab of muscle.

"Jaylen!" I shouted. "Get down here!"

My best friend didn't respond. I didn't have time to

"C-can't," he repeated.

"What do you want me to do?" Where was Jaylen? I had told him two minutes. It was way past that, and I could really use his help.

The man dragged his swollen, cracked tongue across his lips. "Can't . . . reach."

Something heavy smacked the back of my head, and a flare of pain lit up behind my temples. My jaw fell slack, my ears rattled, and the room swirled before my eyes.

As I fell forward, collapsing in a heap, I felt the man's fingers digging at my throat.

And then darkness.

Everything black and empty.

My thoughts blank. No dreams. No sounds.

Nothing.

Except for thick nails piercing my skin.

create some rational thought process. Instead of listening to the voice of reason in my head, I rushed toward the man, knelt on the ground, and began tossing rocks off his lower body.

"Are you okay?" I asked.

The guy just moaned.

He was alive and I could help him.

The dude smelled horrible, like a bag of flaming dog crap. As I tossed rocks to the side, I began thinking about internal bleeding and how his organs should've been smashed to bits. Was I making a mistake by clearing the rubble? What if by doing so, I was just speeding up him dying?

The man tried lifting his chest from the floor and struggled a bit, unable to remove the load, but appeared determined to free himself.

"Don't do that," I said, my voice squeaking. "Just lie still while I go get help."

His old flannel shirt, the material all but rotted to pieces, tore away from the ground as he rose up, reveal-ing a pool of dark muck beneath his back. His fingers tugged at my shirtsleeve, the nails impossibly long and his skin so transparent, I could see the brittle tendons and ligaments working beneath.

I had no idea how long he'd been down here, but something told me it hadn't been just a few days. How long, then? Weeks? Months? Without water, he would've died of thirst, not to mention the severe injuries sus-tained from the roof collapse. Those were ribs poking out through his chest! Small red worms pulled back into his open chest cavity as my light washed over them.

"Can't," the man whispered, opening his mouth, revealing black teeth and gray-colored gums.

The word caught me off guard. "What did you say?"

One

"We should go into business together," Charlotte said.

I lifted my attention from the salad I was picking at—I would have preferred something with more substance, but it was almost three months since Carrie had been born, so it was time to get serious about shedding the rest of the baby weight—and stared at her across the table. "What?"

"I need a job if I'm going to stay in Sweetwater."

She didn't add that so did I, but it was implied. Or if it wasn't, I knew it. I couldn't loaf forever.

She continued, "I could get my real estate license and we could work together. As a team. That's a thing, right?"

I nodded. It was a thing. Not everyone is good at everything, and not everyone is good at the same things, so a real estate agent who likes to take listings might work with a real estate agent who likes to work with buyers, and split the money they make between them. That way they both get to do what they like, and they both make money.

I had no idea what I liked. I'd had my real estate license for going on two years, but I hadn't managed to sell more than a handful of properties in that time. I just didn't seem to be very good at it, and I was constantly distracted by other things. My husband, my baby, murder…

As a result, I was usually thrilled when I landed any client, and couldn't care less whether it was a buyer or a seller. The idea of having to share the commission I made with someone else was frightening, when I made so little as it was.

And aside from that, what if Charlotte turned out to be a better realtor than me? Then I'd feel even worse about myself and my career choice than I did now.

But of course I couldn't tell her that. She had enough to deal with, between her impending divorce and custody battle, her kids, and her parents. She didn't need to hear that I didn't want to work too closely with her.

So— "It isn't as easy as it looks," I said instead. "You know how, when you watch *House Hunters* on HGTV, the buyers always pick one of the three houses at the end of the show?"

Charlotte nodded.

"That doesn't happen in real life. Sometimes you show them dozens of houses, and at the end of it, they don't like any of them, and they decide they're just going to rent for a while. And then six months turn into a year, and by the time their lease is up and they're ready to buy something, they've met another realtor in line for coffee, and they don't call you back. He gets their business. And you did all that work for nothing."

Charlotte stared at me.

"And it takes time to get a real estate license. At least three or four months of classes. If you started now, you wouldn't be licensed until the summer."

"That won't work," Charlotte said. "I need to make money *now.*"

I tilted my head to look at her. "Problem?" She had moved herself and the kids in with her parents, in her childhood home, and it wasn't likely that they were charging her rent. In fact, they were probably thrilled to have her back home, after almost a decade in North Carolina. And I'm sure they were delighted to spend more time with their grandchildren.

"Richard is refusing to give me any money," Charlotte said, her voice tight. "He put a freeze on our accounts, and he shut down my credit card."

Richard is the soon-to-be-ex, and father of the children. That's probably obvious.

"Can he do that? They're his children, too. Isn't he responsible for them?"

"He's waiting for the judge to rule on the alimony," Charlotte said.

"And until then he expects you to live on air?"

"I'm sure he's not expecting it." Her voice was dry. "He just doesn't care."

"But they're his children!"

"He has a new mistress," Charlotte said, "and a new baby on the way. And she's a big deal in Charlotte."

Yes, Charlotte had spent the past ten years in Charlotte. That's called irony. Or something.

"Well, you're a big deal here," I told her. "And the fact that his floozy is a big deal in Charlotte doesn't mean that Doctor Dick doesn't have to provide for the children he already has!"

"Tell that to his lawyer," Charlotte said.

"Have you talked to Catherine about it?"

Catherine McCall is Charlotte's lawyer, and also my sister. When Charlotte first arrived back in Sweetwater, she wanted to hire my brother Dix—her high school boyfriend—to represent her. (My entire family, present company excepted, is lawyers.) But Dix, like most men, is squeamish when it comes to nailing another man's scrotum to the wall for child support. Catherine has no such qualms. She would have had my own ex-husband, Bradley Ferguson, singing soprano if I'd allowed it back when he'd dumped me for his paralegal. (At the time, trying to keep my dignity seemed like a good idea. I've since learned that you can't eat dignity, and besides, he didn't deserve any consideration from me. And while that's all water under the bridge now, the knowledge still stings.) However, I had every confidence that Catherine could do to Doctor Dick what I hadn't allowed her to do to Bradley. And I was looking forward to watching.

"We have to wait for the hearing," Catherine said.

"When's that?"

"Next month," Charlotte said. "The 18th."

"That's almost four weeks away!"

She nodded. "I know."

"What are you supposed to eat in the meantime?"

"We're not starving," Charlotte said. "My parents are taking care of us."

"Well, of course they are." It had been more of a rhetorical question. How did Doctor Dick expect his wife and children to survive until the divorce was final and the settlement decided, if he wouldn't give them any money? Charlotte had never had a job. She'd married Doctor Dick straight out of college and started popping out babies.

"But that's why I need to make some money," Charlotte said. "I can't let my parents continue to pay for everything. They have their own retirement to think about. But I've looked for work everywhere I could think of..."

I nodded. She had asked Dix and Catherine for a job in the law firm. She had asked my mother's best friend Audrey for a job at the boutique. She had probably visited every medium-to-high class establishment in Sweetwater looking for employment. I'm sure she wasn't looking forward to starting on the low-end places. Waitressing and cleaning and working the register at the local Walmart...

"We could flip a house," someone said. It took me a second to realize the voice was mine. And maybe it had sounded strange to Charlotte, too, because she stared at me.

"What?"

I took the thought out and looked at it. "We could flip a house. Buy it, renovate it, and sell it. We could easily do that in the time it would take you to get your real estate license. Less."

It would give me something to do, too. I could bring the baby. And I'd have a house to sell once the renovating was done.

"Like *Fixer-Upper*?" Charlotte said doubtfully.

"Sort of." I mean, Chip Gaines actually knows what he's doing. Neither of us had a clue. "More like Joanna Gaines without Chip."

"Decorating?"

"A little more than decorating. But we could look for a house that doesn't need a lot of heavy-duty renovating. Just cosmetics, you know? New paint, new tile, new light fixtures. And we'd hire people for all the difficult stuff. Like..." I thought about what would go into renovating a house, even one that didn't need much heavy-duty reno, "we could order a new kitchen from Home Depot or Lowes, and they'd install it for us. That way we wouldn't have to worry about installing cabinetry or countertops. Or plumbing. Or electrical work. We'd get a plumber or an electrician for that. We'd just have to worry about tiling the backsplash and painting the walls."

"Wouldn't that cost more?"

Yes, of course it would. "But we wouldn't electrocute ourselves. Or accidentally nail-gun our fingers to the wall. We'd only have to do the easy stuff. Like painting." It's hard to kill yourself with a paintbrush. Practically impossible, probably.

"I could paint," Charlotte said.

I could, too. I mean, how hard could it be? And laying tile, while it looked tedious, didn't seem like it would be all that difficult to handle, either.

"We just have to find the right house. Something not too expensive—since we'd have to buy it—in a good location, and in pretty good condition. We wouldn't want to take on too much our first time."

Charlotte shook her head. "Would we be able to get a loan to buy a house? Neither one of us has a job."

"This is Sweetwater," I said, "and I'm a Martin. I'm sure I could find a bank who'd give me a loan."

There have been Martins in Sweetwater for more than two hundred years. It's not like we aren't a good risk.

"You'd probably have to put the mansion up as collateral," Charlotte said.

I stared at her, aghast. "Have you lost your mind? I couldn't do that!"

Physically couldn't, I mean. All I did was live in it; I didn't own it. It wasn't mine to collateral with. And I'm sure Mother—who did own it, but didn't live in it—wouldn't hear of me taking out a home equity line on the ancestral home.

"You're not a Martin anymore, either," Charlotte pointed out, and I sucked in an offended breath.

"I'll always be a Martin!"

"You know what I mean," Charlotte said, and of course I did, even if I didn't want to admit it.

"You have a point. Everyone in town knows I married Rafe. I'm probably *persona non grata* now. At least with the bank."

While Rafe and I live in the Martin mansion, my husband grew up in the trailer park on the other side of town. And in addition to that, he had a… let's call it a checkered past, including a stint in prison and ten years undercover for the TBI, rubbing elbows—and other things—with the criminal underclass. None of that is a secret. And he was working for the police department now, which probably wasn't a point in our favor, either. Everyone knows that law enforcement doesn't pay much. So no, maybe I wouldn't be able to waltz into the nearest bank and get a loan just on the strength of my maiden name.

We sat in silence for a moment or two. Next to me, baby Carrie sucked on her pacifier and looked around with long-lashed blue eyes. She has my eyes but her daddy's coloring, and the bright blue was startling against her dusky skin and black curls.

"I don't have any money," Charlotte said.

I shook my head. That's what had started this part of the conversation. "I don't, either. I should have had Catherine squeeze Bradley for more, but I didn't. Although it's moot now, anyway. He's making license plates in Riverbend Penitentiary." And had no money to spare.

We sat in silence another minute.

"Dix has money," I said. "And Catherine. And Mother. Maybe one of them would give us a loan."

Charlotte looked dubious. "Dix and Catherine have children of their own to raise. I'm not sure they have any extra money for something like this."

Maybe not. And like Charlotte's parents, Mother had retirement to worry about. Not that she'd ever been anything but retired. But she still needed money to live.

"I could ask Darcy," I said. "She inherited a little money from her parents."

Money I'd borrowed and given back once before. It was hard to say whether this situation would be more or less risky than that one. But at least no one would try to kill either of us at the end of it.

"How much would it take?" Charlotte wanted to know, a wrinkle between her brows.

I turned it over in my head. "It would depend on the house.

As long as we could get a loan for the mortgage, we'd only need twenty percent for a down payment. We might even be able to get a construction loan, where the renovation costs are built into the loan on top of the value of the house the way it is when we buy it. Then we'd only need the down payment for that one loan, and no renovation costs, since they'd be part of the loan."

"Plus enough money to keep up with the monthly payments," Charlotte said.

I nodded. "But we could probably use the loan for that, too."

"Use the loan to pay for the loan?" She wrinkled her nose.

"It would only be for a couple of months. If we hurried, we could get the house on the market by the end of the spring season. Three months from now, maybe. May? As long as we found a house that didn't need a whole lot of fix-up—mainly cosmetics—and we worked fast."

I was starting to get into this idea. It sounded like it would be fun. I could see myself doing the Joanna Gaines thing—making decorating decisions and looking fabulous—while the house turned gorgeous around me.

"Do you have a house in mind?" Charlotte asked.

I didn't. I'd seen a lovely little Victorian cottage recently, that needed renovating, but it wasn't for sale, and was also a bit stigmatized by having had the bodies of two women in the basement for more than fifteen years.

"I'll have to see what's available. Maybe we can go look at houses tomorrow."

"Shouldn't we make sure we'd be able to buy one first?" Charlotte asked.

I supposed we probably should. "I'll talk to Darcy. And if that doesn't work, I'll talk to Dix and Catherine and Mother. And call you when I know something."

Charlotte nodded. "I should get back home. My mother's been babysitting long enough."

"I should get back, too." I lifted my napkin from my lap and dropped it next to my plate. "I'll let you know what I find out."

We walked out together, me hauling the car seat with the baby in it, and parted ways on the sidewalk outside the restaurant, which happened to be the Café on the Square in downtown Sweetwater. When Charlotte walked to her car, I walked next door, opened the door into Martin and McCall Law Offices, and greeted my sister. "How would you like to invest in my latest business venture?"

Darcy looked up from the computer. "You have a business venture?"

"I just came from having lunch with Charlotte," I said, and put the baby carrier down on the floor. "Doctor Dick has frozen her accounts and canceled her credit cards, and he isn't giving her any money. Charlotte says he's waiting for the judge's decision on what he's supposed to pay. And meanwhile, Charlotte doesn't have an income, or any way to feed her kids."

Darcy nodded. "That's too bad for Charlotte, but giving your friend money isn't what I'd consider a business venture."

"I wouldn't ask you to do that." I shrugged out of my coat and draped it over the back of a chair. "We want to renovate a house. Find one that doesn't need a lot of fixing up, polish it, and put it back on the market. And make a profit. I'd have a house to sell, and we'd both make some money. And you too, if you wanted to go in with us."

Darcy contemplated me, her head tilted.

She's my father's daughter, my half-sister, but she looks nothing like me. Dix and I take after Mother's family, the Georgia Calverts. Darcy doesn't honestly look a lot like Catherine, either, although Catherine takes after the Martins.

Darcy looks like Audrey, tall and coltish, with hints of Dad in the mouth and jawline, but mostly she just looks like herself. Or Rafe. She's related to him, too, through her mother. And looks more like his sister than mine, although what they are, is some sort of second cousin a few times removed. Rafe's grandmother, Mrs. Jenkins, and Audrey's mother Oneida, were sisters.

"Do you know anything about renovating?" Darcy asked.

"I know about real estate."

She nodded.

"And Rafe renovated Mrs. Jenkins's house in Nashville."

"But he won't be renovating this one."

No, he wouldn't. But I could ask him questions. "We'll hire people to do the difficult stuff," I said. "I'm not going to attempt plumbing or electrical work. I'm going to be looking for something that needs mostly cosmetic updating to be pretty. Surely we'll be able to sand floors and paint and hang wallpaper."

Darcy nodded. "It sounds like fun, but I already have a job."

"I'm mostly interested in your money," I confessed, and watched her eyebrows arch. "I thought I would just be able to go to the bank and get a loan, on the strength of being Savannah Martin, but Charlotte pointed out that I'm Savannah Collier now, and the Collier name doesn't have that kind of cachet in Sweetwater."

Darcy's lips twitched.

"We'd pay you back, of course. With interest. Or a percentage of the profits, or whatever you wanted."

"What if you don't make any money?" Darcy asked.

I blinked. The idea that we might not make a profit hadn't occurred to me.

It took me a second to figure out what I wanted to say. "I'll make sure that doesn't happen. I'll find us a house that's priced well enough that it won't."

"I'm not sure you can guarantee that," Darcy said, and of course she was right.

"I'll pay you back, Darcy. If I take your money and you don't get it back, plus a profit, when we sell the house, I'll pay you back somehow. It might take me longer—" would undoubtedly take me longer, "—but I'll pay you back."

"Don't worry about it," Darcy said. "The risk of losing your principal is part of the risk of investing. How much do you need?"

Just like that? Must be nice. "I have no idea," I said. "It would depend on the house. I'll have to take a look and see what's out there. But I'd be very careful about how much we paid, and how much work it would need."

"I'd want to see the house before you bought it," Darcy said.

"Of course." I nodded. Several times. "I'll go home and see what's available. I'll contact both you and Charlotte with what I discover. Tomorrow's Saturday. Maybe we can go looking."

"I'm having dinner with my mother," Darcy said. "I'm free until then."

"I'll let you know." I picked up my coat again.

Darcy eyed me. "You don't want to see your sister or brother? Or brother-in-law?"

I shook my head. Now that she had agreed to provide the money I needed—we needed—I had no reason to involve my brother or other sister. Especially since they'd probably try to talk her out of it, if they heard what I'd talked her into. "I've already seen the sister I came to see."

Darcy's lips curved. "I know what you're doing," she told me, "but I still like to hear you say that."

I shoved one arm into the coat, and then the other. "You are my sister. You're just as much my sister as Catherine."

"I'm half as much your sister as Catherine," Darcy corrected.

Maybe so. Technically. But— "Still my sister. And more likely to give me money than Catherine."

"I don't have three kids and a mortgage," Darcy said.

"Not yet. But soon." I grinned at her and picked up the baby carriage. "I'll talk to you tonight. Keep your fingers crossed that I find something good."

"I believe in you," Darcy said. And then she went back to the computer, and I went back outside to the car and headed home.

Two

When Rafe came through the door, it was after seven, and I was sitting at the island in the kitchen with my laptop open in front of me. Pearl the pitbull was snoozing on her pillow by the back wall, twitching occasionally in sleep. Carrie was sitting in her bouncy seat kicking her feet and batting at brightly colored animals hanging from the handle, and on the stove, Bolognese sauce was simmering and water was on the boil, waiting for me to toss in a couple handfuls of linguine. A tray of garlic toast was sitting on the counter, waiting to go in the oven.

Then Pearl raised her head from the pillow and started rumbling in her throat. I glanced at her. "Did you hear something?"

The stub of her tail slapped against the pillow once, and she turned her head to fasten her eyes on the door. When the key slid into the lock, she gave a single bark.

"It's just Rafe," I told her. "No need to go crazy."

By then, she'd figured that out for herself, and was settling back down, her stubby tail wagging and her jaws split in a doggie grin, but she wasn't barking anymore.

Rafe stepped through the door and shut it behind him, and bent to give her a scratch behind each ear before turning to me. "Sorry I'm late."

"It's no problem," I said, as I looked him up and down. "At least you let me know."

As usual he looked better than anybody had a right to. Faded jeans clinging to long legs and a black leather jacket stretching across broad shoulders and tapering to a narrow waist. I couldn't see what was under the jacket, but I knew. I had to clear my throat before I added, "I ate a couple hours ago. I kept the sauce warm for you. It'll take ten minutes to boil more pasta and heat more bread."

"Just enough time for me to get a shower." He glanced at the heat in my cheeks, and grinned. "Wanna come upstairs and wash my back?"

I smiled back. "You have no idea how much I'd like that. But with the baby…"

He nodded, and came a couple steps closer. "Hi there, pretty girl." He reached out and ran the tip of his finger down Carrie's cheek. She gurgled. At three months old, she was already a confirmed daddy's girl.

Rafe turned to me. "And you're pretty, too." He bent his head and fitted his lips to mine. By the time he straightened, my head was swimming and I had to unclench my hand, one finger at a time, from the leather.

"You sure you don't wanna join me upstairs?" He winked.

"I would love to join you upstairs," I said, and it was God's honest truth. "But I can't just leave Carrie to fend for herself. If you can hold off an hour, maybe…"

He grimaced. "I'd rather get the stink off now."

Somehow, I was sure there was no stink. His body is perfect in every way, including that one. However— "I'll have food ready for you when you come back down. And you can tell me about all the excitement." And then we could have sex—not in the shower—later. After Carrie was asleep.

He nodded. "I'll be back in a few."

"I'll be here," I said, and watched him walk across the room and into the hallway before I slid off the chair and padded over to the stove to crank the heat up to high.

By the time he came back downstairs, the linguine was draining in the colander, and the Bolognese was bubbling. I told him to take a seat at the counter, and then I went to doctor his plate the way I knew he liked, with a sprinkling of parmesan and a bottle of beer. Red wine would go better with the Italian food, but as he'd told me once, he'd spent a couple of years eating meals provided by the Riverside Penitentiary, and he wasn't picky.

When I turned around, plate and beer in hand, he had pulled my laptop over so he could look at what I was doing. He arched a brow. "Looking to leave me?"

"Of course not." I nudged the computer back out of the way and put the plate and bottle in front of him. "Charlotte and I are talking about renovating a house. She needs money. Her husband has frozen their accounts and canceled her credit card."

"I bet he hasn't frozen his own account," Rafe said, picking up his fork.

I leaned my elbows on the counter and shook my head. "I'm sure he hasn't. But Charlotte probably doesn't have an account of her own. Or if she does, it was an account he funded, so she could have some spending money. She hasn't worked since she married him."

"She's worked," Rafe said, twisting linguine around his fork. "She just didn't get paid."

Point to the man with the bare feet. Charlotte had taken care of Doctor Dick's children, and probably Doctor Dick's house and yard and laundry and meals, not to mention Doctor Dick's sexual needs. Or at least some of them. And now the bastard had cut her off without a penny.

"We had lunch earlier today," I explained. "Charlotte suggested that maybe she could get a real estate license and we could work together. I guess she thinks maybe I'm doing better than I am."

Rafe chuckled, but didn't say anything.

"When I pointed out how long it would be before she'd start earning money, we came up with the idea of flipping a house instead. I've been looking at the options."

"Come up with anything?" He wound another forkful of pasta and conveyed it to his mouth.

I made my way around the island. "If you don't mind eating and looking, I'll show you."

He swallowed. "Sure. I don't guess Scotty Junior's house is on the market?"

The house I mentioned earlier, the lovely little Victorian cottage with the remains in the basement.

I shook my head. "I wouldn't want to buy that, anyway. It's going to be a long time before anyone in Columbia forgets what was hidden there. It would be almost impossible to sell."

Rafe nodded, and picked up a piece of garlic bread and bit into it. It crunched, and the smell of garlic butter wafted my way. My teeth watered, even though I'd eaten my share—or more—of garlic bread earlier.

"These three are what I came up with." I ran my finger over the mouse pad. "Here's a cute little mid-century ranch in Sunnyside, with all the original features."

I showed him a picture of a low-slung brick one-story before I started scrolling through the interior shots. "The price is a little high for a fixer-upper, but it's a nice neighborhood. Big yards. And if we kept a lot of the original features, like this pink tile—"

Rafe winced.

"—and the knotty pine kitchen cabinets, we could bill it as

mid-century chic."

"Most people don't feel like mid-century chic means a knotty pine kitchen," Rafe said. "Not these days."

No. "But at this price, we won't have the money to redo two bathrooms and the kitchen. And mid-century is popular."

Rafe didn't say anything, just focused on winding linguine around his fork, and I sighed and moved on. "Here's another little Victorian not too far from the Mason house, but without the stigma of bones in the basement. Nice front door. Nice fireplace mantel in the parlor. Unpainted, which is always a bonus. The tile on the hearth is ugly, but it wouldn't be hard to replace it. Someone already ripped out the original tile and replaced it with this ugliness, so I wouldn't feel bad about taking it out again. It isn't original. The kitchen would need redoing, and the bathroom..."

I scrolled through the pictures.

"Lotta work," Rafe said. "And only one bathroom? That could be a problem."

It could. People these days like to have more than one potty.

"Anywhere in the house you could add one?"

"If I sacrifice one of the bedrooms," I said. "Turn it into a two-bedroom, two-bath house, instead of a three-one. That would give me somewhere to put the laundry room, too. Right now it's in this shed addition off the original back door..."

I scrolled through the pictures until I got to the shed addition, and watched another flicker of pain cross Rafe's face. "You don't like the idea?"

He glanced at me. "That's gonna turn into a lot of money, darlin'. Redoing the kitchen and existing bath, adding another bath and a laundry room. That means moving plumbing and electrical. And if you're tearing off the laundry room, you're not only not adding square footage, you're taking it away."

True. And the smaller the house was, the smaller the out-price—the price we'd be able to get for it after it was finished—would be. I gnawed on my bottom lip. "I think the roof needs replacing, too. And the area isn't as nice as Sunnyside. It would probably be harder to sell."

"What else did you find?" Rafe asked, and picked up his fork again. "Where are you getting the money for this, by the way? We don't have much."

"Darcy's going in with us," I said, while I brought the next listing up on the screen. "She has a job, so she won't be doing a lot of the work, but she's footing the bill."

"Nice of her."

"She loves me," I said, and Rafe grinned.

"Yeah. She does."

"And I won't ask you to help, either. You've already got a job, and I know you've got your hands full. We're hoping to find a house that mostly needs cosmetic renovation, so we can do a lot of the work ourselves."

Rafe nodded. "I'll go take a look with you, give you an idea what you're looking at as far as work. But I don't think I'm gonna be a whole lotta help after that."

"Just looking at it and helping me pick the right house would be great," I said. "Here's the last one."

It was a much more recent construction, built in the last twenty years, and situated in a subdivision of similar cookie-cutter houses on the north side of Columbia. It hadn't weathered the time as well as the other two. Rafe took one look at the exterior shot and shook his head.

"No?" I pulled up the interior pictures. "Are you sure? It isn't bad inside."

"Laminate flooring," Rafe said, pointing to it. "Plastic molded tub, pressed wood cabinets, quarter-inch drywall…"

"You mean, it's badly constructed?"

"Cheap," Rafe said. "At least those knotty pine cabinets were solid wood. The clawfoot tub in the Victorian was cast iron. The walls were real plaster. This is all cheap materials."

"But if we tore it all out and put in real hardwood floors, and ceramic tile, and solid wood cabinets…"

"Like putting lipstick on a pig, darlin'."

"Oh." I sank my teeth into my lip. "Then I don't know what to do. These were the only three possibilities I could find on the MLS…"

The MLS is the Multiple Listing Service, where all the realtors share their listings with each other. Outside the MLS, the options are severely limited.

"Craigslist?" Rafe suggested.

"Do people sell houses there?" If so, I wasn't proud. I'd buy a house on Craigslist. I mean, I was a professional. I had all the required forms and knew how to fill them out. Where most people could get in trouble buying a house on Craigslist, I actually knew what I was doing.

He shrugged. "Ain't there a tax sale tomorrow?"

"Is there?"

"I heard something about it," Rafe said.

"At the meeting?"

The reason he was late for dinner was a last-minute meeting called at the police department that he'd been required to go to. He hadn't told me anything about it, other than that he'd be late, so it seemed like a reasonable question.

He grinned. "No, darlin'. Earlier this week. Extra cops directing traffic around the courthouse on Saturday morning."

"Is that where the sale is taking place? On the courthouse steps?"

"As far as I know," Rafe said. "Tax sale. Courthouse."

"Do you know what time? Or what's going to be auctioned off?"

He shook his head. "I'm sure there's a website."

I was sure there was, too, and was already Googling. "Here we go. Ten o'clock tomorrow. Two properties." I rattled off the addresses. "Do either of those sound familiar to you?"

"South J Street is near downtown," Rafe said. "I think it's by the railroad tracks. Didn't used to be the nicest area back when I was running the streets, but that coulda changed in the past ten years. Not sure about Fulton."

I had already found South J Street on Google Earth and was waiting for the streetscape to populate. When it did, I tilted my head from one side to the other. "Hard to see, with the vegetation." The picture obviously hadn't been taken recently, since the yard was almost covered in foliage. You don't get that in February in Tennessee. "Looks like it could have potential, though, if I'm looking at it right. Another little Victorian cottage. Might be some original features inside."

He glanced up from the plate and over at it. "Might not."

No, it might not. And if they were, they might be in as bad a condition as the previous little Victorian we'd looked at.

Nonetheless, I gave the picture a longing look. "It probably wouldn't be a good idea to go over there now."

Rafe glanced at the clock on the stove. "It ain't that late."

"It's dark," I said. And while it was still before eight, he had already had a long day. It was something he didn't point out, but something I should keep in mind, as a good wife. "Maybe we could make it over there tomorrow morning instead." When the sun was up and we could see what we were looking at. "Before the auction."

"Better to do our snooping in the dark," Rafe said, "if it involves breaking and entering."

Yes. But— "It won't. I have a key."

He arched that brow at me. "How'd you get a key to a house you didn't even know was coming up for auction until fifteen minutes ago?"

"It's called a HUD key," I said. "Or at least that's what Tim calls it." Tim is—or was—my broker at the real estate agency I worked for in Nashville. Since I hadn't moved my license anywhere else, I guess he still was, technically, my broker.

Not that any of that mattered to what we were talking about. "When a house goes to foreclosure, the Department of Housing and Urban Development changes the locks, so the previous owners can't get back in. But then there's a parade of other people through the house. It has to be winterized, and inspected regularly, and once it goes on the market, realtors come and go. It's much easier with a universal key."

"Makes sense."

"LB&A had one, and one day I made a copy of it, so I wouldn't have to borrow the office key every time I wanted to take somebody into a foreclosed property. It was inconvenient. Much easier to have my own."

His lips twitched. "Sure."

"I still have it. So we won't be breaking and entering. It's legal to enter as long as I have a license and the key."

"Ain't that a shame," Rafe said. "But we can pretend. Be almost like old times, wouldn't it?"

I guess it would. "If you're willing to cut your evening short, I'm certainly not going to try to stop you." It would give me the time tomorrow to show Darcy the place before the auction. "But you really don't have to. You've had a long day already, and…"

"It ain't likely to take long." He pushed his empty plate away. "I'll go get dressed."

He padded barefoot toward the hallway. I rinsed the plate and put it in the dishwasher, considered the pots and pans on the stove and decided they could wait until we got back, and went to the foyer to get my coat and boots, and Carrie's pink winter suit and the car seat.

By the time Rafe came back into the kitchen, in socks and boots and a sweater and jacket, Carrie and I were dressed and ready to go. Pearl was thumping her stubby tail hopefully against the pillow, and looked crestfallen when I told her, "Sorry, baby. We're going to look at houses. You wouldn't enjoy it."

"Bring her," Rafe said. "If I'm right and South J still ain't the nicest place, she could come in handy."

"I guess it doesn't matter. Nobody will be there to see us. And it'll make her happy. C'mon, Pearl. Car ride."

Pearl jumped to her feet, all quivering excitement. When Rafe grabbed her leash from the hook next to the door, the little bit of her tail that's left wagged so hard the entire back half of her body moved from side to side.

"Good girl." He opened the back door. "Let's go."

Pearl bounded past him into the dark, barking joyously, and then came back to circle him, making sure he was making progress toward the garage and the car. I stopped long enough to lock the door and then followed, with Carrie's car seat over my arm.

When the mansion was built, around 1840, give or take a year, people had carriages, not cars. By the 1900s, that had changed, and the old carriage house was converted into a garage at some point before I was born. Rafe opened the bay where the Volvo was parked—the chrome on his Harley-Davidson caught the light from the next bay over—and then the front passenger door of the car for Pearl. When we have her with us, she rides shotgun while I stay in the back with the baby. I mostly trust Pearl around Carrie, but it makes me feel better not to take any chances. Pearl had a rough life before we rescued her, and until I'm sure she won't suddenly lose her mind and attack Carrie, I don't leave the two of them alone together, even in the backseat of the car.

So we made ourselves comfortable, and Rafe backed the car out of the garage and headed down the driveway around the corner of the mansion and toward the street.

"Nice night for a drive," he told me as he took the turn from the driveway onto the Columbia Highway heading north.

I suppose it was. A little cold, but not freezing. Clear, so we could see the stars, and a pale sliver of moon to the east. "It was nice of you to offer to come with me."

"Can't let you have all the fun," Rafe said, and focused on keeping the car on the road while Pearl sat up on her haunches, panting excitedly, next to him.

We were on J Street in Columbia about fifteen minutes later, cruising between small Victorian cottages and bungalows sitting close together on narrow, city-sized lots. Here and there, a porch lights gleamed, but more often, there was just the blue flicker of a TV from behind half-drawn curtains.

"Don't look much different from what I remember," Rafe said, peering left and right.

It didn't. Or at least it didn't look much different from what he'd told me to expect. The street had a rundown and sort of desolate air. There was trash piled up at the gutter here and there. The cars were all older, past the first bloom of youth, nothing new or shiny. The houses were on the small side and not well kept. They must have had some individuality originally—all Victorian cottages and Craftsman bungalows— but at this point, they'd all taken on the same air of quiet desperation. If someone ever decided to take a chance on the area, it had the potential to turn into something nice. But no one had so far, and I didn't think I wanted to be the first.

"I'll have to search recent sales in this area," I said, as Rafe pulled to a stop in front of a small white cottage with peeling paint and dark windows. "Just in case this goes for a song tomorrow. If we can get it cheap enough, there might still be some money to be made."

Rafe nodded. "Let's take a look." He opened his car door as Pearl watched him, wagging eagerly.

I unfolded myself from the car and grabbed the car seat while Rafe clipped the leash to Pearl's collar. And off we went, across the sidewalk, through the gate, and up the walkway to the house. I stumbled over an out-of-alignment brick, and almost took a nosedive.

"Here." Rafe reached back and took the car seat out of my hands. "You take the dog."

We made the exchange, and kept going. Rafe didn't stumble over anything, of course. His night vision is far superior to mine.

"The porch is rotten," he informed me as he climbed the steps. "Be careful."

I nodded, focused on where I was placing my feet. I wasn't really worried, though. If the steps had held him and Carrie, they would probably hold me no problem.

I dug my keychain out of my purse and sifted through for the HUD key in the dark.

The house was late Victorian, and would probably have had a nice, ornate wooden door when it was first built, with a window in the top half.

If it had, that door was long gone. Someone had replaced it with a standard builder grade metal door. Not only did that mean there was no original door here to restore, it also meant that I and Charlotte, or whoever ended up renovating this place eventually, would have to spend money on a better door than was here now.

So my mental tally added the cost of a new and fancy front door in addition to what it would cost to rebuild the porch and deal with the landscaping. We hadn't even gone inside yet, and the renovation costs were mounting.

"I'll go first," Rafe told me. He held his hand out for the key. I handed it to him and watched as he inserted it in the lock and twisted.

Nothing happened.

He tried again. "You sure this is the right key, darlin'?"

"It's supposed to be the right key," I said, and took it back so I could hold it up to my eyes to peer at it. "Yes, it's the right key."

"It ain't working."

"Try it one more time." I handed it back to him, and he tried it one more time, and shook his head. "Sorry."

"Well, damn. I mean… darn."

It was so dark on the porch that I almost couldn't see his lips curve. "Good thing I don't need a key, ain't it?"

It was. A very good thing. "Need anything from my purse?"

He shook his head. "No, darlin'. I got my own."

Of course he did. I watched as he dug in his pocket, and pulled out a skinny black case, and then I watched as he turned his back to me to fiddle with the lock. After a few seconds he straightened and pushed the door open. And walked in, feeling for a light switch on the wall inside the door.

I opened my mouth to tell him that the power would be off, that part of the procedure of prepping a foreclosure is turning off the power and water, but before I could say anything, the lights flashed on and practically blinded me. I squeezed my eyes shut, but not before a room full of furniture had imprinted itself on my retinas. Sofa and chairs in front of the fireplace, small TV in the corner, old shag rug, books on the shelves, an ashtray full of cigarette butts…

Three

"Shit!"

Rafe flicked the light switch again and plunged the room back into darkness before he turned toward me and pushed me ahead of him through sheer force of personality. He didn't tell me to "*Go, go!*" but I heard it clearly in the back of my head, and in his voice.

I dragged Pearl across the porch toward the stairs just before Rafe stumbled over her, and he shut the door behind us. "Here." He handed me the car seat with the baby. "Go. I'll lock the door."

"Are you sure we shouldn't just...?" *Get out of here, and stand not on the order of our going?*

"It'll only take a second. Go get in the car."

Yessir. I scrambled back down the rickety steps and across the uneven brick pavers, while Pearl panted in the lead. She probably thought this was some sort of fun game, instead of us trying desperately not to be caught breaking and entering an occupied dwelling. By the time I reached the car, Rafe was already beside me, and took the car seat out of my hand. "I got this. You deal with Pearl."

His voice was calm, but he didn't waste any time getting the back door open and the car seat fastened on the base.

I dealt with Pearl—"Go on, baby, back in the car!"—and left the leash dangling when I shut the door behind her and scurried around to the other side. Rafe ran around the other way, and we tangled for a second in front of the doors before we made it to our respective doors. His arm squeezed my waist on its way past, but I suppose it could have been accidental. Then again, maybe not.

I crawled into the back seat and shut the door behind me while he threw the car into gear and peeled away from the curb. By the time we got to the corner he was laughing. "Been a while since I had to book it out of a house in advance of a shotgun blast."

"First time for me," I said, sitting up and straightening my coat.

He grinned at me in the mirror. "Coulda been worse. At least my pants weren't down around my ankles this time. Makes it easier to run."

I could imagine that it would. "When you say down around your ankles… are you referring to the saggy fashions you wore in high school, or the fact that you would have been nailing some poor teenage girl to the wall when her daddy came home?"

He chuckled. "Mostly the latter. But the pants I wore back then didn't make it any easier to get away."

No. "Just out of curiosity," I said, "how many times did you have to hike your pants up and get out in advance of some outraged father's shotgun blast?"

"I don't think it happened more'n once or twice, darlin'."

He'd slowed the car down now, that we were a couple of blocks away from the… let's call it a crime scene, and were cruising at an unobjectionable speed along dark streets. "There was this girl named Rhonda…"

"Of course there was." I made a face, while I flipped

through the Rolodex in my head to try to place Rhonda. "I don't think I remember her."

"No reason why you would, darlin'." His voice was easy. "Sorry about that."

"Rhonda?"

He chuckled. "No. I shoulda thought to knock on the door first, to see if the place was empty."

"It was supposed to be empty," I said. "Why would you question it, if the house is going to auction tomorrow?"

It was a rhetorical question, and he didn't answer it. "Anyway," I added, ""I don't think anyone was home, so chances are, even if you had knocked, you wouldn't have gotten an answer."

"I oughta know better, though. Guess I'm outta practice."

"Since nobody was home," I said, "hopefully they'll never realize we were there." And would have no reason to test the doorknob for fingerprints. His are on record, so would show up in a search. "Or did you take the time to wipe the doorknob before you left?"

"'Course, darlin.'"

Of course. "Well, then we probably don't have anything to worry about."

"Let's hope not." He didn't sound all that worried. "You wouldna wanted that house anyway. Too much work."

I nodded. "Did you see that ugly tile around the fireplace? It was worse than the tile in that picture we looked at earlier."

"And while you prob'ly coulda gotten it cheap, nobody woulda wanted to pay much to live on that street once the house was finished. No matter how nice it looked."

True. "I guess the problem wasn't my HUD key after all."

"Don't seem that way," Rafe said. "I guess whoever lived there prob'ly found the money to pay off the lien. Or maybe they're just hanging on as long as they can, hoping that whoever buys the house tomorrow won't evict'em. Somebody could be picking it up for a rental or something."

Maybe. I didn't think I'd have it in me to evict anyone, and I wasn't looking to pick up a rental anyway, so at this point it didn't matter. It was on to the next one, and better luck next time.

"Gimme the key," Rafe told me a few minutes later.

We were parked outside another little house, this one a few decades younger. Post-WWII, at an (educated) guess, with a more recent addition tacked onto one side. Like the other house, it was painted an uninspired dirty white, but other than that, it didn't look like it was in terrible shape. There was no porch, just a concrete stoop, so we didn't have to worry about sagging boards, and the front door, painted a boring brown, at least had some promising flourishes.

"Roof looks pretty good," Rafe remarked, staring up at it while I dug the keychain back out of my purse. "No holes that I can see. Gutters need cleaning out. I can see things growing up there."

I nodded. I could, too. Visibility was better here—no one had broken half the bulbs in the streetlights—so we were able to get a halfway decent view of the place.

"The lot's bigger than the other one," Rafe added. "And the neighborhood's nicer."

It was. Not only were the streetlights intact, but there were cheerful porch lights up and down the street, and everything looked mostly well maintained and cared for. The house we were sitting in front of was the worst-looking of the bunch, and that's always a good sign when you're looking to renovate something.

"Here you go." I handed the keys across the back of the seat. "Go make sure it's empty."

He opened his door. Pearl perked up, and then drooped sadly when he told her, "No, girl. You have to wait."

He closed the door behind him.

"He'll be back," I told her, as I watched him cross the patch of dead grass in front of the house and step up on the low stoop. He applied his knuckles to the door, and I could hear the sound of the knock even with the car windows shut. Definitely wood, that door. Another point in the house's favor.

Rafe waited half a minute, and when nothing happened, he inserted the key in the lock. A few seconds later, he turned and waved to me. Everything must be working the way it was supposed to this time. It was a nice change. I unfolded myself from the car, took Carrie's car seat in one hand and Pearl's leash in the other, and made my way across the dead lawn to the house.

There was no electricity on here, and Rafe's Maglite lived in his company car—a beat-up Chevy the Columbia PD let him use in lieu of the Harley-Davidson—so we inspected the house by the light from Rafe's phone. It didn't take long. The place was small. A combination living room/dining room in the front, with a kitchen behind, followed by a bathroom and two small bedrooms. The addition looked like it might have been intended to be a den, with double French doors out to a small concrete patio in the back, and I looked around at it. "If we could get a bathroom in here, it would make for an OK master suite."

And that would turn the property from a two-bedroom/one-bath house to a three-bedroom/two-bath house, thus increasing the price exponentially.

Rafe nodded. "You'd have to hammer up the concrete, though. Could be expensive."

It could. The addition was a step down from the rest of the house, and it had a concrete floor under the carpet. In looking at it now, I wondered whether maybe it wasn't so much an addition as a garage conversion. "Maybe we could raise the floor and put the plumbing underneath."

Rafe gave it a dubious look. "Prob'ly end up with a step-up if you did."

Probably. But it might still be worth doing, if it was cheaper than taking a jackhammer to the floor.

Inside the main part of the house again, I glanced around the smaller of the bedrooms while Pearl sniffed the carpet. "All in all, this isn't too bad. New carpet—unless there are wood floors underneath…"

"This age house, there could be," Rafe said.

I nodded. "I'll never understand why anyone would cover perfectly good hardwoods with carpet, but I guess some people like something soft to walk on."

"Or lie on," Rafe said, with an exaggerated leer that made him look positively devilish in the light from the phone.

I laughed. "No way am I having sex with you on this. Not in someone else's house we've broken into, with the baby and the dog in the same room."

"Rain check, then." He shone his light around the walls. "But yeah. It don't look too bad. Get rid of the rug, tear down that ugly border, paint the walls, update the fan, and you're done in here. The front didn't look bad, either. Most of your money…"

"Darcy's money."

He nodded. "Darcy's money would need to go to the bathroom and kitchen. And this master suite conversion, if it works out to do it."

"Would you care to estimate how much money we're talking about, to do this right?"

He didn't answer for a second. Counting in his head, I assumed. "Depends on how expensive you wanna get. If you're sticking to mid-grade finishes, nothing designer, and maybe you work with the kitchen cabinets—replace the doors rather than the whole box, or you just paint'em if they don't look too bad..." He named a figure that seemed ridiculously low. "That's if you do a lot of the work yourselves. If you don't, maybe double it."

"Double it, then."

He chuckled, and I added, "Not because I'm not willing to do the work. But we'll probably have to hire people to do things you could handle yourself. And I'd rather over-estimate than under-estimate and then not have enough."

He nodded. "Guess you'll have to do some figuring on what you can pay for the house, and what you have to put into it, and what you think you can get for it afterwards, before tomorrow morning."

I guessed so. "If you've seen enough, we should go." So I could do the research I needed to, and still leave room for that rain check.

I turned Pearl away from the enticing carpet smells and headed toward the door, peering into the bathroom as we went. "This doesn't look too bad. New tile and new fixtures. But at least it isn't a big bathroom. And I've seen worse kitchens. The layout is good. It—"

I stopped with a squeak, as a big, black figure appeared in the doorway between the kitchen and dining room.

"Hands up!" it boomed, taking a very businesslike stance, legs wide, pointing something at me.

Pandemonium ensued, of course. Pearl went crazy, lunging for the figure and barking. It was all I could do to hold on to her leash.

Rafe, meanwhile—probably afraid the man with the gun was going to use it on Pearl or me, or Carrie—stepped in front of us. "Law enforcement!" his voice boomed. "Lower your weapon!"

For a second, life seemed to hang in the balance. And that second went on a lot longer than seconds should. But after an eternity, the figure in the doorway relaxed. Enough that I didn't feel like death was imminent.

"That you, Collier?"

"Yes," Rafe said, his voice tight. "Put the damn gun away."

"Sorry." The guy in the doorway didn't sound sorry, but he holstered the weapon. "What are you doing here?"

"The house is going up for auction tomorrow," Rafe said, his shoulders still tense. "My wife wanted a look."

"And you couldn't do it during daylight?"

"Got called into a late meeting." He finally relaxed enough to take a step out of the way. With a glance at me, he added, "Savannah, this is Officer Carl Enoch from the Columbia PD."

"Nice to meet you," I said politely, although between you and me, it hadn't been a pleasure at all. "Do you live nearby, Officer Enoch?"

Surely we hadn't tripped any kind of alarm coming in here? Surely Rafe would have noticed, even if I might not.

"Down the street." Enoch nodded in what I assumed was the direction of his house. Beyond the den to the north. "I saw the door hanging open, and figured I'd see what was going on."

Pearl was still rumbling deep in her throat, the short fur at the back of her neck bristling, and Rafe took a step closer to her. "Maybe we should take this outside. Give the dog a chance to breathe."

That must have made sense to Enoch, or maybe he just wanted to put some distance between himself and the growling pitbull, because he nodded and stepped backward, out of the doorway. Rafe took the car seat with Carrie out of my hand and nudged me on my way. I heard his footsteps behind me as I headed for the front door.

Enoch had made it off the stoop and into the grass, and in the better light out here, I saw that he was around Rafe's age, with sandy hair and a buzz cut. He was still wearing his uniform, weapon's belt and all. There was a truck parked at the curb, blocking the Volvo. I was surprised neither one of us had heard it approach.

Rafe came through the door behind me, and put the car seat down. I smiled politely at Enoch for the few seconds it took Rafe to lock the door and turn back to me with the keys. "Here you go, darlin'."

I took the keys and he took Pearl's leash out of my hand. Pearl had stopped growling, but the fur on the back of her thick neck was still bristling.

"So you're looking to buy the place?" Enoch asked, looking from Rafe to me.

"A friend of mine is looking for a fixer-upper," I answered. "We thought this might be a nice house to renovate and put back on the market."

"You have a lot of experience with renovation?" His lips twitched like he thought it was funny.

"I'm a real estate agent," I said. "My experience is mostly with buying and selling." And I didn't have a whole lot of that. "But I know how to paint and decorate." So did Charlotte. "And it's a cute little house." Although it could do with a facelift.

Enoch nodded. "It's been sitting empty for a few years. I'm surprised it's taken this long for the city to foreclose on it."

He didn't wait for me to answer, but turned to Rafe. "The meeting tonight… anything to do with the Morris trial?"

Rafe shook his head. "That was before my time. I don't know nothing about it. The meeting was all about Laurel Hill."

Enoch looked enlightened. I wasn't, but I decided not to

expose my ignorance, and instead ask Rafe later.

"Anything to it?" Enoch asked.

"I'll be heading down there tomorrow," Rafe answered. "I guess we'll find out."

Enoch nodded. "I'll leave you to it. Sorry to have interrupted."

He exchanged a nod with Rafe, and a glance with me, and then he moved his truck out of the way while we got the dog and the baby situated in the Volvo. By the time Rafe slid behind the steering wheel, the truck was on its way down the street.

"Laurel Hill?" I asked, as I made myself comfortable in the back seat. "Who's she?"

Rafe's lips twitched in the mirror. "Nobody, darlin'. It's the name of a wildlife area in Lawrence County."

"Oh." *That* Laurel Hill. Fifteen thousand acres of horse trails, ATV roads, lakes, and trees. "What's that got to do with you?" We were in Maury County. North and a bit east of Laurel Hill.

"Joint taskforce," Rafe said, as he put the car in gear and we rolled off down the street after Enoch's truck. Up ahead, he was pulling into a driveway on the right, a few houses up from ours. Or the one that might be ours after tomorrow.

"What kind of joint taskforce?"

"Lawrence, Lewis, Giles, and Maury," Rafe said.

All counties, all in a cluster down here in Southern Middle Tennessee.

"Why do you need a joint taskforce?"

Rafe hesitated. "Talk has it there's a group of some sort meeting in Laurel Hill some weekends."

"I'm sure there are a lot of groups meeting in Laurel Hill on the weekends." Hunters and fishermen and family reunions and ATV riders and what have you.

"Not like this one," Rafe said. "Nobody's really sure

whether they're Neo-Nazis or militia or Antifa or what, but we're thinking they could be a problem if they're left alone."

Yes, I could see where they might be. None of those are types you want wandering around in your backyard.

"The sheriffs for Lewis and Lawrence contacted Bob," Rafe said, meaning Bob Satterfield, the sheriff of Maury County and my mother's boyfriend. "Bob called Tammy and got her involved."

"And Tammy—I mean, Grimaldi—got you involved."

Tamara Grimaldi is the chief of police for Columbia. She's also a good friend of ours—maid of honor at my wedding—in addition to being Rafe's boss and my brother Dix's girlfriend. Or almost-girlfriend. Semi-girlfriend. Something in the girlfriend line.

He nodded. "And then Sheriff Jackson down in Giles wanted in. And given Giles's history..."

Yes, indeed. The city of Pulaski in Giles County was the birthplace of the Ku Klux Klan. If anyone had a vested interest in rooting out racists in our midst, it was the sheriff of Giles County.

"How did you find out about this?"

"I found out when Tammy called me in to her office and told me," Rafe said, taking a right on the Columbia Highway—or in this case the Pulaski Highway—going south toward Sweetwater and the mansion, and beyond that, to Pulaski. "She found out from Bob. And Bob found out from Lewis and Lawrence."

Or their respective sheriffs. "And who told them?"

"Seems somebody reported it to the Wildlife Resources Agency," Rafe said. "They passed the message on to law enforcement."

"So you're working with the park rangers, too?"

"I'm working with everybody," Rafe said.

Not with Enoch, it seemed.

"It's a shame that Clayton isn't around anymore," I said.

Clayton had been one of Rafe's students at the TBI. My husband had spent the past year teaching him and two others about undercover work, along with other useful skills such as lock-picking, hand-to-hand combat, and spotting someone tailing them. But at the end of December they had graduated, and had started the new year being assigned to different TBI offices across the state. Jamal was still in Nashville, working under Wendell, who had been Rafe's handler during his own undercover days, while José had ended up in Memphis and Clayton in Chattanooga.

José, as his name suggests, was Hispanic. Wendell and Jamal were both black. Neither of the boys would be a good choice for infiltrating a white supremacy group. But Clayton... Clayton was a stringy white kid with a skinhead haircut and tattoos up and down his arms, who had come to the attention of the TBI when he got swept up in a sting on a chop shop. He favored wife-beater tank tops—not that he had a wife, or even a girlfriend that I knew about, and he certainly wouldn't beat her if he did—and faded jeans that practically fell off his bony hips, and he'd look just right waving a flag with a swastika.

The corner of Rafe's mouth turned up.

"And you already thought about that," I said.

He glanced over at me. "I get paid for thinking about that, darlin'. Thinking about that's my job."

So it was. I settled back in my seat and let the world go by outside the window while he gave some thought to his situation, and while I did the same to mine.

The little house we'd just come from on Fulton Street had potential. It wasn't a Victorian or Craftsman or anything like that, so the finishes were pretty plain—no original fireplace tile or mantels, no ornate crown molding or transoms—but it was in decent shape and didn't look like it would take an extraordinary amount of time or money to renovate. It was small, for one thing, and wasn't falling down, for another. I liked the street. The fact that a cop lived there meant it was probably pretty safe—and it had seemed safe, too, when we'd been there, other than the sudden appearance of the man with the gun. The neighbors looked out for one another—or at least Carl Enoch looked out for them—and that was a good sign, too.

All that remained now, was figuring out how much we could afford to pay for it, based on how much Rafe estimated it would take to fix it and the price I thought we might get after it was renovated and back on the market.

Oh, and to tell Darcy to meet me over there at the crack of dawn tomorrow, so she could yay or nay the purchase before the auction.

While I was at it, I should probably contact Charlotte, too. She'd be getting her hands dirty fixing the place up, so even though her opinion mattered less than both mine and Darcy's—mine because I understood real estate and the market, and Darcy because she was footing the bill—I should give Charlotte a chance to give input, as well.

In fact, I might as well do it now, since I wasn't doing anything else.

I fished my phone out of my purse and started texting.

By the time we reached the mansion, both Darcy and Charlotte had responded to my RSVPs with agreements to meet me at the property at eight-thirty the following morning, and Rafe still hadn't said a word.

"You OK?" I asked him when he'd slotted the Volvo back into the garage-cum-carriage house, and he was releasing Pearl from the front seat while I resleased Carrie and her car seat from the back.

"Yes, darlin'." He shot me a quick smile. "Just thinking."

"That you might get Clayton involved?"

"It's something to think about," Rafe said, "once I figure out who he'd need to get involved with." He took the car seat with the baby out of my hand. "C'mon, darlin'. You owe me a rain check."

So I did. "Just let me get Carrie changed and fed and into bed, and then I'm all yours."

"That's what I like to hear," Rafe said and whistled for Pearl.

Four

Eight-thirty the next morning found me back in Columbia, waiting for Darcy and Charlotte to show up.

I was alone: Rafe had a date with Tamara Grimaldi and the joint sheriffs of Maury, Giles, Lawrence, and Lewis, to trek through Laurel Hill in the company of a park ranger. Because Bob was busy, Mother was at loose ends, and had offered to stay with Carrie and Pearl while I went to the auction. So she was currently hanging out at the mansion, petting an adoring Pearl and watching Carrie kick her feet and gurgle, and I was here, on Fulton, getting my first look at the place in daylight.

It didn't look too bad, all things considered. Fulton Street was just waking up, this early on a Saturday. A few curtains were open, more were still closed. An older woman walked a small dog with short legs down the other side of the street. A couple of houses up on my side—or the side I hoped would be ours—two kids were playing behind the fence in a front yard.

The house we were trying to buy looked pretty decent in the morning sun. Still a little run-down, with uninspired paint and vegetation in the gutter, and a little sad, with no curtains to brighten the windows, but in halfway decent shape. The roof looked good. The windows were intact. There was no visible sagging. It was what I'd told Charlotte we should look for: a house that mostly needed cosmetic updates.

A car turned the corner down at the end of the street and I watched as my sister's blue Honda made its way toward me and parked behind the Volvo. A second later, Darcy swung her long legs in snug jeans out of the driver's seat and strode over to me. "Good morning."

"Morning," I said.

She smiled and looked around, into the back seat of the Volvo. "No baby?"

"Mother offered to stay with her. Bob's off on a field trip with Rafe and Grimaldi and the sheriffs of Lawrence, Lewis, and Giles."

Darcy arched her brows, and I explained what was going on.

"That's not good," she said.

"Tell me about it." And upon consideration, which I had done on the way over here, Rafe was probably the last person who should be involved in trying to eradicate a group of white supremacists. Or the first person, from a different perspective. But he was involved, whether I liked it or not, so it didn't matter one way or the other whether it was a smart move. And I could just imagine his reaction if I suggested that he recuse himself because the job was too dangerous.

Darcy turned to the house. "This it?"

I nodded, just as another car turned the corner at the end of the street. We watched as Charlotte's minivan came toward us and turned into the driveway. The door opened and she hopped down. "Morning."

"Good morning," Darcy and I echoed.

Charlotte came over and stood next to us, peering at the house. "Is this it?"

"This is it." I put on my metaphorical realtor hat and took a breath. "As you can see, it isn't in terrible shape. The roof looks good. The gutters need to be cleaned out, but hopefully we can get away with not replacing them. We'll need to do some landscaping, but there aren't any big trees that need to be taken down, or anything like that."

They both nodded.

"The street looks good. Old people feel safe enough to walk their dogs and mothers leave their children unattended in the yard. There's a cop a few doors down."

"Which cop?" Darcy asked.

I told her. "Does Nolan know him?"

Patrick Nolan is Darcy's boyfriend, and also an officer with the Columbia PD.

"If he does, he's never mentioned him," Darcy said. "But it's a good sign, that there's a cop on the street. The neighborhood must be safe."

"Exactly." I beamed at her, because she got it. "Ready to go in?"

She nodded. Charlotte did, too, and I led the way up to the door while I fished my keychain out of my purse. "This would be the living room/dining room combination," I told them after I'd unlocked the door and waved them both inside. "The kitchen is through that door on the left."

"It isn't very big," Charlotte said, looking around. "It would be hard to get a sofa and chairs as well as a dining table in here."

She had a point. The living/dining combo was considerably smaller than just the dining room at the mansion, and the same was probably true for the Victorian Charlotte's parents lived in, in downtown Sweetwater.

Then again, the dining table at the mansion can seat sixteen. There would be no need for that kind of thing here.

"At most, you'd probably have six people living here. Two parents in the master, two kids in each of the other bedrooms.

More likely there would be less. Two parents, or maybe just one, with two or three kids."

Charlotte nodded. So did Darcy.

"It would be a little tight, but we could fit a dining room table down at that end." I pointed. "Or here's another option. We knock out most of the wall between the dining room and kitchen, which won't give us any more space, but it'll make it seem more open, and maybe we can add an island with seating, and avoid the table altogether. They do that on HGTV sometimes."

"How much is that going to cost?" Darcy asked, squinting at the wall.

I had no idea, and told her so. "It depends on whether it's load-bearing, first of all. If it is, the opening either has to be smaller, or we have to pay to put a beam up in the ceiling. That count run into some money. But if it's just a matter of ripping and tearing, we can probably do it ourselves." Although we'd need to get someone in to reframe the opening and deal with the electrical wires and outlets.

She nodded.

"The kitchen needs updating." I led them through the doorway that might be going away and into the compact U-shaped kitchen. "It has a lot of cabinets and counter-space, though, for being a fairly small room. Rafe suggested that we could save money by refacing the cabinets—putting new doors on them—instead of replacing everything. They look solid, so it's worth looking into."

"New appliances," Charlotte murmured, and I nodded.

"New countertops. New flooring. New sink and faucet. New drawer pulls and cabinet handles." That, on its own, could run into some money.

Darcy calculated in her head and mentioned a figure that sounded mostly on target. We moved on to the bathroom and the two bedrooms, and finally to the addition. By the time we were done, Darcy had come up with an idea of what the renovations would cost, that meshed reasonably well with the figure Rafe had mentioned last night. And while it wasn't exactly pocket change, it didn't sound too bad, either.

Granted, my only expertise came from watching *Flip or Flop* on television, but it was something.

"So what do you think?" I asked when we were back outside on the stoop and I had locked the door behind us. "It's your money, Darcy. And—" I turned to Charlotte, "your time and effort. I like it. I think if we could get it for fifty or so, we'd stand a good chance of making money."

"Fifty dollars?" Charlotte said.

"Fifty thousand. Tax auction bidding starts at the amount of taxes owed. In this case, it's probably around ten grand."

Darcy's eyes lit up, and I shook my head. "We won't get it for that. The houses often go for close to market price. On the market, this might go for sixty or even seventy thousand. But there'll probably just be investors at the auction, and they like to get things cheap. So we could get lucky. Not that lucky, though. But lucky enough to pay ten or twenty thousand under market value."

"I think I'd be OK up to sixty thousand," Darcy said. "After we put the money into it—if you're right about the amount—and if you're right about the... what did you call it? Out-price?—we stand to make somewhere around seventy thousand."

"A bit less, after realtor fees and other closing costs. I'd do that part for free, of course, since I'll be getting a third of the profits, but we still have to pay the other agent. So maybe sixty." If I was right and all the numbers lined up.

"Twenty thousand each," Darcy said. "Not sure it would be worth the risk for any less than that."

No. It was easy for me to feel confident, since all I had to put up was some time and effort. If this blew up, Darcy would be the one with egg on her face. So if she wanted to stop the bidding at sixty thousand, that's what we'd do.

"Ready to get this show on the road, then?"

They both nodded.

"Want to drive together? That way we don't have to worry about finding parking for three cars."

"Is it safe to leave the cars here?" Charlotte wanted to know, with a glance at her late-model Town and Country. I didn't think the minivan was in any danger of being stolen—most car thieves don't go for mom-vans when they commit grand theft auto, and they don't tend to commit grand theft auto at nine on a Saturday morning in a nice, residential neighborhood, either—but of course I didn't tell her so.

"If it makes you feel better," I said instead, "you can drive. But you have to come back here after the auction to drop us off."

"I'd have to come back here after the auction either way," Charlotte said. "I have car seats in the back."

Come to think of it, so did I. "I think it's up to you," I told Darcy, the only one of us who hadn't produced offspring she was ferrying around in her car.

She sighed. "First my bank account and now my car. Where's it going to end?"

"Hopefully on the courthouse steps." I headed toward the Honda. "C'mon. We don't want to be late. You can ride shotgun, Charlotte."

"That's OK," Charlotte said. "I'll take the back. You sit up front with your sister."

We arranged ourselves and Darcy put the car in gear and headed down the street toward the courthouse.

"How'd it go?" Rafe asked several hours later, when he came home, sweaty and out of sorts, from spending the best part of the day walking and climbing all over Laurel Hill.

I was back in the kitchen, this time with the computer open to tile choices, and I beamed at him. "It went well."

He took his leather jacket off and hung it over the back of a chair. "Got the house?"

I nodded. "It took some doing, but we did. Eventually."

One guy had kept the bidding going much longer than I'd wanted—I suspected at that point he was doing it just to drive the price up, although that could have been my imagination—but eventually he gave up, and we were the proud owners of a fixer-upper on Fulton Street.

Or we would be, once Darcy got to the county clerk's office on Monday with the check.

"Good for you," Rafe said.

"I guess it is." We'd come in under Darcy's top price, if a few thousand above where I'd wanted to be. But if my calculations were right, and the renovation costs didn't go over by too much, we should still be able to make a decent profit.

His lips curved. "Cold feet?"

"Yours or mine?" He was in the process of peeling off his socks, from which I deduced that he'd probably gotten wet at some point.

He nodded when I said so. "There was a creek. I had to make it to the other side."

"Just you?"

"Most of the others are old," Rafe said. "And Tammy's a girl. I volunteered."

"I'm not sure Grimaldi would appreciate you calling her a girl." Or Tammy, for that matter.

He smirked. "I wouldn't do it to her face."

"That's probably safer. So did you find anything interesting on the other side of the creek?"

He made a face, but I wasn't sure whether it was because of the wet feet or the subject matter. "A sort of half mask someone had left on the ground. Printed with the bottom half of a skull."

"Lovely," I said. "Although there's no law against running around in the woods wearing a skull mask. There could be lots of reasons for that."

He arched a brow and I corrected myself. "Maybe not lots. But it could be kids playing or something like that."

"Not with what else I found," Rafe said.

"What was that?"

"Bullets. Lots of'em."

I wrinkled my brows. "Who'd dump a bunch of bullets in the woods?"

"They didn't dump'em," Rafe said. "They used'em. For target practice, prob'ly. And when it was time to leave, they didn't pick'em all up. Either 'cause they couldn't find'em, or because they just didn't care about being stealthy."

If they'd been meeting for target practice, and they'd been wearing skulls over the bottom halves of their faces, I think stealthy was out the window. I mean, yes… they'd clearly taken some pains not to be recognized if they were seen. Hence the masks. But getting together in a popular wildlife area less than an hour and half's drive from Nashville, wearing skull masks and shooting guns, wasn't exactly inconspicuous. If they wanted to stay out of the public eye, there were better places they could hide to do their business.

"No clues as to who they are or where to find them, I guess."

He shook his head. "They didn't leave calling cards. But now that we know they meet there sometimes, we can keep an eye on the place. And maybe catch'em next time."

"You can't arrest them, though," I said. "Can you? I mean,

it's a wildlife area. Shooting is allowed. And there's no law against shooting while wearing masks." At least as long as they didn't try to shoot people.

"But we can figure out who they are and follow'em home. And then keep an eye on'em."

Right. In case they decided to do more than shoot at targets.

"But they weren't there this weekend?"

He shook his head. "The rangers are keeping an eye out. But if they were there last week, we're thinking it might could be a week or two before they're back."

"If they come back at all."

"No reason they wouldn't," Rafe said. "Nobody bothered'em this time. They'd prob'ly feel safe coming back."

Maybe so. Although for the next week, that left him, and Grimaldi and the sheriffs, with nothing to do but wait and see.

"So you got cold feet?" He came back to the part of the conversation that had been derailed by the discussion of the creek and what had been on the other side of it.

"Not so much cold feet," I said. "I'm glad we got the house. But the whole thing is scarier now that reality's set in. It was fun while we were talking about it, but now that we actually have to do something, I'm not sure I know how. I've never renovated anything before. Bradley's townhouse was new when we moved into it. My apartment was a rental, so I couldn't do anything there, and you'd already done all the work on your grandmother's house by the time I moved in."

He nodded.

"The mansion's been the same for a hundred and eighty years. But this house is on me. Darcy's putting up the money and Charlotte's willing to help with the work, but I'm going to have to be the one to tell them both what to do. And what if I don't know what I'm doing? What if I forget to turn off the power, and someone gets hurts?"

"You won't," Rafe said.

Maybe I wouldn't. But— "What if I choose the wrong wall color or bathroom tile, so nobody wants to buy the place, and we don't make any money and Darcy doesn't get her investment back?"

"She'll still love you," Rafe said.

Yes, of course she would. At least I hoped she would. But— "I want this to be a success. Charlotte needs the money. I could do with another property to sell. And I don't want to fail my sister."

Rafe shook his head. "You won't fail, darlin'. You know what people are looking for. You know the paint color and tile to pick. Worst case scenario, you'll make a little less than you hoped you'd make. But nobody's gonna die because you were negligent, and you're not gonna fail."

"Famous last words," I said.

He grinned. "How about I get changed, and we drive over to Home Depot and look at paint and tile? And then I'll take you to dinner. How does Cracker Barrel sound?"

Cracker Barrel sounded great. "I love you," I said.

The grin widened. "I love you, too. Gimme five minutes." He disappeared down the hallway while I closed the laptop and prepared to go.

Five

At nine on Monday morning, Darcy and I met at the county clerk's office in downtown Columbia. By ten after, the deed was done and the house was ours.

"Go to work," Darcy said, handing me the receipt. "It's all yours."

I took it. "It's yours, but I'll accept the baton. Thank you."

She smiled. "It's my pleasure. Especially since you're going to take my money and turn it into more money."

"You aren't worried that I'll do something stupid and lose it?"

"Why would you?" She shook her head. "This is your business. You know what you're doing. I'm not worried."

Good. That made one of us.

"But I do have to get to work," she added, "or your brother's going to fire me."

"Our brother," I said. "And he won't fire you. You're his sister."

"It still doesn't always feel that way," Darcy admitted. "I know it. Theoretically. I just don't always feel it."

I wrinkled my brows. "Dix is being nice, isn't he?"

She grinned. "Of course he's being nice. He was nice before we found out we were related, too."

"You don't feel unwelcome or anything?"

She shook her head. "No. It took your mother some time to warm up to me, but I guess that's understandable."

Maybe. Although if you ask me, it had taken Mother a bit longer to warm up than it should have. It wasn't like she was the only person whose husband had a child from a previous relationship. Rafe did, too.

Granted, I knew about that before I married him, while Mother had found out about Darcy thirty-two years after Catherine was born. But that's no reason to lace your afternoon cup of tea with brandy and be rude to your husband's daughter. None of what happened was Darcy's fault.

Anyway, Mother had come around. She was nice to Darcy now, and had made up with Audrey, Darcy's mother and Mother's best friend—and between you and me, I think it was the fact that Audrey hadn't told Mother the truth in thirty-three years of friendship that had hurt more than the fact that Dad hadn't been a virgin when they got married.

"You and Audrey doing all right?"

"We're doing fine," Darcy said. "I really have to go, Savannah. Are you starting the work on the house today?"

I nodded. "Time is money. I'll call Charlotte and have her meet me over there. We'll put in a couple of hours of scraping wallpaper and ripping up carpets. And I need to rent a dumpster. Hopefully they'll be able to deliver it quickly."

"I'll do that," Darcy said. "I'll be the one paying for it anyway."

"Thank you. Tell them to put it in the driveway if they can—if not, we'll probably have to get permission from the city to leave it on the street—and to get it there as soon as they can."

Darcy said she would, and gave me a hug. "I'll talk to you later."

"I'll be here," I said, although of course that wasn't entirely accurate. I was on my way to my car just as Darcy was on her way to hers.

Until a familiar voice spoke my name. "Hello, Savannah."

"Oh." I stopped and looked up. "Hello, Todd."

It was always a bit awkward to run into Todd. I'd known him most of my life. He was Dix's best friend and Bob Satterfield's son, and he'd been my boyfriend in high school. He'd wanted to be my boyfriend more recently, too, and had proposed marriage not all that long ago. He had not taken it well when I'd chosen to attach myself to Rafe instead.

But things were better now. Todd had gotten involved with a woman named Marley Cartwright after I took up with Rafe, and they were engaged as of Christmas, so I was able to muster a genuine smile. "How are you?"

"Good," Todd said.

He looked good. Of course, he'd always looked good, if you like the type. Tall and fair, in a well-cut gray suit and conservative tie, he was the very image of a Southern gentleman—and a successful attorney.

Todd's an assistant DA for the county. He and Marley met when he tried to prosecute her for the murder of her son, who—it turned out—wasn't dead but kidnapped. And speaking of getting over things… I really admired Marley for putting that behind her and forgiving Todd. He'd had some fairly compelling circumstantial evidence on his side, admittedly, but still. It was big of her.

"How's your fiancée doing?" I asked, and Todd grimaced.

"Throwing up."

My mouth dropped open, I admit it. I hiked my jaw back up. "Marley's pregnant?"

Was that why he'd proposed? I'd thought he'd gotten over me and found someone else, but if they were only getting married because Marley was expecting, that was a very different story.

"I had no idea," I said. "Congratulations."

"Thank you."

He didn't sound thrilled, I had to say. Admittedly, it was hard to know for sure without looking at him closely, and I didn't really want to do that.

"How far along?" I asked, thinking maybe the answer would give me some inkling.

"Three months," Todd answered.

So she'd have been around six weeks along at Christmas. Just enough time to realize that she was pregnant.

I pasted a bright smile on my face. "A summer baby."

Marley would be miserable during her last few months, poor thing. Summer in Middle Tennessee can be hot and humid and uncomfortable under the best of circumstances, and when you're carrying another small human around inside you, plus some extra weight, it doesn't help. I'd only been five and six months pregnant last summer—Carrie had been born in late November—but I'd been panting a lot, too.

Todd nodded grimly. Or maybe the grimness was in my head. But he wasn't smiling, and was showing none of the euphoria of the usual expectant father.

"On your way to work?" I asked, since further talk of the pregnancy was likely to make matters worse.

He nodded. "What about you? What are you doing here so early on a weekday?"

"We bought a house at auction on Saturday," I said, "and had to go to the county clerk's office this morning to pay for it."

"You and Collier?" He looked around, probably for Rafe.

I shook my head. "Darcy paid for it. Charlotte and I are going to fix it up."

"Something I should know about?" Todd asked, a little coyly, I thought.

And since I was afraid he might be thinking that I was dumping Rafe and moving out on my own, I wanted to nip that thought in the bud ASAP. "Charlotte needs to make some money. I need to get established with real estate here, if we're staying. And renovating can be fun." At least I hoped so.

Todd nodded, and his face gave nothing away, so maybe he hadn't been secretly hoping that I'd dumped Rafe, etc. He wasn't supposed to be hoping that, being newly engaged to a lovely pregnant woman, who had adored him—and forgiven him for trying to convict her of murder—long before he decided he liked her.

If he did in fact like her, and hadn't proposed just because she was pregnant.

I wrenched my thoughts away from that path a second time as Todd asked, "Where's the house?"

"Fulton Street," I said, and watched his brows lower. He didn't say anything, though, so after a few seconds, I broke the silence myself. "Something wrong?"

"No," Todd said, but didn't sound entirely sure.

"It looks like a nice street. Well-maintained houses. Not upper-class, you know, but nice. And there's a cop living down the street. Carl Enoch. If there's a policeman living there, I'm sure it's safe."

Todd nodded, but still didn't look convinced.

"Are you sure nothing's wrong?" I asked.

He seemed to shake it off and gave me a faint smile. "I thought I heard something about Fulton Street recently. But I can't remember what it was. I could be wrong."

I nodded. "Speaking of hearing of things... has anyone— has your dad—told you about Laurel Hill?"

"Yes," Todd said and firmed his lips together in a tight line. "The DA's office will be ready to prosecute if anything happens in our jurisdiction."

Good to know. Laurel Hill was out of their jurisdiction, of course, so anything that happened there would be under Lawrence County's district attorney, but if any of the bastards—excuse my French—turned out to live and breathe in Maury County, and they stepped a toenail over the line, it sounded like Todd and his boss would be all over it.

He glanced over his shoulder toward the entrance to the DA's office, also located on the square. "I should go."

I nodded. I should, too, so I could call Charlotte. "It was nice to see you."

"Likewise," Todd said. "Take care."

He turned and walked away. I did the same, and when I got to my car, parked under the Martin and Vaughan mural, and turned back, he was on his way through the door into the office. He didn't turn to look around, which I told myself was a good thing. He wasn't still hung up on me, and he hadn't gotten engaged to Marley for the wrong reasons.

Charlotte met me at the house on Fulton Street after lunch, dressed in designer jeans and a designer T-shirt, with hundred-dollar sneakers on her feet. I guess she imagined she looked like Christina el Moussa—Christina Anstead now—but to be honest, it was an invitation to disaster, since none of her clothes were likely to survive the day in the same shape they were now.

I squinted at her. "Are you sure you want to wear that?"

She squinted back. "What's wrong with it? You're wearing the same thing."

Yes—and no. My jeans had a maternity panel across the stomach, because I couldn't button the waistband of my regular clothes quite yet. And while they were a decent quality, they weren't designer. Rafe doesn't make enough money to keep me in designer jeans—which is fine by me—and besides, these were maternity clothes. I'd thought I'd only be wearing them for six months or so. It had turned out to be a little longer than that—my stomach was refusing to flatten to its former proportions—but that also meant it wouldn't be a terribly big deal if I ruined them, since I wouldn't be needing them much longer. And my T-shirt, unlike Charlotte's, had no elegant Double-C emblem on the chest.

"That's a Chanel T-shirt," I pointed out, as if she needed to be told. "We're going to be doing dirty work. It could get ruined."

"Richard bought it for me," Charlotte said. "I don't care."

She might care when it came time to replace it, and all she could afford was Walmart brand T-shirts, but I let it go without further discussion. It wasn't like I hadn't warned her, after all.

"Did you leave the kids with your mother?" I asked instead.

She has two, a boy and a girl. Both of them several years older than Carrie. Two and four, if memory served, or maybe closer to three and five now.

She nodded. "Is she going to be all right?"

She glanced at Carrie, kicking her feet in the car seat over my arm.

"She'll have to be." Since I wasn't about to dump her on my mother for hour upon hour every day—not that Mother would allow that to happen. She's happy to baby-sit once in a while, when she doesn't have something better to do, but she has already raised her own brood and doesn't want to be responsible for mine. "I'll give her to Mother whenever we're doing something that wouldn't be good for her—" like sanding floors or painting or anything else that might compromise her tiny and sensitive respiratory system, "but she'll be fine here for the next couple of hours. I have to feed her soon, anyway."

Charlotte nodded and looked at the house. "What do you want to do today?"

"I thought we'd start with something simple," I said. "There's wallpaper in the den and the bathroom that we have to scrape off, and a border along the ceiling in one of the bedrooms that has to come down. And if we have time after that, we can try to tear out the carpets. I don't want to rip out anything else until we have a dumpster to put it in."

"Will we have a dumpster?" Charlotte asked.

"Darcy is arranging for one. I'm not sure when it'll get here. But we can get started while we wait."

I headed for the front door. Charlotte followed obediently.

The dumpster arrived before we were finished for the day. The wallpaper task turned out to be a lot more arduous than I think either of us had expected—I know it took more time and effort that I thought it would—and as a result, we were still scraping at four o'clock, when the sound of a large engine sounded outside.

I put my scraper down on the edge of the sink and shook out my hand in relief. It was cramping from being wrapped around the edge of the scraper for so long, and I was pretty sure I was getting a blister in the middle of my palm, too. "Sounds like the dumpster might be here."

"Go and sign for it," Charlotte said. She was standing up to her ankles in wallpaper scraps in the tub. "I'll keep scraping. We're *so close* to being done…!"

We were pretty close to being done. The den floor was covered in shreds, and we had a wall and a half—the half being the part above the tub in the bathroom—to go.

"I'll be right back." I headed out of the bathroom, down the hallway through the kitchen, and across the living room and out, where I greeted the truck driver. "Is that my dumpster?"

"Your name—" He consulted a clipboard he was holding, "Darcy Corcoran?"

I shook my head. "Darcy's my sister. I'm Savannah Martin. Collier. But you're in the right place."

He raked the yard and street with a glance. "Driveway?"

"For the dumpster? Sure." I'd made Charlotte park on the street just in case we got lucky and the dumpster arrived today.

"By the X." He thrust the clipboard at me. I located the signature line and scribbled my name there.

"When are you coming back for it?"

"Check the copy." He took the clipboard back, tore the carbon off, and handed it to me. I retired to the front step and perused the copy while he got back into the truck and reversed into the driveway. The dumpster slid off the back of the truck and hit the concrete with a bang, and then the driver threw the truck into drive and rolled off down the street with a merry *beep-beep* of the horn. I opened the door and went back inside.

"All set. We keep it for thirty days unless we fill it up and need it emptied sooner. If so, we call."

Charlotte nodded. She was on her toes in the tub, taking wild swipes at the ceiling.

"Give me that," I said, reaching for the scraper. "I'm taller than you. I'll do it."

Charlotte stepped out of the tub, catching her breath. "Tomorrow I'm bringing a step stool."

Good idea. I intended to finish scraping the last of the wallpaper before we left today, but there would surely be other uses for a step stool later. And a ladder. If nothing else, we needed it to clean out the gutters.

Over the next hour we finished dealing with the wallpaper and gathered it into a couple of lawn and leaf bags we tossed in the dumpster on our way out. The plastic was an extra step, but there was no top on the dumpster, so if we got a storm anytime in the next month, the shreds could be whipped out of the dumpster and end up all over the neighborhood. That wasn't likely to endear us to the neighbors, so the bags seemed like a good idea. And I'd made sure to buy the biodegradable kind, so it could be worse.

The following day we started on the carpets, and then the mats under the carpets, and the furring strips holding the carpets to the floors, and the millions and millions of staples that had to be pried out individually, by hand, because if we left them, they'd tear up the sandpaper once it was time to sand the floors. And then there was the textured finish on the ceilings we had to scrape off, since nobody wants popcorn ceilings anymore.

By the time that job was over, the week was getting close to an end, and we were both in pain. My shoulders and arms were screaming from hours and hours of holding them aloft, scraping at the ceiling. I had calluses on my knees from prying tacks from the floor, and blisters on my hands from both. My nail polish was chipped, and two of my nails were broken.

Charlotte was no better. She stood in the middle of the floor with her hands on her hips, with chunks of plaster and dust turning her hair white, and looked around at the empty living room with an expression of loathing on her grimy face. "It's been less than a week, and I already hate this house."

"The hardest work is done," I told her, wondering whether I looked as bad as she did. Or maybe even worse. The plaster had mixed with the sweat at her temples and turned into paste. "From here on out, it'll be better."

She didn't look like she believed me.

"I swear," I said. "It gets easier. We've done most of the tear-down. Tomorrow, we can start building up the floor in the den, to make it level with the rest of the house, and then the plumber can come and rough in the new bathroom. Or maybe we have to build the walls first. I'm not sure. I'll ask Rafe."

Charlotte nodded. "This is a lot more work than I thought it would be."

It was more work than I'd thought it would be, too. Or if not exactly that, it was more work than I'd been prepared for. I knew it took time and effort—and money—to renovate a house. I just hadn't quite understood what it would take to actually do all the work with my own two hands.

"Think of the money," I advised her. "In a month or two, when we're done, it'll be worth it."

"If you say so," Charlotte said, and turned to the door. "Is that a car outside? Who's coming?"

I had no idea. "One of the neighbors? Or your mother or mine, coming to see what we're doing?"

It probably wasn't Rafe, since the workday wasn't over yet and he'd still be dealing with keeping the peace at the Columbia PD.

"Looks like some guy," Charlotte said, peering out the grimy window. "You go talk to him. You're married. I don't want anyone to see me like this."

She ducked through the doorway into the kitchen just as the knock came on the door. I arched my brows—officially, she was married too, even if perhaps she didn't feel quite so married anymore—and went to open it.

The person outside was male, around thirty, and black, dressed in a pair of khakis and a peacoat that looked to be a couple of years out of date. To the best of my knowledge, I'd never seen him before.

"Steve Morris." He put out a hand.

"Savannah Martin," I said. "Collier." I held up my hand to show him the grime coating it, and he dropped his own. "What can I do for you?"

He was dark-skinned but sallow, like he didn't spend much time outdoors. And he obviously subscribed to the Rafe Collier method of haircuts. In fact, he was totally bald, his scalp gleaming, while Rafe at least keeps a half inch or so of scruff covering his head. Trying to avoid those pretty waves he gets when his hair grows longer.

"You're in my house," Steve Morris said.

My stomach did a kind of funny flip, although I kept my voice steady when I told him, "This is our house. My sister bought it at auction last week. Tax sale."

"It was my house first," Morris said.

I put my hands on my hips. "Well, it's our house now. If you wanted to keep it, you should have kept up with the tax payments."

"I had other things to worry about," Morris said grimly.

"That's too bad. But it isn't my problem."

He smirked. There's no other word for it. "I'm about to make it your problem, sister. Have you ever heard of a statutory right of redemption?"

Vaguely, in the back of my head, I thought I had. Maybe in real estate school? Or even longer ago, in pre-law? Something about a year-long redemption period and ten percent above the sales price...

"No," I said, thinking that if I told him I had no idea what he was talking about, he'd explain it to me, and I wouldn't have to dig up the elusive memory.

"It means I have twelve months after my house is sold to pay you back the money you paid for it, and get it back."

"Plus ten percent," I said, as the details slid back into my head and realigned themselves.

He nodded, even as a shadow of what looked like vexation moved across his features. I guess he hadn't expected me to know that.

"We paid fifty-seven thousand for the house. An additional ten percent makes it over sixty." Although that didn't cover the cost of the dumpster, or the work we'd already done. Or the materials we had ordered, and the fees we'd paid. Not to mention the plans we'd had, which had been free, but which I was loath to give up. "Are you sure it's worth it to you?"

"It's my house!" Morris said.

"Not anymore. It's our house now."

He didn't answer, and I added, "If you have sixty thousand dollars, you could just buy another house. There are several other properties on the market you might like."

He scowled at me. "You a real estate agent, or something?"

I smiled sweetly. "I am, as a matter of fact. I'd be happy to help you look for something else."

"You can help me by getting out of my house!" Morris snarled, his face turning brick red with anger.

I shook my head. "Sorry. As I said, it's our house now. You can't just come back here and tell us to leave. If you want to invoke your statutory right of redemption, there are proper channels for that. But until you do, we own the place, fair and square."

He scowled at me, his brows lowered and his fists curled, breathing through his nose. It made him look like he wanted to punch me—he probably did want to punch me—and I decided it would be best if I removed the temptation.

"Sorry, Mr. Morris, but until you talk to the court, there's nothing I can do for you."

I moved to close the door, bracing myself in case he tried to stick his foot in the gap to stop me.

But no, he didn't. I got the door into the frame with no resistance, and turned the lock so I could be sure to keep him out.

"This ain't over," he told me through the wood.

I didn't answer, just stayed where I was and listened to his footsteps walk away. A few seconds later there was the sound of an engine starting and then fading away down the street. I turned to the doorway into the kitchen, where Charlotte was staring at me with huge eyes. "Oh, my God, Savannah!"

I nodded. It was an oh, my God sort of moment.

"What he said…" Charlotte said, "is it true?"

I thought it was. What little bit I could remember about it told me it was. But I didn't want to rely on what might be a faulty memory.

"We need to talk to Catherine or Dix. Or Jonathan. Someone who knows the law better than I do. I never graduated from law school." And the education I'd had was several years in the past. We needed updated information.

"Now?" Charlotte said.

"The sooner, the better."

I turned to the tiny coat closet in the corner of the living room. We'd left our stuff in there this morning so they wouldn't be covered with the same plaster dust the two of us were covered with.

"I have to go get my kids," Charlotte said, watching me pull the door open. "Mom's had them all day."

My mother had had Carrie all day, too. I hadn't wanted to expose the baby to the flying plaster dust. But under the circumstances, she'd just have to wait another fifteen minutes.

"I'll take care of it," I told Charlotte as I handed her her coat. "Go home and relieve your mother."

I yanked my own coat off the hanger and stuck one arm through the sleeve. "I'll go talk to Dix and let you know what he says. Then we'll figure out what to do from there."

Charlotte nodded. "Is it safe to open the door?"

"I heard him drive away." But that didn't stop me from making sure the stoop and lawn and driveway were empty before I pulled the door all the way open. "Come on. Let's get out of here."

We slipped outside, and I locked the door behind us while Charlotte peered worriedly up and down the street. "Savannah?"

"Yes," I said and turned to the car.

"If he's right…? What are we going to do?"

We'd probably have to give him the house, and take the loss on the money we'd spent on it so far. It wasn't a huge amount beyond the purchase price plus ten percent, but enough that I hated to lose it. "I don't know," I said. "One thing at a time."

Charlotte nodded, but she was still looking worried when she buckled herself into the minivan and took off down the street.

Six

"We have a problem," I announced to Darcy thirty minutes later, after I had driven to Sweetwater, found a parking spot on the square, and stalked through the door of Martin and McCall Law Offices.

She looked up from the computer. And while her lips twitched, she didn't comment on the fact that I looked like I'd been standing under a congregation of birds. "What kind of problem?"

"Someone's trying to take our house," I said.

She took her hands off the keyboard and leaned back, folding them in her lap. "The guy from the auction?"

There had been maybe twelve guys at the auction. Most of them had started bidding with us. All but two dropped out by the time we got to fifty thousand. One dropped out at fifty-three. The last guy kept the bidding going all the way up to fifty-seven before he gave up, and as I may have mentioned, I think he was doing it just to drive the price up. At that point he had probably figured out that we wanted the house and would keep bidding, so he jacked the price up by a couple thousand just so we'd end up paying more.

Now that she'd brought him up, I considered the possibility. One that hadn't occurred to me until Darcy said something. Would he benefit in some way if we lost the house?

It would probably give him satisfaction, if I was right and he had taken the trouble to make sure we'd overpay for the house, even when there was nothing but spite in it for him. And of course it was possible he was in league with Steve Morris.

That's if the man who had come to the door was actually Steve Morris. He hadn't shown me any kind of ID.

If it came to that, he might not even have told the truth about owning the house before us.

Maybe it was all one big elaborate hoax to freak us out and make us willing to take a cash settlement for the house. Maybe by tomorrow we'd hear from someone else, like the guy from the auction, who'd be willing to pay us fifty thousand to spare us the trouble of dealing with Steve Morris and his right of redemption.

But just in case that didn't happen, and Steve Morris was who he said he was, and he really did want his house back, we should clarify this whole right of redemption thing before we went any further.

"We need to talk to Dix," I said. "Or Catherine or Jonathan. Anyone who's here and available." And who would know more about it than me.

"Dix is here. And not with a client." Darcy unwound her long legs from under the desk and got to her feet. "Come on back."

I followed her toward the door to the inner sanctum.

"No baby today?" she asked over her shoulder.

I shook my head. "I left her with Mother. We've been scraping popcorn off the ceilings, and I didn't want her to have to deal with the dust." Or the pieces of plaster falling all over her.

Darcy nodded as she legged it down the hallway toward

Dix's office. On the right, Catherine's office door was open, with the light off—she wasn't there—and Jonathan's was closed. He was either consulting with someone or working quietly.

Or he wasn't here either, and had shut his door before he left.

Dix's door was open, and the light was on. The man himself was sitting behind the desk tapping away on the computer. When Darcy knocked on the doorjamb he looked up, and his lips twitched. "Sis. What happened to you?"

"Flock of seagulls," I said, inaccurately. "We have to talk to you."

I pushed past Darcy and made a beeline for the chairs in front of the desk.

Dix's brows arched, but he took his hands off the keyboard and leaned back in his chair. "Something wrong?"

"Nothing you need to worry about." I made myself comfortable while Darcy strolled over to the chair next to mine. Dix winced when my posterior hit the navy leather of the chair, and I rolled my eyes. "Don't worry, I won't ruin your precious leather. It's mostly the top of me that's dirty. I didn't sit in plaster."

"Sheila picked out those chairs," Dix said, and left it at that. "So what can I do for you?"

Sheila was Dix's wife, until she was murdered a year and a half ago, so now I felt bad. But saying I was sorry was only going to make it worse, so I didn't. "You know about the house we bought," I said instead, as Darcy folded one long leg over the other.

He smirked. "You mean the house Darcy bought."

I resisted the temptation to treat him to another eye-roll. "Yes. That house. Charlotte and I were over there this afternoon, scraping popcorn from the ceilings, when there was a knock on the door. This guy was outside. Said his name was Steve Morris and it used to be his house."

Dix dropped his hands back on the keyboard. "That's easy to check, anyway. What's the address?"

I gave it to him, and waited for him to access the tax records for the county. After less than a minute, he nodded. "The previous owner of the house at that address was named Steven Morris."

Yes. But— "That doesn't mean the guy who came to the door was Steven Morris," I said. "He didn't show me ID. From that standpoint, he could have been anyone. And everyone who knows how can look up that information. You just did, in about thirty seconds. Someone else could have, too. The courthouse records are public."

"Any reason to think it isn't him?" Dix wanted to know.

I had to admit there wasn't. "If he says he's Steve Morris, he's probably Steve Morris. But—"

"If he's Steve Morris, and it was his house until you bought it, he has a case."

"Even if the house has been sitting there for three years and he could have come back to it at any time before he lost it?"

"Even then," Dix said. "When a house is sold at foreclosure, the previous owner has a year to buy it back. It's called a statutory right of redemption..."

"Thank you, I know." And if I hadn't, Steve Morris would have told me.

"Then why are you asking me?" Dix wanted to know, a touch of irritation in his voice.

I took a breath. And another. "Sorry. I'm just a bit stressed out. I remember learning about a statutory right of redemption, either in pre-law or Real Estate 101. But it's been a while, and I wanted to talk to someone who knows more about it than I do."

My brother looked slightly mollified at this blatant petting of his ego.

"Go on," I told him, laying it on even thicker. "Educate us. If you tell me something I already know, I'll be quiet."

He snorted, but went on. Addressing himself pointedly to Darcy. "A statutory right of redemption is good for a year. The previous owner has to pay back the full purchase price of the house, plus ten percent—"

Darcy turned to me. "Ten percent isn't enough to cover our costs, is it?"

I shook my head. "Not between what we've spent and the deposits we've made. We'd be in the hole a couple thousand at this point."

Darcy winced and turned back to Dix. "Go on."

"There's not a lot more to say," Dix said. "He has to file a motion with the court and pay them the money. Once that's done, the house is his, and you're out of luck."

There was a moment's silence while we all processed this unflinching statement of facts.

"Any way around it?" Darcy wanted to know.

"None that are legal," Dix answered.

"If he happened to die…" I said.

They both turned to me, wide-eyed.

I scowled. "I'm not going to kill him, for God's sake. It was just a question."

Dix didn't look like he quite believed me, but he answered anyway. "If the motion has already been filed, it's too late to do anything. Even if he turns up dead tomorrow, as long as he started the process, his estate will get the house."

"What if he didn't file the motion?"

It was Friday, and it had been after four when he'd showed up at the house. Now it was almost five. Maybe he hadn't had time to make it to the bank and the clerk's office before they closed for the weekend.

"If he didn't," Dix said, "then you own the house until Monday. Assuming he files then."

"And if something happens between now and then?"

"If you're planning to murder the guy," Dix said, "I don't want to know about it."

"I told you I'm not." I glanced at Darcy. "I suppose we could try to talk to him. See if maybe he'd let us keep the house in exchange for a cut of the profits?"

Darcy didn't look happy about that idea. "Those profits are getting sliced thinner every single day."

They were. Although none of us had—or could have—anticipated this. "Tell you what. He can have my profits. I don't care. Rafe makes enough money to take care of us. I live for free. And I'll still have a house to sell. Maybe I can get a buyer out of it, or something, to recoup some money that way."

"I didn't mean that you should work for free," Darcy said. "Just that it's starting to look like less and less of a viable investment."

It was. And I saw her point. However— "A smaller percentage of something is better than a bigger percentage of nothing. And if he takes the house, we get nothing. We might as well see what we can salvage."

Darcy looked reluctant, but she nodded.

"How do you plan on finding this guy?" Dix wanted to know. "Did he leave you his address? Or telephone number?"

He hadn't, and that meant this situation had just gotten even more difficult.

"Local motels?" Darcy suggested.

It was a possibility. Although chances were the staff at the local motels weren't going to tell us whether Mr. Morris was a guest there. That probably went against their rules and regs.

Besides, if he was from Columbia, or had lived there for a while, he might have friends he was staying with. And we had no idea who they were.

"I don't know what to do," I admitted.

None of the others seemed to, either, so we sat in silence a minute.

"Maybe we just carry on as if nothing's wrong until we know better?" Darcy suggested. "Go back to work tomorrow, and wait to hear from Mr. Morris or the county clerk?"

That might be the best thing. Steve Morris didn't know who we were, either, or where to find us, so if he wanted to talk to us again, he'd show up back at the house.

It would put a damper on the renovations, of course, since it would be hard to be gung-ho about painting and tiling when we didn't know how long we'd own the house... but it sounded better than doing nothing. At least if Morris showed up, we'd get a chance to talk to him again.

"Patrick is working tomorrow," Darcy said. I nodded. "I'll meet you over there. Say nine?"

Nine would be fine. Rafe was traveling down to Laurel Hill with the sheriffs and Grimaldi again, so I was at loose ends, too. Might as well work. "I'll see you there," I said.

"Close up and go home," Dix told her. "It's almost five."

She nodded, and unwound herself from the chair. "Savannah?"

"I need a minute."

She arched her brows, and so did Dix, but neither of them said anything. Darcy walked into the hallway and closed the door behind her, and Dix watched me, turning a pen over and over between his fingers. "Something we didn't cover?"

"Not about this." I grimaced. "I feel bad for talking Darcy into it now."

"I don't imagine you had to twist her arm that hard," Dix said dryly.

Well, no. I hadn't. But that made it even worse. She was my

sister. She'd given me the money without a second thought, just because I'd asked. And now it looked like she might have lost some of it.

But that wasn't what I'd wanted to talk to him about. "I ran into Todd the other day."

Dix's eyebrows moved infinitesimally.

"He told me that Marley's pregnant."

Dix nodded.

"Is that the only reason he proposed?"

The eyebrows shot up, and I elaborated. "I know in the beginning, she was in love with him, and he mostly used her to distract himself from the fact that I'd gotten involved with Rafe."

The corner of Dix's mouth curved, and I scowled. "Don't look like that. I know I sound conceited, but it's true. He wanted to marry me. I said no. And then he took up with Marley, mostly as friends, I think. Or maybe friends with benefits. Or at least they developed into that."

"That's fair," Dix said.

"Marley was in love with Todd while he was still a little bit hung up on me. I thought that changed. But he didn't sound very excited about the baby. So now I'm worried that he proposed for the wrong reason."

"Is it wrong to propose because you made your girlfriend pregnant?" Dix asked.

"It is if you don't want to be married to her!"

"Maybe he's hoping it'll turn into more."

I felt the air go out of me. "So you're saying he only proposed because she's pregnant?"

"I don't know why he proposed," Dix said. "We haven't talked about it."

I stared at him. "What do you talk about?"

He didn't answer, and I added, "You spend time together,

don't you? Don't you talk about things?"

"The weather," Dix said. "Sports. The girls." His daughters, Abigail and Hannah. "He mentions Oliver sometimes. Sometimes we talk about work."

I threw my hands up. "I can't believe it. He's your best friend. He's newly engaged. You haven't dissected his relationship with Marley?"

"Guys don't do that," Dix said.

I scowled at him. "You're no help."

"Why do you care? You have Collier. It shouldn't matter to you why Todd's marrying Marley."

"I like Marley," I said. "I don't want Todd to hurt her. He's already tried to prosecute her for murder."

"And she's forgiven him for that. Obviously."

Yes, obviously. But that didn't mean I'd be OK with him hurting her again.

Dix shook his head. "Leave it alone, Sis. It's their business."

It was their business. But I liked Marley. "Maybe I'll give her a call and invite her to lunch one day." And pick her brain about their relationship.

"You do that," Dix said. "But if you do, I don't think you ought to ask her whether he only proposed because she's pregnant."

No, probably not. "It's probably not a good time, anyway. Todd said she's throwing up. It would be better to wait until she's through the first trimester and can eat again."

"Sounds like a plan," Dix said, and glanced at his watch. "I hate to cut this short, Sis—" His tone told me clearly that he was happy for the excuse, "but it's after five. I gotta go pick up the girls."

I got to my feet. "I have to go get Carrie, too. And Pearl. Mother's been taking care of them today."

"Don't let Mother see you like that," Dix said, giving me a

once-over.

"If I go home and shower and change, it'll be even later when I get there. I'll take my chances."

"Don't say I didn't warn you," Dix said and reached out to turn off the computer. "Let me know how it goes with the Morris guy and the house."

I told him I would, and then I headed for the back door while he finished his tasks for the day.

Bob Satterfield's house, where Mother lives in sin with the sheriff, is located just a block or two off the square. It took me no more than a minute to drive there, once I got into the car. And Dix was right, when Mother opened the door and got a look at me, she winced like she were in pain.

"Darling…"

"I've been scraping popcorn off the ceiling," I said, for what felt like the umpteenth time that day. "I'll go home and take a shower before Rafe gets there."

Mother nodded, reassured. "You don't want your husband to see you like that."

Actually, my husband had seen me look worse than this. My husband had seen me at my absolute worst, and covered with drywall and blisters wasn't it.

Mother, of course, looked spotless. She'll be sixty on her next birthday, and doesn't look a day over forty-eight or so. It takes considerable work to maintain the illusion, but it seems like she enjoys it, so maybe it doesn't feel like work. Her hair was tinted its usual soft champagne color, her makeup was spotless, and she was dressed in wool slacks and a silk blouse. There were no spit-up spots on the blouse and no doggie drool on the pants. She didn't look like a woman who had spent the day with her three-month-old granddaughter and a slobbering pitbull.

"How do you do it?" I asked, and she gave me a look out of blue eyes the same color and shape as mine, but more expertly made up.

"Willpower, darling."

Willpower. I obviously didn't have willpower enough to stop the baby from spitting up on me and the dog from drooling, but if she'd worked out how to do it, then more power to her.

"I'll get your things," Mother said and click-clacked her way down the hardwoods of the hallway. "Just stay where you are."

Although she didn't say it, I deduced she was afraid that if I came farther into the house, I'd leave flecks of wallpaper and plaster dust behind. So I grabbed Pearl's leash from the hook by the door and fastened it on her collar—she had come bounding out to greet me, or to protect Mother, when I rang the bell—and raised my voice. "I'll take the dog to the car and be back for Carrie."

"Yes, darling," Mother's voice wafted back to me from the parlor.

I let Pearl tinkle on the grass and got her situated in the front seat. By the time I got back to the door, Mother had Carrie bundled into her coat and ready to go. I flung the suitcase sized diaper bag over one shoulder and threaded the car seat handle over the other arm. "Thank you for taking care of them today."

"It was a pleasure," Mother said, and sounded like she meant it. "Did everything go well?"

For a second I thought about telling her about Steve Morris and the right of redemption, but then I decided against it. There was nothing she could do about it, and nothing to be gained by sharing the news. So I just smiled. "Fine. We got all the popcorn off the ceilings. The carpets are out. The wallpaper's down. We can start building things back up."

"Wonderful, darling." She smiled back. "And Charlotte's helping you?"

"She's working as hard as I am," I said. "She needs this money badly."

Mother nodded. "What are you and Rafael up to tonight?"

Rafe would probably be up to the usual, no pun at all intended. But other than that, our lives were pretty boring right now. Our personal lives, anyway. He had plenty of excitement on the job, and I had Steve Morris and the house to worry about, but with an almost-new baby in the house, our partying days were over. We usually conked out in front of the TV by ten o'clock.

How the mighty have fallen.

"Not much," I admitted. "What about you?"

"Bob and I are having dinner at the Wayside Inn," Mother said with satisfaction. It's her favorite restaurant, and I'm sure she kept Bob busy taking her there. Hopefully he liked it, too, and didn't just put up with it because she did.

"Have a good time." I turned on my heel before she could suggest that we join them. Or maybe she wouldn't. She'd spent all day with my daughter; she was probably ready for some peace and quiet, and adult conversation.

"Do you need me to take the baby tomorrow too?" she asked behind my back.

"We're done with the scraping," I told her, after I'd made my way across the porch and down the couple of steps to the walkway. In the car, Pearl was fogging up the window. "She should be OK coming with me tomorrow."

Mother nodded. "Just let me know, darling. Bob's going to be busy all day again."

"Rafe, too. They're going back to Laurel Hill."

"I can't imagine what's so interesting down there," Mother said, a little peevishly.

I gathered Bob hadn't told her what was going on. Not in enough detail to make her worry, anyway. And since he hadn't, I decided it wasn't my place to do so, either. "Have you ever been to Laurel Hill?"

"Of course, darling," Mother said. "We took you kids down there a few times when you were small."

'We' being her and my dad, I assumed. Not her and Bob.

"We could always take a drive over ourselves, if you wanted. And see what's going on."

The creeps in the masks, if they were there this weekend, weren't likely to be interested two white women with blond hair. And they'd have their hands full with the combined power of the sheriffs, Tamara Grimaldi, and Rafe, anyway.

"Aren't you working on the house?" Mother asked.

Actually, I was. Or would be. And besides, Rafe wasn't likely to be happy if he ran across me and Mother in Laurel Hill while he was there. I didn't think Bob would be, either. "Maybe some other time."

"Of course, darling," Mother said. "Have a good evening."

I wished her the same, and then I carried my daughter to the car, and drove her and my dog and myself home, to wait for my husband.

Seven

When Rafe ambled through the back door a little after seven, the chicken enchiladas were about ready to come out of the oven, the condiments—chopped tomatoes, guacamole, shredded cheese, and sour cream—were nestled in a line of small blue bowls along the counter, and the Spanish rice had almost finished steaming.

"Wow," I said, looking him up and down as he shut the door behind him.

He shot me a grin. "Evening, darlin'."

"Yes," I said. "It is."

The grin widened. "'Scuse me?"

"Nice to see you, too."

That didn't make much sense, either. But it was nice to see him. Very nice. And not just because he's my husband and I love him, but because he was dressed head to toe in SWAT black, only missing the body armor, and looked good enough that I forgot all about the food. The way that tight black T-shirt molded to every muscle in his arms and chest, and stretched tight across his shoulders, had my mouth watering for reasons that had nothing to do with the enchiladas. Not to mention the way those black cargo pants hugged his thighs and butt, and molded to…

But I digress. When he came closer, and then bent to fit his lips over mine, my eyes rolled back in my head, and if it hadn't been for the arm he snaked around my waist, I would have dribbled into a puddle on the floor.

"Hungry?" he asked against my mouth.

My eyes were closed, but I managed a confirming murmur. "M-hm."

"For food?"

That, too. But it was far distant to the other appetites.

"We could go upstairs, and—"

The baby cooed. My eyes popped open, and he grimaced. "Guess not."

"Parenthood," I told him, and scooted away so I wouldn't fall into temptation to attack him again. "Keep your clothes on."

He arched a brow. "I wasn't thinking I'd eat dinner in the altogether, darlin'."

"I meant keep them on rather than getting a shower. If you can wait an hour or two, until the baby's asleep, I'll help you take them off later." With my teeth, if he'd like.

A cocky smirk made it look like he'd heard the part of the sentence I hadn't spoken out loud. It wouldn't be the first time he'd read my mind. He didn't comment, though. Just said, "Yes'm," while his eyes laughed.

"SWAT team?" I asked, my cheeks still a little hot, as I started to dish up the food, and as Rafe sauntered over to where Carrie was sitting to greet her.

He nodded, eyes on the baby. "Just in case."

I thought about asking in case of what, but I figured I knew. They were going back to Laurel Hill tomorrow. And depending on what they found, a SWAT team might come in handy. "Do you think there's anything to worry about?"

I was hoping he'd say no, that a bunch of wannabe storm

troopers running around a wildlife preserve preparing for a war they had no chance of winning, wasn't a concern. He didn't.

"They obviously got firepower," he said instead, straightening, "if the bullets we found were anything to go by. They got semi-automatic weapons, so if they put a finger on the trigger, the gun'll spew out bullets till the magazine's empty. Most of'em, when it comes right down to it, maybe ain't likely to aim at another human being and squeeze the trigger. But there's always one or two."

Yes. In any crowd, there's always one or two. And that one or two, with a semi-automatic weapon, could do a lot of damage in a short time.

And he'd been practicing tonight to walk into the line of fire of that one or two.

I swallowed. "You'll be careful, won't you?"

"I'm always careful, darlin'." He gave me a grin, and I smiled back, in spite of knowing for a fact that no, he wasn't always careful.

And then he glanced at Carrie and added, "I got more reason to be careful now than I used to."

Good. "I know it's your job," I said, as I put two plates of enchiladas and rice on the table. "I know someone's got to do it. But I'm not real happy that it has to be you."

He gave me a level look as he took a seat on one of the stools at the island. "Who better'n me, darlin'?"

Well, nobody better than him. For a lot of reasons. But the reason why he (and the sheriff of Giles County) had to do this, was the same reason I was worried. So I guessed we were at an impasse.

"Eat," I told him, trying to put some levity in my voice. "You'll need your strength for later."

"Yes, darlin'." He smiled at me, but as he picked up his

fork, he added, "For what it's worth, I don't think you have to worry about tomorrow. Even if they're there, we ain't gonna be engaging with'em. Just make note of where they are, what they're doing, and seeing if maybe we can follow a few of'em home, to get a bead on who they are."

I nodded. "That makes me feel better."

"Good." He drove the fork into the enchiladas. "So what's going on with you?"

I opened my mouth to tell him about Steven Morris's visit and the fact that we might lose the house before we'd even gotten properly started on the renovations—but not soon enough that we hadn't spent too much money—but then I rethought the impulse. He had other things to worry about, and in the scheme of things, they were more important things. He didn't need my worries on top of his own. So I just told him that we'd gotten to a point where all the popcorn was off the ceilings, and the wallpaper was down, and the carpets were up, and we were ready to start putting things back into the house again. "If you can spare an hour on Sunday to go over there, I wouldn't mind getting your opinion on what we should do next. Unless you're busy tailing neo-Nazis by then."

"I might be busy tailing neo-Nazis. But if I'm not, then I'll go over with you and take a look."

"I appreciate it," I said.

So we ate, and talked—about innocuous things, no more neo-Nazis or rights of redemption—and then I cleaned up the kitchen while he spent time with Carrie, and after we fed the baby and put her to bed, I took his clothes off—not with my teeth—and we made love. And the next morning, he kissed me goodbye like he didn't have a care in the world, and since he didn't seem worried, I pretended I wasn't either, just told him to be careful before I waved him off and got ready to get Carrie and myself over to Fulton Street.

When I got there, Darcy's blue Honda that was parked at the curb, but there was no sign of Charlotte's minivan. I pulled up behind her and cut the engine, and faced her across the roof of the car. "Morning."

She opened the back door before I could get around to the other side, and unhooked the baby carrier from the base. "Hello, gorgeous."

The compliment was directed at Carrie, not me. My daughter blinked up at her, and showed off a big, gummy smile.

"You didn't have to wait outside, you know," I said. "It's your house. You could have gone inside."

"I don't have a key," Darcy said, looking up from the baby.

Well, of course. "I'm sorry. I should have given you a spare when I had the locks changed on Tuesday. We have a couple of spares inside. I'll get you one."

"How far have you gotten?" Darcy wanted to know, peering into the dumpster as we made our way up the driveway and toward the door. "We were too preoccupied last night to talk about it."

"Oh." Yes, of course we'd been. "We've taken down the wallpaper, the popcorn on the ceilings, and ripped up the carpets. The plastic shower surround still has to go, and the toilet and bathroom vanity—they're both old and ugly, so we need to replace them—but since there's just the one bath, we're leaving them as long as we can, so we have a bathroom to use while we're here."

Darcy nodded.

"There's a cabinet maker from Leiper's Fork coming on Tuesday to talk about putting custom cabinet fronts on the existing cabinet boxes; that way we won't have to worry about replacing the cabinets themselves. They're solid wood and they go all the way up to the ceiling, so we can save some money by keeping them and just adding new doors." And hardware. And counters. And a sink. And tile on the backsplash. And new appliances. And flooring.

There were plenty of other things to spend on our money on in the kitchen, and every little bit of savings we could manage would help.

I dug my key out of my purse while I continued. "Maybe I should have called last night and told him not to come. Just in case the house isn't ours anymore by Tuesday. It's just that he's really busy—I called him on Monday, and this Tuesday was the earliest he could come out—and I didn't want to miss the chance to talk to him."

Darcy nodded. "Have him come out and take a look. Get a quote. Just hold off on committing to anything until we know how the Steve Morris situation is going to work itself out."

Good idea. "You're smart," I said, and inserted the key in the lock.

Darcy grinned. "You would have thought of it too, if you hadn't been so rattled."

Maybe so. I turned the key, withdrew it, and pushed the door open. "It's just that I feel guilty, you know? I got you into this..."

And then I stopped, when a breath of cold air hit me in the face. "Why is there a draft in here? Did we accidentally leave a window open?"

Hard to see how we could have, when it was February and cold outside. I certainly hadn't opened any windows yesterday. But maybe Charlotte had, and then Steve Morris's appearance had made her forget to close it again.

"God," I said, "I hope we haven't been ripped off."

Houses under construction are easy pickings for people looking for stuff to fence for a quick buck. Tools, materials, even copper pipes are worth good money. And since houses under construction just sit empty at night, they're easy to get into, too.

"Not sure we have anything worth ripping off," Darcy said behind me, but I didn't listen, just charged into the house. The kitchen looked OK. Everything that was supposed to be there was still there. Same with the bathroom. Nobody had ripped a hole in the wall to get to the plumbing pipes, and the window above the toilet was shut. The draft was still blowing down the hallway, though, from somewhere in the back of the house. I followed it past the two small bedrooms and into the garage addition.

At that point, I'll admit I was starting to get an uncomfortable feeling in the pit of my stomach. I'd been here before, once or twice. Or not here, specifically. But the situation felt familiar, if not exactly comfortable. By the time I turned the last corner and peered into the big room in the back, and saw the figure lying on the floor, it almost didn't come as a shock at all.

At least not until I looked closer and saw the handle of the screwdriver that stuck out of his chest like the hilt of a knife. At that point I'll admit to a wave of nausea and lightheadedness.

I fought them both back. There was no time for vapors.

There was no question who it was, of course. Not only did I recognize him, and the clothes he'd worn yesterday afternoon, but there was a certain inevitability to this.

Not that I'd been expecting it. Of course not. But if anybody was going to turn up dead—murdered—in our house-under-renovation, of course it would be Steve Morris.

"Don't come in here," I told Darcy, who had followed me down the hall. I glanced at Carrie, still in the carrier over Darcy's arm. "I don't want her to see this. I have no idea whether she'd have any idea what she'd be looking at, but I don't want to scar her for life."

Darcy arched her brows and put the carrier carefully on the floor just outside the door before she stepped down into the garage.

"Oh," she said after a second, sounding remarkably calm. "Steve Morris, I presume?"

I nodded. "You presume right."

There was a pause while Darcy looked at him. "I guess that's one of our screwdrivers? If that's what it is? A screwdriver."

I confirmed that it was, indeed, a screwdriver, and that it did belong to us. Or it belonged in the garage at the mansion, at any rate.

"I had dinner with Patrick last night," Darcy said, "after he got back from the SWAT thing. We spent the night together."

OK. Not that I'd been in any doubt that my sister was sleeping with her boyfriend.

And then I realized why she'd mentioned it, and my stomach sank. Yes, of course we'd be considered suspects in this. It was our murder weapon and our crime scene, and Morris had been threatening to take it away. We'd better make sure we had alibis.

I'd better make sure I had an alibi, after the discussion with Dix yesterday.

"Rafe was home by seven," I said steadily. "We were together after that. In the same room. Until he left this morning."

So that was the two of us taken care of. And I didn't think I had to worry about Dix. Given his outraged reaction to my suggestion that something might happen to Steve Morris, I didn't think my brother had driven over here to do this.

Darcy eyed the body. "Any idea when he was killed?"

Not without going closer and touching him, and I had no intention of doing that.

"Sometime overnight. He broke in, clearly—" One of the small panes in the fifteen-light French doors had been broken, right next to the handle and lock. That's where the whistle of cold air was coming from. "—and he probably waited until it was dark to do it. It's the kind of neighborhood where people pay attention to what's going on. If he used to live here, he would have known that."

Darcy nodded. "Not in the past thirty minutes, though?"

No. Probably not in the past thirty minutes. So we were both alibied.

"I should call it in," I said, looking around vaguely for my phone

"I'll do it," Darcy said, reaching in her pocket. "You said Rafe's on his way to Laurel Hill with Chief Grimaldi, so it won't do you any good to call either of them. They have other things to worry about."

They did. And yes, that had been my intention, to call my husband or Grimaldi directly. When you have a straight line to the top, why not use it?

"I'll call Patrick," Darcy said, but before she could suit action to words, a voice behind us asked, "What's going on here?"

It didn't, as you might suspect, belong to Charlotte, but it was familiar nonetheless. I pasted a smile on my face and turned, not sure whether this was going to turn out to be good or bad. "Officer Enoch. What are you doing here?"

"Saw the door standing open," Enoch said. "Thought I'd make sure everything was OK."

He glanced at Darcy, and then beyond us to the body. His shoulders stiffened and his eyes turned cop-flat. "What happened?"

"We just got here," I said. "We opened the front door, felt a draft, and followed it back here. He must have broken the window, reached through and unlocked the door, and gotten in that way."

Enoch glanced at the back door and then returned his attention to the body. "Did either of you touch him?"

We both shook our heads. "We haven't been any closer to him than we are right now." Which was a good ten feet away. It was a big room.

Enoch walked over the body. He didn't touch it, though. There was no point. I could see from where I was standing that life was extinct. Steve Morris wasn't breathing.

Enoch squatted next to him for an up-close look. "Do you recognize the murder weapon?" he asked after a moment.

I looked at it again, sticking out of the center of a brownish red stain on Steve Morris's blue shirt. "Yes." My voice sounded like it came from far away. "It's one of ours. The last time I saw it, Charlotte was using it to unscrew the ceiling fan."

A couple of days ago now. I couldn't rightly remember where it had spent the time since, but it was a certainty it had stayed in the house. Neither of us would have had a reason to take it home.

Enoch glanced up at the hole in the ceiling where the (really ugly) ceiling fan had been, and back at me. "Charlotte is your friend with the brown hair?"

I nodded.

"Where's Charlotte this morning?"

"She hasn't gotten here yet," I said. My voice still sounded weird, at least in my ears.

"Did she call to say she'd be late?"

No. But… "We didn't plan to meet at a certain time."

Next to me, Darcy shifted her weight, and I glanced at her. She looked back at me, and I remembered that, yes, we had indeed arranged to meet at a certain time. "Around nine?" I'd said, and Darcy had nodded.

And then the reason for Enoch's line of questioning penetrated, and I turned my attention back to him. "You can't be serious! Charlotte wouldn't have done this!"

Enoch just looked at me, and I added, "She lives thirty minutes away, in Sweetwater, with her parents and children. She had better things to do last night than to hang around here. We finished work around four yesterday, and went home."

Or at least she'd gone home. I hadn't. Not until later.

But there was no point in telling Enoch that. The whole right of redemption situation would only make us—and Charlotte—look more suspicious.

"We left at the same time," I said. "I saw her get into her car and drive away."

Enoch didn't say anything to that.

"We were just about to call 911," Darcy added, "when you showed up. Would you like us to do that now, or will you take care of it?"

"I'll take care of it." Enoch looked her up and down. "Haven't I seen you before?"

"I'm dating Patrick Nolan," Darcy said. "Lupe Vasquez's partner."

"And what's your connection to—" He gestured; it took in the house, the dead body, and me, "all this?"

"I put up the money for the house," Darcy said steadily. "Savannah's my sister."

Enoch looked at me, and back at Darcy. "Don't you mean sister-in-law?"

I shook my head. "She's Rafe's second cousin once or twice removed," which explained the resemblance, "but my sister."

Enoch thought about it for a second, and then shrugged, like it didn't matter. And for his purposes, it didn't. "I have to call this in." He reached for the phone in the holster on his belt, but before he could pull it, there was a sound in the front of the house, followed by rapid footsteps coming down the hallway. Instead of the phone, Enoch smoothly pulled his gun from the holster and, putting himself between Darcy and me and whoever was coming, moved into firing stance, legs planted and gun trained on the doorway.

Eight

Charlotte stopped in the doorway with a startled squeak, her lips forming into an O and her eyes widening. Enoch's finger twitched on the trigger, and I took a step forward before I made myself stop.

"I think it's safe, Officer. You can put the gun away."

He shot me a look like he didn't like me telling him what to do, but I guess he saw the absurdity in keeping a pistol trained on a twenty-eight-year-old mother of two who looked about as threatening as June Cleaver, because he lowered the weapon.

Charlotte looked beyond him to me and Darcy. "Savannah! What's going on?"

And then she saw the dead body, and her eyes bugged out and her cheeks turned pale. "Oh, my God. Is that—?"

"Dead body," I said, before she could speak Steve Morris's name and let on that we knew who he was. Enoch hadn't asked that question yet, and if he did, of course I'd answer truthfully. But until then, it didn't seem like a good idea to volunteer the information that Morris was trying to take our house away. Enoch might get ideas about motives for murder. "We should get out of here. The longer we stay here, the more DNA we're dropping on the crime scene."

Enoch nodded, holstering the gun. "Yes. Out. You can wait

in your cars while I call this in."

No problem. "Come on." I nudged Charlotte out the door ahead of me, while Darcy brought up the rear. We scooped up the baby seat with Carrie on the way past, and headed out. The last thing I saw was Enoch pulling out his phone before we passed out of sight.

We ended up in the Volvo. Charlotte started to ask questions as soon as we'd left the den, but I shushed her until we were outside. There, I snapped Carrie's seat back into the base while Darcy crawled in next to her and Charlotte opened the passenger door. Since only the driver's seat was available, I made myself comfortable there. It was my car, so maybe it made sense.

Charlotte still looked a little pale. "Was that who I think it was?"

"The guy from yesterday," I said. "Steve Morris."

"And he's dead?"

"I didn't touch him, but he looked dead." I met Darcy's eyes in the mirror. "I'd be very surprised if he turns out to be alive."

"Where did the cop come from?"

"He lives down the street," I said. "He showed up when Rafe and I were here last Friday night, too. And pointed his gun at me. Pearl went ballistic, and Rafe wasn't too happy, either."

I turned to Darcy. "You mentioned Lupe Vasquez. Something going on?"

"Who's Lupe Vasquez?" Charlotte shot in.

I turned to her. "She's Nolan's partner. Nolan is Darcy's boyfriend."

"I asked them about Enoch," Darcy said. "After you mentioned what happened when you and Rafe were here. They both said they knew who he was. Lupe said he's asked her out a couple of times."

"They've gone out?"

She shook her head. "She said he isn't her type."

"What's her type?" I mean, on the surface of it, she could do worse than Enoch. He was decent-looking, gainfully employed, and he owned a home. All the things Mother had taught me to look for in a man.

"Not a cop," Darcy said with a grin.

"Ah." Yes, when you're in that line of work, it's probably nice to go home to someone who isn't steeped in the same kind of world.

"How did he get in there?" Charlotte asked.

We were back to Morris again, I assumed, since Enoch had found the door open and walked in. Both last Friday night and this morning.

"One of the panes in the fifteen-light door was broken. I guess he waited until dark, snuck around the back of the house, busted the window, reached through and unlocked the door, and came inside."

"And someone stabbed him," Charlotte said with a shudder.

I nodded. "With one of our screwdrivers. The one you used on the ceiling fan a few days ago."

We sat in silence a moment. In the backseat, Carrie gurgled.

"You didn't come back here after we left yesterday," I asked Charlotte, "did you?"

She shook her head.

"Can you prove it?"

A flush of red rose in her cheeks, the first sign of color I'd seen in her face since Enoch pointed his gun at her. "Are you insinuating that I might have killed him?"

"Of course not," I said. "Although someone else might. Because someone did. Someone who was in our house last night along with Steve Morris. That—" I nodded to the house, and the crime scene inside, "wasn't an accident. Someone picked up that screwdriver and stabbed him with it deliberately."

I waited a second to let that sink in before I added, "I was home with Rafe last night. Darcy was with Nolan. They both work for the police department, so we both have solid alibis."

"It sounds like you're saying you think I killed him," Charlotte said steadily.

"I'm not." I refrained from rolling my eyes, but it took effort. "I know you wouldn't kill anyone. But the murder weapon—"

"The screwdriver," Charlotte said.

I nodded. "It probably has your fingerprints all over it. You used it a couple of days ago. Between that and the fact that he was threatening to take our house back, you had means and motive. If you can't prove that you were somewhere else when he was murdered, someone could make a good case that you killed him."

There was a moment's silence. "I didn't," Charlotte said.

"Of course you didn't," I answered, while Darcy added, "No one thinks you did."

"*He* might think so." Charlotte directed a scowl at the house, and at Enoch, behind the wall.

I nodded. "He might." In fact, he had intimated as much. "Although it won't be his case. Enoch's an officer. They don't investigate murders. The police department will send out a detective." And not Rafe, who had his hands full in Laurel Hill. "That's why it would be good if you could prove that you were somewhere else when it happened."

"I'll talk to my parents," Charlotte said, and in the rearview mirror, I saw Darcy's brows wing up.

I looked away from her and to Charlotte. "When you say

you'll talk to your parents... are you saying that you weren't home last night?"

Because if she had been, what would be the point of talking to her parents? If she'd been there, naturally they'd say that she'd been there.

"I was home most of last night," Charlotte said.

"When were you not home?"

She squirmed. "I put the kids to bed and went for a drive."

There was a beat of silence.

"A drive?" I said.

Charlotte nodded, her cheeks pink and her lips pressed together.

"Tell me you didn't drive here."

She didn't, and I added, "You didn't drive here, right?"

"I drove past here," Charlotte said.

"Why would you...?!" I stopped myself and lifted a hand. "Never mind."

"I was upset," Charlotte said, "OK? This isn't a big deal to you." Her glance over her shoulder took in Darcy. "You've got money, and husbands, or boyfriends. You're all set. I don't have either. My husband cheated on me and won't pay alimony, and the kids and I have to eat. I need to figure my life out. I thought renovating this house was going to take care of that. But then that... that *man* showed up, and said he was going to take the house away...!"

I nodded sympathetically while I thought that, at this point anyway, chances were that we didn't have to worry about that anymore. Now that Steve Morris was dead, and probably before he'd had time to take steps to invoke his statutory right of redemption, chances were the house would remain ours.

Although this didn't seem like an opportune time to mention that. Charlotte might appreciate hearing it, but with Morris lying dead in the den, it seemed a bit tactless.

"Did you happen to notice anything when you drove by last night?" Darcy wanted to know. "A car? Anyone breaking in? Someone walking down the street?"

She shook her head. "Everything looked normal. Lights on on the porches. TVs on. The old lady was walking the little dog. I didn't see anyone else."

"What time was it?" Probably too early for B&E. If Morris was going to break into our house—even if he might have thought of it as his own house—he probably would have waited until most people were in bed.

Or at least that's what I would have done, had it been me.

"Ten?" Charlotte said, and made it a question. "Ten-thirty?"

So the small dog had probably been out for a tinkle before bed.

"Did the lady with the dog see you?"

"Probably," Charlotte said. "I mean, she was right there." She pointed up and across the street.

"Good."

She squinted at me. "What's good about it?"

"If she saw you, she can tell the police that you just drove by. You didn't stop or didn't leave you car. If you didn't leave your car, you couldn't have killed Morris."

Charlotte nodded, sinking her teeth into her bottom lip and looking pensive.

We seemed to be at the end of this particular subject, unless we wanted to go back to the beginning and hash it out again. And I didn't see the need.

"So what's Nolan up to today?" I asked Darcy, to have something else to talk about while we waited.

She shrugged. "Just the usual. He and Lupe are patrolling."

"What about Rafe?" Charlotte asked.

"He's down in Lawrence County, at Laurel Hill Wildlife Area, with Tamara Grimaldi and Bob Satterfield and the sheriffs of Lawrence, Lewis, and Giles."

Charlotte arched her brows, and I added, "Rumor has it there's a neo-Nazi group meeting down there on the weekends. They're trying to figure out if it's true, and who those people are."

Charlotte stared at me. "Are you sure your husband should be part of that?"

Because he was the kind of person those kinds of people targeted? "When the police come to arrest them, I don't think they're going to care about the skin color of the cop holding the handcuffs. Besides, Sheriff Jackson in Giles County is black, too."

More black than Rafe, in fact, since Rafe's mother had been as blond and blue-eyed as I am.

"Still," Charlotte said. "Aren't you worried?"

Of course I was worried. I was always worried. But I'd been more worried when he'd gone undercover as Ry'mone the gun dealer, with saggy pants and dreadlocks and a gold front tooth, and put himself in the middle of a brewing gang war. Not to mention when he'd dressed up as Jorge Pena, international hit man—the same hit man who had been hired to kill him—and walked into the middle of Hector Gonzales's South American Theft Gang.

And if he'd survived those, he'd survive this.

"He'll be fine," I said. "They're just looking around. They did it last weekend, too. Nobody was there then. If somebody's there now, they'll keep them under surveillance and probably follow some of them home. If not, they'll go back next weekend."

Charlotte nodded.

"Anyway, he was wearing soft clothes—not that he ever wears anything but soft clothes, really—so it isn't likely that anyone's going to look at him and think, 'there's a cop.' He doesn't look like law enforcement."

More like the other type of person who frequents a police station.

Darcy hid a smile, and I smiled back in the mirror. "You know it's true. He's getting a little older, but other than that, he still slides right in with the gang bangers and drug dealers and thieves."

"I'm not arguing," Darcy said. "Although for the record, he looks more like a TV criminal than a real one. Most real criminals are ugly. He's not."

No, he wasn't. But he still carried that edge of danger with him. That sense that if you did something he didn't like, he had the capacity to hurt you.

Not that he'd ever hurt me, or Darcy or Charlotte, or anyone else who didn't deserve it. But the capacity was there, and palpable.

Outside on the street, an unmarked sedan pulled past us, executed a neat turn, and parked in front of the house on the other side of the street. A man got out, and I groaned.

"What?" Charlotte said, while behind us, Darcy smirked.

"That's Detective Jarvis. It figures he'd be the one to get this case."

Charlotte looked from him—early forties, slick, dark hair, trench coat; the stereotype of the TV detective—to me. "Don't you like him?"

"I don't dislike him," I said. And amended it to, "I used to dislike him. He's the one who had Beulah Odom exhumed last fall."

Charlotte's eyebrows rose, and I continued, "I guess that's probably unfair. Mrs. Otis Odom, Beulah's sister-in-law, wouldn't accept that Beulah had died from a heart attack, so she talked Chief Carter into ordering an exhumation. Jarvis just got the job of standing next to the digger."

"Beulah owned the restaurant on the Columbia Highway?"

I nodded. "Now Yvonne McCoy owns it, which was part of what upset the Otis Odoms, and the reason why Mrs. Otis Odom wanted Beulah exhumed. She was trying to prove that Yvonne killed Beulah."

"And did she?" Charlotte looked fascinated. Meanwhile, Jarvis crossed in front of the Volvo, without realizing that we were here, and walked across the lawn and into the house.

I shook my head. "Of course not. It's possible someone did, but it wasn't Yvonne. The second autopsy was inconclusive." Just as the first one had been.

After a second, I added, "I personally think that if anyone did it, the Otis Odoms probably did. I don't think they realized that Beulah had written a will leaving the restaurant to Yvonne. But I don't know if anyone will ever prove it. Or if there's anything to prove. It might just have been a heart attack."

Charlotte nodded. "So Detective Jarvis…"

"Couldn't arrest Yvonne. He doesn't like her much, though. A few weeks ago, he and Rafe cooperated on a case, or two cases that turned out to be related, and we met him at Beulah's Meat'n Three to talk about things. Jarvis and Yvonne took one look at each other and bristled. Do you remember Yvonne?"

Charlotte nodded. "Slutty redhead with big boobs and a thing for Dix."

Which would naturally bother Charlotte, who had been dating my brother in high school. That was a long time ago, though.

"She slept with Rafe once," I said. "As far as I know, she never slept with Dix. And she's not a slut. Just a bit less worried about the proprieties than some of us."

Some of us who, frankly, had been a little too worried about the proprieties. Speaking mostly about myself here, although Charlotte hadn't been a whole lot better.

"If you say so," Charlotte said.

"I do say so. I like Yvonne. Anyway, she and Jarvis don't get along. But since she's not involved in this, that shouldn't matter for our purposes."

I glanced at the house, where Jarvis had disappeared.

"Is he good at his job?" Darcy asked, and I moved my attention from the front door to the rearview mirror to meet her eyes.

"Hard to say. He solves cases and makes arrests. Hopefully he arrests the right people. Although he's obviously a little hung up on Yvonne..."

"Do you think he'll look past Charlotte and try to figure out if someone else killed Morris?" Darcy asked, putting it all on the table with cheerful efficiency.

Charlotte gasped and lost some color. I shrugged. "I hope so. He didn't seem unreasonable when I spoke to him about that other case. We'll just have to hope for the best. And if he doesn't look like he's going to investigate well enough, we can always do some investigating of our own."

Neither of them looked particularly pleased about that idea.

"Hey," I said, "it beats going to trial for a crime you didn't commit."

Up at the house, the door opened again, and Jarvis came out, followed by Enoch. They looked around for a second, and then Enoch indicated the Volvo. Jarvis scowled at it—at us—before he stepped off the porch and stomped across the grass.

"Here we go," Darcy said.

Nine

I opened my car door and gave Jarvis my best smile. "Good morning, Detective."

He grunted. "What are you doing here, Mrs. Collier?"

"It's my sister's house." I indicated Darcy, who had followed my example and gotten out of the car. "Do you know Darcy? She's dating Patrick Nolan."

"I know Patrick," Jarvis said, with a nod at Darcy. "Pleasure."

He didn't sound like he meant it, but I guess he found himself in a tough position, and didn't really appreciate it. Here I was: Rafe's wife and Chief Grimaldi's good friend. And there Darcy was: my sister, Rafe's sister-in-law, and Patrick Nolan's girlfriend. Jarvis couldn't really treat either of us like the suspects he probably felt like we were, since our friends and significant others would have something to say about it.

"And this is our friend Charlotte," I said, as Charlotte belatedly—and reluctantly—opened the passenger door and swung her legs out. "Darcy bought the house, and Charlotte and I have been working on renovating it."

Jarvis glanced at Charlotte, nodded, and turned his attention back to me. "Tell me about this morning."

"There's not much to tell," I said. "I got here about forty-five minutes ago. Darcy was waiting outside. She doesn't have a key."

Jarvis nodded. His face didn't change, but I could tell he was thinking. Maybe about the fact that the back door had been open, or at least accessible. Or maybe just about the fact that Morris hadn't had a key, either.

"We changed the locks on Tuesday. I should have made sure Darcy got one of the new keys, but I didn't. So she was waiting on the sidewalk when I pulled up."

Jarvis nodded.

"We went inside. And felt a draft—from that broken pane of glass in the den—so we walked through until we found... him."

"Did you know him?" Jarvis wanted to know.

I shook my head. "No."

Charlotte twitched and gave me a surprised look over her shoulder, which totally made me look like I was lying.

"He showed up here yesterday afternoon," I told Jarvis, "just before we were done for the day. Around four. Knocked on the door and waited for me to open it. Said his name was Steve Morris and that this used to be his house."

Jarvis nodded.

"I have no idea whether he was telling the truth. No reason to think he wasn't, I guess—" Except for that half-formed theory that he might have been working for the other bidder at the auction, "but it was the first time in my life I'd seen him, so he could have been anybody."

I glanced at the house, where Enoch was still waiting on the stoop. "Did he have ID on him?"

"Yes," Jarvis said.

"And is he actually Steven Morris?"

Enoch nodded, but Jarvis—who couldn't see him—said, "I'm the one asking the questions here, Mrs. Collier."

I refrained from rolling my eyes. "What else do you want to know, Detective?"

"Did either of you see Mr. Morris again?" He looked from one to the other of us, and seemed unaware that he had now confirmed the victim's identification.

"Between yesterday at four and this morning?" I shook my head. "No. I left and went home. Stopped off at the Martin and McCall office on my way, to talk to Darcy, and then picked up my daughter from Sheriff Satterfield's house—you know that my mother's living with the sheriff, don't you?—and took her home. Rafe got there a little after seven, and we spent the rest of the night together."

The name dropping was almost indecently heavy, and Jarvis must have noticed, because he grimaced.

"I stayed at work until five," Darcy said, without being asked. "I went to my mother's house and had dinner with her and her aunt. Then I went home, and Patrick met me there after the SWAT practice."

"I guess you didn't go to Laurel Hill with the others this morning," I said, and Jarvis gave me a flat look.

"Someone has to stay and deal with the things that happen here, Mrs. Collier."

Like this. He didn't say it, but it was implied. It was also implied, somewhat, that my husband and Tamara Grimaldi had no business gallivanting off to Lawrence County when there were crimes happening here in Columbia.

"Of course," I said. "And we're happy to have you."

He didn't snort, but I got the feeling he wanted to. "What about you?" He turned to Charlotte. "Did you see Mr. Morris after you left the house yesterday afternoon?"

Charlotte shook her head. Her voice was almost inaudible, and she had guilt written all over her face and posture. "I went home. I'm staying with my parents in Sweetwater. My husband…"

She swallowed.

Jarvis waited, and eventually Charlotte pulled it together. "The kids and I left my husband over Christmas. I have two. A boy and a girl. We've been staying with my parents since. My mother was watching the kids while I was here, working. We had dinner together, and then I put the kids to bed…"

She trailed off. Jarvis nodded. "And then?"

It was obvious that there was more. Instead of ending the statement with a solid period—she'd put the kids to bed; the end—Charlotte had left the sentence sort of hanging. It was not surprising at all that Jarvis probed further.

"I went for a drive," Charlotte said reluctantly.

"A drive." Jarvis's tone was flat, and said nothing at all. And that in and of itself said a lot. "Did you talk to anyone during this drive? Stop for gas or a drink somewhere?"

Charlotte shook her head, her eyes wide.

"Do you know when he was killed?" I asked, just as much to take Jarvis's attention off Charlotte as because I'd like to hear the answer.

Jarvis shook his head. "That'll be up to the medical examiner. Best I can determine, between four o'clock yesterday and nine this morning."

Between the time I'd seen him drive away yesterday, and when we'd found him on the floor this morning, in other words.

Or maybe it was between when he showed up here, and when Enoch had seen the dead body. Maybe Jarvis wasn't ruling out the possibility that Morris never left yesterday, and we were all lying.

"He really did leave last night," I said. "If you check with the neighbors, someone might have seen him drive away. But if we'd decided to kill him—and we had no reason to—we wouldn't have left him on the floor in the den until this morning."

Jarvis didn't sound surprised. "What would you have done? Come back in the middle of the night to get rid of him?"

"Of course."

"You don't think it might have been smarter to leave him here and make it look like he'd broken in overnight and been murdered by someone else?"

I suppose it might have been smarter. But to be honest, if we'd killed him, I'm not sure we'd have thought of it.

"We didn't do anything to him, Detective," I said firmly. "He was here. I watched him drive away. We locked the door, we left, and we didn't see him again until this morning."

"And he was dead," Darcy added, since I hadn't made that clear.

Jarvis nodded, but not in a way like he believed us. "I know how to get in touch with the two of you." He looked from me to Darcy. "You—" He turned his attention to Charlotte, "—I'll need contact information for, in case I need to talk to you again."

Charlotte gulped, but managed to rattle off the Albertsons' address and her cell phone number. Jarvis took them down in his little notebook.

"You're free to go," he told us. "I'll be in touch if there are any more questions."

And there surely would be, because I didn't think he was finished with us. We were the obvious suspects, and Charlotte, at least, didn't have an alibi. No, this wouldn't be the first time we spoke to Jarvis, singly or together.

"There are a couple of spare keys on the kitchen counter," I said, "if you'd like to lock up when you're done. And if you wouldn't mind taping something in front of that broken windowpane, too, when you're finished processing the scene.

We probably shouldn't leave it open for anyone else to walk in."

Jarvis sighed. "I'll take care of it."

"We appreciate it. We'll get out of your way now." And make room for the crime scene van and the vehicle from the morgue.

Jarvis nodded. "I'll be in touch."

He headed back to the house. Enoch fell in behind him, respectfully.

We waited until they'd both disappeared inside and shut the door behind them before I glanced at Darcy. "Your house?"

She lives in Columbia, much closer than Charlotte or I, and I wasn't quite ready to go our separate ways yet.

She nodded, and we separated into our respective cars. Charlotte and I tailed Darcy over to her small rental on the other side of town.

"I think that went fairly well," I said fifteen minutes later, when we were sitting in Darcy's breakfast nook with cups of coffee in front of us and Carrie cooing in the car seat on the bench next to me. "Or as good as we can expect, anyway. He didn't arrest anyone."

"He wanted to," Charlotte said darkly.

I shook my head. "I don't think so. Not yet. He'll need more evidence before he can arrest anyone. Right now he doesn't know enough."

"He knows that Morris is dead," Charlotte said. "On our floor with our screwdriver, that has my fingerprints all over it. What more does he need to know?"

"Motive?" Darcy suggested.

"We had motive. He was taking the house."

"Jarvis doesn't know that," I said.

"Are you sure?" Darcy asked. "He didn't ask us what Morris wanted when he showed up yesterday afternoon. Why do you think he didn't?"

Good question. It would have been logical for Jarvis to wonder about that. But—

"It can't be because he already knows. How would he?" We hadn't told him, and Morris wasn't talking.

"Maybe he found out some other way," Charlotte said.

"How?"

"I don't know. Maybe Enoch knew? If Morris used to live in our house, maybe he and Enoch knew each other. Maybe Morris stopped by Enoch's house last night after he left ours, and he told Enoch what he was doing there. And this morning Enoch told Jarvis."

Huh. "But if Jarvis knew that Morris wanted to take his house back, don't you think he would have mentioned it?"

"Maybe he was waiting to see if we mentioned it," Darcy said. "And since we didn't, he knows we're trying to hide something."

Maybe.

"This whole thing doesn't make any sense to me," I said. "I know what Morris said, but the house sat empty for three years before the city foreclosed on it. If he wanted to keep it, he could have come back to it at any time during those three years. Why wait until it sold?"

"Maybe there was something in the house that he wanted," Charlotte suggested. "Maybe he'd hidden something there, and for as long as he owned the house, it was safe, even if he didn't live here. But once the city foreclosed and we got the house, he was afraid that whatever it was would be discovered. So he needed to get the house back."

It's probably telling that my first thought was dead bodies buried in the basement. Not that there was a basement. Just a small crawlspace.

"We've been tearing things out all week. Don't you think

we would have found whatever it was by now?"

"Depends on what it was," Charlotte said.

"What do you think it might be?"

She shrugged. "Could be anything. Maybe he was a bank robber. Or a jewel thief. Maybe there's a fortune in gems hidden in the house."

"I don't think he'd leave anything like that sitting around if he wasn't here," Darcy said. "Why wouldn't he take it with him?"

No idea. "Maybe we should look into bank robberies and jewel thefts in this area three to four years ago."

"I can ask Patrick," Darcy said. "He was on the police force back then."

"Did you tell him about Morris last night?"

She shook her head, her cheeks turning pink. "I was going to, but then he got here and we got busy with other things."

I nodded, even as I hid a smile. "I was going to tell Rafe, too. But then he walked in wearing that SWAT outfit, and the thought blew right out of my head." Until later, but by then I'd decided to keep my mouth shut, since his case involving the neo-Nazis was more important than my little problem.

Of course, now my little problem had turned into a much bigger problem, and I would have to tell him—if Jarvis hadn't already done it for me—but if he did, at least Rafe could tell him, in all honesty, that I hadn't made a big deal out of Steve Morris showing up.

Charlotte looked from one to the other of us. "SWAT?"

"The Special Weapons and Tactics team at the Columbia PD. Rafe and Darcy's boyfriend are both on it."

"I know what a SWAT team is," Charlotte said irritably. ""This is Maury County. What do we need a SWAT team for?"

"At the moment, I'm thinking the neo-Nazis. Although you never know when a SWAT team might come in handy."

Charlotte rolled her eyes.

"They're nice to look at," Darcy said mildly, "if nothing else."

Yes, they were.

"Is there anything we can do," Darcy wanted to know, "other than wait and see what conclusions Detective Jarvis draws?"

"We could do a little investigating of our own. Or at least we could try to shore up Charlotte's alibi, in case she needs it." I turned to her. "Are you sure you didn't stop anywhere last night? Did anyone see you who could prove that you weren't on Fulton Street when the murder went down?"

Charlotte shook her head. "But I wasn't on Fulton Street when the murder went down."

"How do you know?" My eyes narrowed. "You didn't go inside, did you?"

"Of course not," Charlotte said, with a guilty little wriggle.

I stared at her. "Oh, my God. You went inside the house and you didn't tell us?"

"It was just for a minute," Charlotte said.

I threw my hands up and turned to Darcy, who said calmly, "Anything else you haven't shared?"

Charlotte shook her head.

I took a deep breath—in through the nose, out through the mouth—and forced myself to calm down. "Why did you go inside?"

"I'd lost an earring," Charlotte said. "I wanted to see if it was there."

An earring? Had she even been wearing earrings yesterday?

I thought back, but couldn't rightly remember. I'd been leaving mine off this past week, along with every other piece of jewelry I customarily wear. All except my—plain, unadorned—

wedding band. There's no point in trying to look fancy when you're scraping popcorn off the ceiling and tearing out drywall. It wasn't like we had cameras following us around, after all.

"What did it look like?" I asked, at the same time as Darcy said, "Did you find it?"

Charlotte shook her head to Darcy and told me, "Diamond studs. Richard bought them for me last year."

And she was still wearing them? I would have pawned those the first chance I got. Especially given how hard up for cash she was, and how Richard wasn't giving her any.

"I'm sorry," Darcy said.

"Did you look everywhere?" I added. Partly because I hated the idea that she'd lost a valuable earring—valuable because it had the potential to put food on the table for a while, not valuable because it came from Doctor Dick—and partly because I wanted to hear whether she'd truly been through the whole house. "Even the den?"

We hadn't done any work in the den on Friday, but Charlotte nodded.

"I assume Steve Morris wasn't lying dead on the floor when you were there?"

"No," Charlotte said.

I gave her a narrow look. "You aren't lying to us, right?"

She shook her head.

"Because you sound like you're lying."

"I'm not lying," Charlotte said. "He wasn't dead on the floor when I was there."

"Was he dead somewhere else?"

"Of course not!" Charlotte said.

"And he didn't show up while you were there?"

"No," Charlotte said.

I leaned back, just as my phone rang, and I reached for my bag instead. "Well, at least we know that the murder happened after… when did you say you were there? Ten?"

I fished the phone out of my bag and put up a finger to stall the conversation. I already knew who was calling, so there was no need to look at the display. "Hi," I said brightly. "I didn't expect to hear from you so soon."

"Jarvis?" Darcy mouthed. Charlotte sat up a little straighter.

I shook my head, as my husband's voice said, with no further introduction, "What the hell, Savannah?"

Ten

"It wasn't my fault," I said.

"Glad to hear it."

I made a face, but there wasn't much I could say to that, so I didn't try.

"As it happens," Rafe continued, "I ain't upset that you found a dead body. I ain't even surprised. Not like it's the first."

No, it wasn't. I've found more than my fair share. Although it was perhaps a little disconcerting that he'd gotten so used to it that it wasn't even a surprise anymore.

"I didn't particularly appreciate hearing about it from Paul Jarvis, though," he added. "Some reason you didn't call me?"

"You're in Lawrence County," I said. "Dealing with more important things."

"Not sure I'd call'em more important, darlin'." So at least I'd gone from Savannah—something he usually only calls me on serious occasions—to the more casual *darlin'*.

He continued, "Somebody was stabbed to death in a house you work in every day. A house where you take our baby to work with you. That's a pretty big deal."

When he put it like that, I guess it was.

"I don't think it had anything to do with us," I said.

"How'd you figure that?"

"We didn't know the guy. He just knocked on the door and…"

"Yeah?" Rafe said when I didn't continue. "Go on. He just knocked on the door and… what?"

I sighed. "That was yesterday afternoon. Hours before he ended up dead."

He didn't answer, but the silence spoke volumes.

"He knocked on the door around four yesterday," I said, resigned. "Told me his name was Steve Morris and that he owned the house before us."

"And the reason you didn't tell me this last night was…?"

"I was distracted by the SWAT outfit. And we didn't know whether he was going to go ahead with—"

I bit my tongue, a second too late, and winced.

"With what?"

I might as well just tell him, because at the rate I was going, he'd have it out of me in another minute anyway. "He said he wanted the house back. That there's a statutory right of redemption period that allows him to pay us back the amount of money we paid for the house plus ten percent, and he'll get it back."

There was a beat. "That true?"

"I checked with Dix," I said. "He said yes."

"You tell Jarvis about that?" Rafe wanted to know.

"He didn't ask."

"You don't think maybe you shoulda told him anyway?"

"No," I said. "It didn't have anything to do with anything. He wasn't killed because he wanted the house back. That would mean that one of us killed him." I glanced from Darcy to Charlotte. "And we didn't."

"You sure about that?"

"Yes," I said. "Of course I'm sure. Besides, we were

together last night. You and I. You know I didn't go anywhere and kill anyone."

"And the others?"

"Darcy spent the night with Nolan," I said. "Charlotte lives with her parents and her kids."

Which was not the same as saying that Charlotte had an alibi, and Rafe has spent enough years deflecting to recognize an evasion when he hears one. "Savannah—"

"She didn't kill anyone, either," I said. "Give me a break, Rafe. You can't seriously suspect Charlotte of stabbing somebody in the heart with a screwdriver!"

He didn't answer that. "You're gonna have to tell Jarvis about this right of redemption business," he said instead. "It's only a matter of time before he finds out about it on his own, and it's gonna look really bad for all three of you if you haven't told him yourselves by then."

I could quite see that, of course. But— "How is Jarvis going to find out? Steve Morris is dead. And we don't think he had enough time to go to the county clerk's office and start the paperwork between the time he left the house and the time they closed yesterday afternoon..."

"That a chance you wanna take?"

He didn't wait for my answer. "I'm gonna tell Jarvis. When he asks you, you better admit to everything."

"Of course I will," I said. "When you say everything..."

I could practically hear his eyes roll. "I mean everything you told me. That he came and said he was thinking about taking the house back. That you talked to your brother, the lawyer, and he told you Morris could do that if he wanted, and there was nothing you could do about it. And that you had no reason to kill him, 'cause you'll get your money back plus ten percent."

"Right." I breathed out. "Good point."

"That's what you told me, ain't it?"

"Yes," I said. "That's what I told you."

"And it's true, right?"

"Yes," I said. "It's true. You can check with Dix."

Rafe made a noise but didn't actually ask me whether Dix would confirm it if he did. "You OK?" he asked instead.

I nodded. "We're all fine. It was a bit of a shock, but compared to, say, Brenda—" The first dead body I'd found, with her throat cut from ear to ear, "there was very little blood. He just had a screwdriver sticking out of his chest—"

Charlotte made a gurgling noise and turned pale. I lowered my voice a degree and continued, "But there wasn't much blood."

"If whoever stabbed him left the screwdriver in the body," Rafe said calmly, "that makes sense. The bleeding would start if the screwdriver was removed."

Good to know. "Anyway. As crime scenes go, it was pretty clean. No signs of a fight; not that it would be easy to tell in that location. He was stabbed in the chest, so he must have known—or at least trusted—whoever stabbed him."

"Or thought it was nothing to worry about," Rafe said, which I guessed brought the suspicion back on us again. Morris would probably not have believed either of us—Darcy, Charlotte, or me—capable of murder.

"What's going on where you are?" I asked, to turn the conversation away from that possibility and onto something different.

"Not much. Not till Jarvis called, anyway. We're just riding around the area on the back of a golf cart. Keeping an eye out."

"You're not on horseback?"

I'd never seen Rafe on horseback. I tried to picture it, and got it to look pretty all right in my head, but there was no denying he looked much better astride the big black Harley-

Davidson he prefers.

"No, darlin'." His voice was dry.

"There are riding trails, right?"

"There are trails. We're driving 'em."

"But you're not seeing any neo-Nazis?"

"Not so far," Rafe said. "The day's young. You want I should come home?"

For my sake? "Not at all. We've got this under control. It's nothing to worry about. You stay where you are and keep looking for bad guys."

He sounded amused. "Sure thing, darlin'. The baby all right?"

I glanced at her. "The baby's fine. Probably getting hungry, though." And maybe wet. "I should go so I can feed her."

"Talk to you later, darlin'. Tammy says hi." He disconnected before I could respond in kind. I dropped the phone back in my purse.

"Well?" Darcy said.

"Jarvis must have called him. Or maybe he called Grimaldi. She and Rafe are together down there. Either way, Rafe found out what happened and wanted to make sure we were OK."

"Was he upset?" The curve of Darcy's mouth gave me the idea that she thought it might be funny if he was, although Charlotte looked worried.

I shook my head. "Not aside from the fact that he thought I should have called him myself, instead of letting Jarvis break the news."

"Can't blame him for that," Darcy said.

I shook my head. "Speaking of… did you talk to Nolan?" He'd probably prefer to be told in person, too, rather than hearing the news from Jarvis. Or through the grapevine.

"On the way over," Darcy said. "He'll be by after work."

We sat in silence a second.

"So what do we do now?" Charlotte wanted to know.

I glanced at Darcy, who looked back at me. The two of us were fine. We had alibis for last night, and I'm sure Jarvis knew that we couldn't have—wouldn't have—killed Steve Morris. I was less sure about his faith in Charlotte.

"I guess we'll wait and see what Jarvis comes up with. If it looks like he's going to be a problem, we'll do what we can to figure out who else would have had reason to want Steve Morris dead."

"How would we do that?"

I had no idea, to be honest. "I guess we have to figure out who Steve Morris was, first of all. And why he left his house sitting empty for more than three years without paying the taxes. Once we know that, maybe we'll have a better idea who would have wanted him dead." If he'd been gone because there was someone here he was trying to avoid, for instance.

"I'll ask Patrick," Darcy said. "He grew up in Columbia. He might know."

I nodded. "And once Jarvis and the crime scene crew is done on Fulton, we can go talk to some of the neighbors. If Morris lived there for several years, some of them must have known him."

We both turned to Charlotte. She said nothing.

"I'm going to take my daughter home," I said, and scooted out of the dinette. "When Jarvis gets in touch, I'll make sure he knows that we'd get Darcy's money back—" or at least most of Darcy's money back— "if Morris decided to invoke his right of redemption. Hopefully that'll take us off the suspect list. If he contacts either of you, make sure you tell him the same thing."

They both nodded.

"How about we meet for lunch tomorrow, and compare notes. Afterwards, we can go over to Fulton and knock on doors if we don't have the information we need by then. Will your mother baby-sit for an hour, Charlotte?"

"I'm sure," Charlotte said, without sounding sure of anything.

"Noon at Beulah's?"

Charlotte grimaced, and I told her, "It's convenient for Darcy." She wouldn't have to drive all the way to Sweetwater. And as an added bonus, we wouldn't have to worry about seeing Dix, Catherine and Jonathan, all the kids, and Mother and Bob Satterfield, at the usual Sunday Brunch location at the Wayside Inn.

"I'll pick you up," I added, magnanimously. "That way you can leave the van and the car seats with your mother. In case she wants to take the kids somewhere."

We agreed to that, and then we went our separate ways. Darcy back into her house after waving us off, Charlotte into the minivan for the drive to her parents' house, and me and Carrie into the Volvo for the trip back to the mansion.

Jarvis called just after lunch. "I wonder if I could bother you to come down to the station, Mrs. Collier?"

"Of course," I said. "You aren't planning to arrest me when I get there, are you?"

He didn't answer that. Not specifically. "It's just to make a formal statement, Mrs. Collier."

"Because if there's a chance I won't be coming home," I said, "I'll have to make arrangements for the baby. Rafe's still in Lawrence County, but I can leave her with my mother or sister. Other sister." Since, if he was planning to arrest me, he was probably planning to arrest Darcy, too.

"Are you going to confess to something that would cause you to be arrested?" Jarvis asked.

I sniffed. "Of course not." I planned to tell him what I hadn't told him earlier, that Steve Morris had threatened to take his house back, but beyond that, I wasn't planning to confess to a thing.

"Then feel free to bring the baby," Jarvis said.

Great. I breathed out. "I'll be there in about thirty minutes."

"I'll be waiting," Jarvis said, and hung up.

When I walked into the police station thirty minutes later, the girl behind the desk—the same girl who had been behind the desk every time I'd been here lately—gave me a smirk. "Your husband isn't here. He and Chief Grimaldi left this morning. Together. In her car."

Her name is Officer Robinson, and she doesn't like me. I'm sure she has a first name, too, and she has probably shared it with Rafe, but she hasn't with me. He has that effect on some women, and this one had taken one look at him the first time he walked through the door, a few days into the new year, and started to ignore me. After a while, the ignoring wasn't enough, and she started making snide little comments. Like this one, insinuating that Rafe and Grimaldi were off doing God knows what, while I was home with the baby, barefoot and, if not exactly pregnant, the second best thing.

Except of course they weren't doing anything they shouldn't be, and I knew it, and Officer Robinson probably knew it too, unless the Laurel Hill taskforce was a secret, and no one had informed her what was going on. If she spent her time behind this desk in the lobby, maybe she didn't need to know what was going on in the wider world.

"I'm here to see Detective Jarvis," I said, without responding in kind. Rafe came home to me every night, not Officer Robinson—and certainly not Grimaldi—so I had no need to stoop to her level. "If you'd let him know I'm here?"

I didn't wait for her to comply, just took my baby in her carrier over to the waiting area on the other side of the room.

Jarvis opened the door to the inner sanctum a minute later, and waved for me. "Mrs. Collier."

I gathered up my coat and the baby again, and followed him through the door and into the bowels of the police station.

I'd been here before, so I knew that Grimaldi's office was the big one at the end of the hall. I'd also seen Jarvis inside one of the smaller offices on the left, and that's where we ended up.

"Have a seat." He gestured to the two cloth-covered chairs in front of the desk while he walked around to the other side himself. I put Carrie's seat on the floor and made myself comfortable on a chair while Jarvis took a seat behind the desk. The swivel chair squeaked when he sat down in it, and so did the leather. "Thank you for coming in."

"I'm happy to help," I said politely. "Have you finished with the crime scene?"

Jarvis nodded. "We won't be releasing it for a few days, though. You'll have to wait until Monday or Tuesday to get back to work."

Fine by me. I wasn't looking forward to going back into the house, and I had a feeling Charlotte might flat out refuse.

"Do you know who killed him?"

"I was hoping you'd help me with that," Jarvis said.

Me? I shook my head. "I have no idea. Until Friday afternoon, I had no idea he existed. I spoke to him for two minutes, and that's it."

Jarvis didn't respond, and I added, "I don't know anything about him other than that he used to own the house and lost it to foreclosure. And that he wanted it back."

Jarvis's eyebrows twitched. "Is that what he wanted?"

"That's what he said. That he used to live there, and he wanted his house back. It doesn't make any sense. If he wanted it, why wait so long? Why not just keep up with the taxes, so he wouldn't lose the house in the first place? Two weeks earlier he could have gotten away with paying six grand in taxes instead of sixty thousand to us."

"Two weeks ago he was in jail," Jarvis said.

My jaw dropped, and I hiked it up quickly. "Jail?"

Jarvis nodded.

"Why?"

"Rape and murder," Jarvis said.

I felt myself turn pale, and it was hard to get my voice to cooperate. "He didn't look like a murderer." Or a rapist.

Not that you can always tell, I guess. But I've met a few rapists, and more than a few murderers. The rapists, to a man, had given me the creeps. The murderers, overall, seemed like normal people, and in most cases, I'd had no idea they were murderers until long after I first met them. But Steve Morris hadn't struck me as either, in the couple of minutes I'd spoken to him.

"He was arrested for the rape and murder of a young woman named Natalie Allen," Jarvis said. "Three and a half, almost four years ago now. It's public knowledge. Her body was discovered a couple blocks away. She lived down the street."

"And Steve Morris killed her?"

"He was the main suspect," Jarvis said. "Close in proximity. Knew the victim. We had a witness who said he'd argued with her. And he had a record for sexual misconduct."

I blinked. "He did?"

Jarvis nodded. "Statutory rape. He didn't have an alibi for the time of the murder, so we arrested him. He's spent the past three years plus in jail, until he was released two days ago."

"Holy shit," I said. "I mean… wow."

Jarvis didn't respond, and I added, "It doesn't sound like you need my help with figuring out who killed him, then. It's probably someone who thought he got away with murder when he was released after less than four years. Have you spoken to the victim's family?"

Jarvis opened his mouth, and I made a face. "Sorry." I couldn't expect him to indulge my inquisitiveness the way Rafe and Grimaldi did.

"Yes," Jarvis said. "They're alibied."

"By each other? Or by someone who can actually be trusted?"

Because family members providing an alibi for each other during the time when their daughter's rapist and murderer was killed, didn't strike me as iron-clad.

"It was the middle of the night," Jarvis said. "It's hard for most people to provide a solid alibi."

It was, admittedly. Unless you happen to share your bed with someone, and Natalie's parents probably did. If Natalie had brothers or sisters, they might, too. But again, those were people I would expect to lie should their spouse or significant other need to provide an alibi.

Jarvis probably wouldn't be amenable to giving me further details, so I resolved to dig up the details on the murder and on the Allens myself, later.

"What I wanted to talk to you about," Jarvis said, "is your friend."

"Charlotte? She wouldn't do anything like this."

Jarvis didn't respond to that. Or at least not directly. "You know her well?"

"My whole life," I said. "We were best friends growing up. She dated my brother Dix in high school."

"But she ended up marrying someone else."

It didn't sound like a question, but I nodded anyway. "She went to college in North Carolina, and met a guy named Richard Whitaker. A doctor." Just the kind of guy she'd been brought up to look for. The same kind of man I'd been brought up to look for, although my expectations had run more along the lines of lawyers than doctors. "They married after she graduated, and had a couple of kids. Then he knocked up one of his clients, and she left him."

"I spoke to her earlier," Jarvis said.

So he had called Charlotte into the police station before me. I wondered what, if anything, that meant. "She must have told you this herself, then."

"Not in so much detail," Jarvis said blandly. "Her husband isn't paying alimony?"

I grimaced. "He's punishing her for leaving. He's the one who cheated, but I guess he expected Charlotte to just put up and shut up. When she didn't—when she took the kids and left—I guess he decided to get her back the only way he could."

"By not paying support?"

I nodded. "He's waiting for a judge to rule on the alimony, he says. In the meantime, Charlotte and the kids are living with her parents, with no money and no job."

"Any reason she hasn't gotten a job?"

"She's tried," I said. "But it's hard. That's why we came up with this idea of flipping a property. Darcy has money. I have a real estate license. And Charlotte is willing to work. It seemed like a good idea at the time."

"Until Steve Morris showed up," Jarvis said.

Yes. Until then.

"How upset was Mrs. Whitaker last night?"

Sounded like Charlotte had filled him on what Steve Morris had threatened to do. No reason I needed to do that, then.

"Not all that much," I said. "We were both surprised, of course. And disconcerted. It came as a bit of a shock. But it wasn't like we'd lose money. He'd have to pay us back for the price of the house plus ten percent if he wanted it back."

"Had you spent the ten percent above the purchase price?"

Jarvis wanted to know.

I made a face. "More or less. "

"So there'd be no profit in it for you."

No. "But we wouldn't be losing money either." Or not much. "So it could have been worse."

"Perhaps not for your friend," Jarvis said blandly. "Your sister would get her investment back. You probably didn't care as long as that was taken care of. But your friend lost the opportunity to make some much-needed cash."

There wasn't much I could say to that—he'd nailed it—so I didn't try. "Did you talk to the neighbors?" I asked instead.

Jarvis nodded. "Mrs. Oberlin saw Mrs. Whitaker arrive when she was out walking Chester before bed. She didn't think anything of it, as she's seen Mrs. Whitaker come and go for the past week."

My heart gave a hard thud, and then another. "Did Mrs. Oberlin see Mrs…. I mean Charlotte, leave again?"

"No," Jarvis said. "Mrs. Whitaker went inside the house. Mrs. Oberlin waited for Chester to take care of business, and went inside her house. When she looked out her bedroom window while pulling the curtains, the minivan was still there."

"But she didn't see Mr. Morris?"

Jarvis shook his head. "What was your friend doing inside the house so late, Mrs. Collier?"

"She said she was looking for an earring she lost," I said.

Jarvis pursed his lips. He opened his desk drawer and pulled out a small plastic baggie. "Is this the earring?"

I leaned forward to peer at it. It was a diamond stud, or at least it looked like a diamond stud, so it matched the description of what Charlotte said she'd lost. I couldn't honestly remember whether I'd seen her wear it or not. It wasn't something I would have worn to renovate a house, but that didn't mean Charlotte wouldn't have. "I guess. Where did you find it?"

"In the den," Jarvis said. "Underneath the body."

Underneath—? "Maybe it fell off earlier in the day, and lay there for a few hours, and then Morris happened to land on top of it."

"Do you remember seeing the earring?" Jarvis asked.

"On the floor?" I shook my head. "No. But I don't know if I went into the den yesterday. We were working in the front part of the house."

"But Mrs. Whitaker went back there?"

"She must have," I said, "if her earring was there."

Jarvis didn't respond to that, just swept the baggie back into the desk drawer. "Anything else you can tell me, Mrs. Collier?"

"Just that Charlotte wouldn't kill anyone. Although I expect it'll take more than just my word to convince you of that."

He didn't say anything, and I added, "Anything else I can tell you, Detective?"

"Not at the moment," Jarvis said. "Your sister wasn't with you at the house yesterday?"

"When Morris showed up? No. But I told her about him. She spent the night with Patrick Nolan, though. He would have noticed if she went someone and killed someone, I'm sure."

"I'm sure," Jarvis said blandly and got to his feet. "Thank you for your time, Mrs. Collier."

"Thank you, Detective." I shrugged into my coat and grabbed the baby carrier. "Let me know if there's anything else I can do to help."

Jarvis told me he'd be sure to do just that, and escorted me down the hallway and into the lobby, where Officer Robinson watched me walk out. She looked gleeful. Maybe she thought Jarvis was building a case against me, and I was about to be arrested, leaving the path to Rafe clear for her. Or maybe she was just looking forward to telling him that his wife had spent several minutes locked in Detective Jarvis's office while Rafe was in Lawrence County. Given the glee with which she had told me that he had left with Grimaldi this morning, I wouldn't put it past her.

Eleven

"Did anything exciting happen?" I asked Rafe a few hours later, when he walked through the back door of the mansion in the late afternoon. "Did you see any neo-Nazis? Get to follow anyone home?"

He shook his head. "Quiet as the grave. Just like last week."

"Maybe they've figured out that you're on to them, and they've found somewhere else to congregate."

He shook his head. "Prob'ly just aren't there every weekend. Once a month or every couple months is enough. If you have weirdos in skull masks running around shooting off guns every weekend, somebody'd get wise and put a stop to it. This way, they skim under the radar longer."

Perhaps so. "I guess you'll be going back next Saturday."

"I imagine I will." He leaned in to drop a kiss on my mouth, and slanted a sideways look at the laptop. "What's going on?"

"I'm researching a murder," I said.

Rafe's eyebrows arched, both of them this time, and I added, "Steve Morris—the guy who ended up dead in our garage conversion overnight—was released from jail a few days ago. That's why he lost the house to foreclosure. He was incarcerated, and was probably saving all his money for his second trial."

"And he got out?"

I nodded. "Hung jury the first time. Acquittal the second. And then he showed up here the next day, wanting his house back."

"Who was killed?" Rafe asked, scooting up on the stool next to me and turning the laptop so he could get a look at the screen.

"A girl named Natalie Allen. She lived on Fulton Street with her family. Nineteen when she died. Rape and strangulation. The body was found a couple of blocks away."

Rafe was scanning the article I had pulled up, originally printed in the local paper. "And Morris did it?"

"That's what the police thought at the time. Jarvis said he had a record for statutory rape."

"There's a database for that. The TBI runs it." Rafe took the laptop away from me, opened up another browser, and started pecking. "Steven with a ph or a v?"

I had no idea, and said so.

"Let's just go with Morris, S." He hit enter, and we waited. Eventually Rafe shook his head. "If he was convicted of statutory rape, it wasn't in Tennessee."

"Another state, then?"

"There's a national registry," Rafe said, and pecked at the keyboard again. We waited. "Any of these guys look familiar?"

He turned the computer toward me. I scanned the row of faces, all belonging to men named Steven or Stephen, or in one case Stefan, Morris. "No."

"Then he don't have a record," Rafe said.

"What does that mean?" Jarvis made a mistake? Or had Jarvis lied?

He shrugged.

"He said the Natalie Allen case was his investigation. And that the evidence pointed to Morris. He should know, right?"

"He should," Rafe agreed. And left it there.

"I don't suppose… Is there a chance Morris was a suspect because he's black?"

"Your guess is as good as mine," Rafe said. After a second he added, "But I don't imagine it hurt."

No. It probably hadn't. Although there had to be more to it than that. Jarvis couldn't just make up a record for sexual misconduct and run with it. Whatever color the suspect was.

"I told Jarvis what you told me to tell him," I said. Might as well change the subject since there wasn't much more to say about Morris's record, or lack thereof, of previous sexual offense. "That we wouldn't have lost any money if Morris took his house back. Although Jarvis made it clear that it didn't absolve Charlotte of suspicion."

"I didn't figure it would," Rafe said and opened the fridge. He peered into it for a second and then brought out a carton of orange juice. He shook it, listening to the juice slosh around inside the cardboard. "Mind if I finish this off?"

I shook my head, and watched his throat move as he chugged the last of the juice and then took the carton to the sink to rinse it before two-pointing it into the recycling bin. When he turned, he caught me looking, and grinned. "Hold that thought, darlin'."

No problem. "I wonder if Todd would share any information from the trial? If I asked nicely? He was still in Atlanta the first time, so he wouldn't know anything about that, but he's here now, and was probably around for this trial…"

It would explain the little double take he'd given me, when I'd mentioned Fulton Street the morning Darcy and I had gone to pay for the house, and I had run into Todd on the square. He'd probably been in the middle of the trial, and thought it was quite a coincidence that we'd picked up a foreclosure on

Fulton.

Maybe Rafe and I could run over to Marley's house, and I could take a look at the two of them and determine what their relationship was like, too, just so I could reassure myself that Todd had proposed to Marley for the right reasons. That way, I could stop worrying about it.

Not that I thought it would be a good idea to mention any of that to Rafe. He's not jealous of Todd, exactly. Certainly not anymore. But he's always had a weird little hang-up where Todd is concerned.

As evidenced by the next words out of his mouth.

"You don't need Satterfield for that. Court cases are public record. If you go to the courthouse and pay a fee, they'll give you a transcript."

"Just like that?"

He nodded. "Can't do nothing about it till Monday, though."

No. I couldn't. "So how would you like to spend the rest of the day?"

He grinned and waggled his eyebrows.

We spent the next morning sleeping in and having a leisurely breakfast together, and then Rafe stayed home with Carrie so I could go meet Darcy and Charlotte for lunch at Beulah's.

"Are you sure you wouldn't like to come?" I asked as I pulled my coat on. "You know Yvonne likes to see you. And the baby."

He smiled, but didn't deny it. "You spend all your time with Carrie, darlin'. I don't. Let me take her for a couple hours and give you a break."

"If you're sure."

He said he was sure. "Your brother's invited me over to watch the game. He won't mind if I bring her. He's already brought up two girls. If I don't know what I'm doing, he will. Your brother-in-law's prob'ly gonna be there, as well, and he has a girl of his own, too. Between us, we'll figure out how to handle one baby."

"I wasn't worried about that," I said. "I assumed you'd know what to do. It just feels weird not to be taking care of her."

But he'd had none of this with David, his son. David had been almost thirteen when Rafe—when all of us—learned he existed. Rafe had missed all those years and milestones. Their relationship was still more big brother/little brother than father and son, although at least they had a relationship now. And anyway, David already had a father in the man who'd brought him up. He didn't need anyone trying to take Sam's place. But if Rafe wanted to spend time with Carrie, on his own and away from me, who was I to complain? He had every right, and every reason.

So I left Rafe the Volvo with the car seat, and called Charlotte to ask if she'd mind picking me up on her way north out of Sweetwater instead of the other way around, and that was that. I kept myself from going over and over the same instructions for how to deal with Carrie if she got hungry, if she got wet, if she fell asleep, if she didn't—and just kissed my husband goodbye. "Have fun. Enjoy the game. Don't drink too many beers."

"Not with the baby in the car," Rafe said and nudged me out the door when the minivan made the turn into the driveway and crunched its way up toward the front doors. "You have fun, too, darlin'. Don't do nothing I wouldn't do."

"At Beulah's? It's not exactly somewhere you go to dance on the tables."

He shook his head. "Although I'd pay to see that."

"When I come home, maybe I'll show you." I waited for

him to shut the door, and then I descended the steps and reached for the car door as the minivan pulled to a stop beside me.

"Good morning."

Charlotte made a sound that most of all sounded like a grunt. I gave her a closer inspection. "You don't look so good. If you don't mind my saying so."

She gave me a look out of bloodshot eyes. The bags beneath could have held groceries for a family for a week. "I didn't sleep well."

No kidding. "Something on your mind?"

I fastened my seatbelt as we rolled back down the driveway toward the road again.

Charlotte rolled her eyes. "Nothing at all. How could you possibly think that?"

I opened my mouth, but she went on before I could say anything, her voice so brittle I half expected it to crack. "Richard called, to ask me whether I'd reconsidered coming home. I said no, and had he reconsidered allowing me access to the bank accounts so I could feed his children. He told me he'd be happy to provide for the children as long as they lived with him. But as I was the one who had taken them and left, he was waiting for a judge to determine what was fair."

"Bastard," I said. "Is he trying to take the kids away from you?"

Charlotte stared out the window at the road with her jaw clenched so hard it hurt to look at it. "It's starting to sound like that. It's the first time he's mentioned anything like that, but it sounds like he's thinking about it."

It did.

"And if he finds out that I'm a suspect in a murder case," Charlotte said bitterly, "what would you give for my chances of keeping them?"

Not much, to be honest. She already had a strike against her by being unemployed and unable to provide for the kids. She didn't have a home of her own, but was living with her parents. The murder would be the final nail in the coffin. "You didn't tell him, did you?"

She shot me a glance. "I'm not stupid. But if I'm charged, he'll find out. You know he will."

I'm sure he would. "We'll make sure that doesn't happen," I said, with more confidence than I felt.

"Yeah?" She gave me another look. "How?"

It was clearly meant as a rhetorical question, because she continued before I had a chance to respond. "That Detective Jarvis called me in to the police station yesterday. And kept asking me questions about Richard and the kids and my 'situation'…" She took her hands off the wheel for the second it took to make air quotes around the word. "—and what I'd been doing in the house on Fulton last night."

I had my own questions about what she'd been doing in the house on Fulton last night, to be honest. The story about the earring was a little too far fetched, and not only because I couldn't remember seeing the earrings in her ears during the day. It didn't make any sense that she'd be wearing diamond earrings to renovate a house, and it didn't make sense that she'd be wearing anything Doctor Dick had given her. It would make more sense that she'd either hock the diamonds or if not that, at least leave them in a drawer so she didn't have to look at them.

But I didn't say any of that. "I spoke to Jarvis yesterday," I told her instead. "I don't think you have to worry about being arrested anytime soon."

"He sounded like he thought I might have done it," Charlotte said.

"He has to keep an open mind and investigate all the

angles. But there are likelier suspects than you."

"Who?" Charlotte wanted to know, as she turned the minivan into the gravel lot that fronts Beulah's Meat'n Three. We bumped over some ruts and rolled into an empty space next to a pickup truck with a Confederate flag sticker glued to the tailgate and a pair of steel balls in a sack hanging from the trailer hitch.

I grimaced at them—what kind of guy finds it necessary to hang a pair of stainless steel testicles from the back of his truck, and what is he trying to prove?—and told Charlotte, "Wait until we're inside. I'll tell you and Darcy the story at the same time. She might have been called in for a second interview, too. We can compare notes over lunch."

I pushed my door open and got out. On the other side of the minivan, Charlotte did the same, and we headed for the entrance to Beulah's side by side.

It's a little old cinderblock building, long and low, that's clearly seen better days, but it's popular with the locals. Mother gives it a wide berth, of course—she's much too refined for Beulah's—but I've always rather enjoyed slumming.

"Have you been here before?" Charlotte asked, glancing around the parking lot.

I looked at her, surprised. "Of course. Haven't you?"

The place has been her since before we were born. Not that I'd spent much time in it growing up. It wasn't the kind of place the Martins frequented. But it wasn't my first time, either.

Charlotte bit her lip. "Is it..." She hesitated, lowering her voice another degree, "—rough?"

Rough?

I bit my tongue on the first, instinctive response that came to mind. Charlotte couldn't help it that she was still stuck with the old mindset I had mostly managed to jettison since I met Rafe.

"If you're looking for bone china and Michelin stars I suppose it is," I said instead. "But it isn't a bar. Nobody's going to get drunk and start a fight."

Certainly not at noon on a Sunday, when the place was likely to be filled with church goers chowing down after the morning service. "It's a perfectly respectable diner. Run by a woman we both went to school with. No worries. C'mon."

Charlotte didn't say anything, but I could see her brace herself when I grabbed the handle and pulled the door open.

The inside of Beulah's looks like you might expect. It's a long, low room with an old-fashioned lunch counter along one side and with a row of booths along the other, looking out over the parking lot. The stools and benches are red vinyl, the table tops speckled Formica with steel edges. It's all very traditional and, in its way, comforting. There's nothing fancy about it at all.

Yvonne was manning the hostess station, and beamed a welcome when she saw me. "Afternoon, princess." And then she looked past me. "Where's your husband?"

"Home with the baby," I said. Or on his way to Dix's house by now, most likely. Kickoff, or whatever it was called, was probably at noon. Truth be told, I wasn't even sure what kind of game they'd be watching. What kind of sport do people play in February?

"Sorry," I added. "I'll bring him next time."

"See that you do." She grinned at me before turning to Charlotte. A second passed. "I know you," Yvonne said.

Charlotte looked pretty deeply uncomfortable. I smiled. "Of course you do. You went to school together. Charlotte was my best friend growing up."

Yvonne nodded. "You dated her brother." She flicked a glance at me.

I nodded. So did Charlotte.

"She's back in town," I told Yvonne, since Charlotte wasn't stepping up and doing her own talking. "Her husband cheated."

Charlotte flinched, but I wasn't sure whether it was because of the cheating or because I'd said it out loud where other people could hear.

I didn't think she had to worry. Nobody looked like they cared much what we were talking about, and I didn't know many of them, so Charlotte probably wouldn't, either. Most of them were a lot older than us. Cletus Johnson, one of Bob Satterfield's deputies, was an exception. He was Yvonne's age, a couple years older than Charlotte and me, and was sharing a booth in the rear with his mother and his two kids. I hadn't seen them—the kids—for more than a year, and they'd gotten much bigger. Cletus's mama looked about the same, at least from what I remembered and what I could see of the back of her head.

Darcy had gotten here before us, and was sitting by the window. I gave her a raised finger—index, not middle—and she nodded. In the booth next to her, a young guy with light brown hair flopping over heavy eyebrows looked from me to her and back, and said something to his companion. I didn't think I'd ever seen either of them before, but I gave them a polite nod anyway before turning my attention back to my own companions.

"Oh, honey," Yvonne said, in response to my remark about Charlotte's marriage, "all men are bastards." She patted Charlotte's arm in commiseration.

Charlotte forced a smile. "Thank you."

"Yvonne's had her own experiences with cheaters," I said. "Remember Darrell Skinner?"

"Wasn't he one of that family who...?" She trailed off without finishing the thought, but I knew what she hadn't said.

Wasn't he one of that family who was murdered last fall?

I nodded. "The youngest son. Several years older than us, though. But Yvonne dated him for a long time."

"A decade," Yvonne said. "More. And he just couldn't keep his pants zipped."

After a second she added a reflexive, "Bless his heart."

Charlotte and I both observed a moment of silence for the dead. "Anyway," I said, "Charlotte's living here now. Doctor Dick's still in North Carolina."

"Nice to have you back home," Yvonne said politely, as the door opened behind us and a couple of septuagenarians walked in. "I guess you're meeting your sister?"

I nodded. "I see her. We'll talk to you later."

"I'll be by," Yvonne said and turned toward the new arrivals. "Welcome to Beulah's. How many for lunch?"

We left her there, and made our way toward Darcy's booth. The two young guys in the next booth watched as we came closer, and I did my best to ignore them, even if it wasn't easy. It was also a little weird, since they were at least four or five years younger than Charlotte and me, if not more, and probably a decade younger than Darcy. I get attention from men sometimes, and I'm sure Charlotte does, too, but they're not usually college kids.

As soon as we slid into the booth across from Darcy, I forgot all about them, though. "Did you get called back in to the police station again, too?" I unwound my scarf from around my neck.

Darcy shook her head. "Did you?"

"Both of us." I glanced at Charlotte. "Not together. Charlotte was there first, I think. Or at least it sounded like Jarvis had already talked to her when he talked to me."

"Any news?" Darcy wanted to know.

And how! "I found out why Morris couldn't keep up with

the taxes and lost the house to foreclosure."

"Why?" Charlotte and Darcy said in unison.

I lowered my voice, since we were in a public place and there was no point in broadcasting this to everyone in Beulah's. "He was in jail!"

There was silence. From the table behind me, too. The two young guys were probably listening to every word we said. I reached for the menus and gave one to Charlotte and one to Darcy. "We should decide what to eat before the waitress gets here."

Charlotte accepted hers obediently, but Darcy said, "What for?"

"Jail? Rape and murder."

Charlotte gasped, and I added, "A rape and murder he said he didn't commit. And a jury agreed with him, because they acquitted him a couple of days ago, and he was let go."

"So he didn't do it?"

I didn't actually know whether he'd done it or not. "He was acquitted. Farther than that, I'm not sure. I'll get the court transcripts on Monday. Rafe said court records are public in Tennessee, and if I go to the courthouse and pay a fee, they'll give them to me. But it may not be that he didn't do it. It may be that he was let off on some kind of technicality. It happens. We won't know until we do a little investigating."

Charlotte shuddered and tried to hide it. "I can't believe he came to the door and you talked to him! And all along he might have been a rapist. And a murderer!"

"I only talked to him for two minutes," I said. "And I wasn't in any danger."

And he wasn't the first rapist or murderer I'd talked to. Although Charlotte might not know that, and I didn't want to make her look at me the way she looked at the memory of Steve Morris. Besides, my experiences with the dregs of society weren't anything everyone in Beulah's needed to hear, either.

"I should have salad," I said, perusing the menu. "I need to get serious about losing the rest of the baby weight."

"You look great," Darcy said, and added, "for having had a baby three months ago."

I hid a grimace. She probably hadn't meant it the way it sounded. "I don't look as good as you." She was tall and slender. I was less tall, and had been less slender even before I got pregnant.

"Yoga," Darcy said. "And I didn't have a baby recently."

"Speaking of that…"

She eyed me across the top of the menu. "I'm not pregnant."

"I didn't think you were. But are you and Nolan at least talking about it?" Because she wasn't getting any younger. Although it would be rude to point it out.

That hadn't stopped me once before, actually, but I was determined not to do it again.

"Yes," Darcy said, with long-suffering patience. "The topic has come up. But we've only been dating six months. It's too soon to have babies."

She turned back to the menu. "If not salad, what are you going to have?"

"Probably salad." I sighed. "The cobbler sounds good, though. It's a good day for cobbler."

"Any day's a good day for cobbler," Darcy said. "If you have salad, maybe you can reward yourself with a cobbler for dessert. I'll help you eat it, so it'll only be half a cobbler."

She moved her attention to Charlotte. "What about you? Want to help us eat a piece of cobbler?"

Behind us, the two young guys struck up another conversation. I guess they'd gotten tired of listening to us talk about food.

"I guess." Charlotte sounded like she didn't care about cobbler one way or the other, which was practically sacrilege. "I should have salad, too. It's more than two years since JR was born, and I've still got baby weight to lose, too."

"JR is your son?"

Charlotte nodded. "Richard Junior. JR for short."

"Cute," Darcy said. "So salads all around, and cobbler for dessert." She sounded happy about it. It was probably the cobbler, although I wouldn't put it past her to be excited about salad.

The waitress materialized beside the table, snapping gum. "Getcha?" The name tag pinned to her ample bosom said Mo, but I remembered her from the competency hearing last year, and knew that her full name was Maureen Boyd.

"How are you, Miss Boyd?" I said politely. "I'd like a sweet tea with lemon and a chef salad, please."

She gave me a look under bushy brows. After a second her eyes cleared. "You're the youngest Martin girl, ain't ya?"

I nodded. I was indeed the youngest Martin girl. "Although I'm a Collier now."

"That's right." She grinned. "You married LaDonna Collier's boy last summer, didn't ya?"

I had. And I appreciated her leaving out the 'good-for-nothing, colored' part between LaDonna's name and 'boy.' And since she had, I grinned back. "It was the event of the season. At least according to my Aunt Regina." Who writes the society column for the *Sweetwater Reporter*.

Maureen put her head back and hooted. "Don't tell the boss I said so, but she has a crush on him."

Oh, I was well aware of that. "Yvonne has a crush on everyone. She likes my brother Dix, too. Speaking of which, this is my sister Darcy. And if you remember me, you probably remember Charlotte Albertson, too."

Maureen nodded. "Ain't seen you in a while."

"I've been living in North Carolina," Charlotte said softly.

When she didn't say anything else, Maureen turned her attention to Darcy. And looked from her to me and back for a second. "Sisters?"

"Same dad," I said. "Different mothers."

Maureen nodded. "I've seen you around. Been here a while now, ain't ya?"

"Three years. A bit more."

"Well, we're happy to have ya," Maureen said. "What'll it be?"

Darcy ordered a salad, and so did Charlotte. "And we're going to split a cobbler for dessert," I told Maureen.

She grinned. "Good choice. Grady's been baking up a storm back there."

I remembered Grady, too, from the hearing. He had also spoken up in Yvonne's favor, and against the Otis Odoms. I should have asked Jarvis, when I had the chance, what—if anything—was going on with that case.

Maureen withdrew to fetch our drinks and put in our orders, and we returned to our conversation. On a totally different topic now. "I never knew Savannah had another sister," Charlotte said to Darcy.

Darcy glanced at me and back at Charlotte. "We didn't know it, either, until last fall. I asked Savannah to help me figure out who my birth parents were. I've always known I was adopted, but I didn't do anything about it as long as my parents were alive. But after they died, and I moved here and started working for the law firm, I thought I'd look into it. I didn't have any other family, and my ex-husband had married someone else, so I was all alone. I thought it might be nice to see whether I was related to anyone else in the world."

"Rafe was busy in Nashville," I added—this had been

during the dreadlocks and gold tooth debacle that Charlotte knew nothing about, so no sense in mentioning it, "and he wanted me to stay down here with Mother, and out of the way of what he was doing, so I thought I'd help Darcy. And we ended up finding out that we were related."

"That's amazing," Charlotte said.

Oh, it was. I grinned at Darcy across the table. She grinned back.

"You don't look much alike," Charlotte added.

No, we didn't. "It's a maternal thing. Darcy takes after Audrey's family. I take after the Georgia Calverts. Same as Dix."

"I remember your dad," Charlotte said, still looking at Darcy. "I guess there's some resemblance…"

"The mouth and jaw, mostly. But she's related to Rafe, too, through Audrey's mother. It's all very tangled."

And this wasn't the time or place to go into the details, especially since Oneida, Audrey's mother, had spent her whole marriage passing for white, and I had no need or desire to broadcast that to everyone at Beulah's. Given that Audrey had opened her home to her Aunt Tondalia—Oneida's sister and Rafe's grandmother—who was as brown and wrinkled as a raisin, I'm sure Sweetwater was catching on, but that was no reason to sit here and announce anything.

"So you used to be married?" Charlotte asked.

Darcy nodded. "In Birmingham. He cheated."

"So did my husband," Charlotte said darkly.

So had mine. "All first husbands are scum."

"Feel free to drink to that," Maureen said, as she stopped beside the table with our glasses. "The food'll be out shortly." She wandered off again.

I lifted my tea. "To better luck next time."

"Better luck next time," Darcy said.

We both looked at Charlotte. She sighed, and raised her glass. "Better luck next time."

We drank.

Twelve

The salads had arrived by the time the Johnson family—Cletus, his mother, and two kids—were ready to take their leave. The kids came bouncing down the aisle first—cute little tykes, a girl with beads in her hair, and a boy in an oversized sports jersey with a number twenty-three on the back—and when the adults came even with us, they slowed down.

"Deputy," I greeted Cletus. "Afternoon off?"

He nodded. "Your husband working?"

There's no love lost between him and Rafe, but I guess they get along better now than they have at any time in the past. There's professional courtesy, if nothing else.

I shook my head. "He has the day off, too. He's over at Dix's house watching the game."

Cletus nodded and shifted his attention across the table. "Darcy. Good to see you."

"You, too," my sister said brightly. Once upon a time, she'd gone on a date with Cletus Johnson. Hopefully he wasn't still harboring hopes in that direction, since Darcy was getting pretty serious about Nolan, at least as far as I know.

Cletus turned his attention to Charlotte, while behind my back, I heard one of the young guys in the next booth say something in a low voice. It was the tone more than anything that caught my attention, because he spoke too softly for me to hear the words. But when I glanced over my shoulder, I saw Cletus's little girl take two steps back from the table, her eyes wide.

At the same time, Cletus drew in a big breath, big enough that the buttons on his shirt strained.

He's a muscular guy. Not quite as tall as Rafe, but stockier, and with a chest and a set of shoulders that are quite impressive. And when he inhales and breathes out through his nose, he looks something like the Incredible Hulk powering up. Brown, not green, but you get the point.

"What did you say to my little girl?" he wanted to know, his voice a deep bass rumble laced with menace.

The young man turned, a cocky smirk on his face. A smirk that faded when he got a load of Cletus towering over him. I could see his throat move when he swallowed. "Nuthin."

"That's not what I heard," Cletus said.

It wasn't what I'd heard, either. Or rather, I hadn't heard exactly what was said, but I'd definitely heard something. And from the little girl's expression, it hadn't been nice. I glanced over at the hostess station, but it was empty. Yvonne must be somewhere else.

Not that Cletus wasn't perfectly able to handle this on his own.

He leaned in, bracing both hands on the table. Muscles bunched under the thin Sunday-shirt, stretching the fabric tight. Just one of his arms was bigger around than the younger man's thigh, and while the kid—because he wasn't much more—wanted to act brave, he shrank back a little before he caught himself.

Cletus's voice was dangerously even. "Did I just hear you call my little girl a jiggaboo?"

A couple of people at the nearby tables gasped audibly, and

started whispering to each other. The young man shook his head. "No, sir."

He couldn't quite wipe the smirk off his face, though. Nervous he may have been, but not so nervous that he didn't think it was funny to hear Cletus repeat the ugly word.

The little girl tugged the back of Cletus's pants, and when he turned around, she whispered something to him. He nodded. "I know, precious. You go on outside with your nana now. Daddy'll be there in a minute."

He waited for Mrs. Johnson to nudge both the kids ahead of her toward the door. The look she turned over her shoulder as she walked away was scared, but it was hard to say whether it was the two young men she was afraid of, or whether she was just worried about what her son might do.

By now, Yvonne had come out of the kitchen and noticed what was going on, too. She said something to Mrs. Johnson as the older woman shepherded the little boy and girl past the hostess stand. Mrs. Johnson responded, and Yvonne took off toward us, the soles of her shoes squeaking on the floor. "What's going on?"

"This… gentleman," Cletus said, "just called my daughter a jiggaboo."

Yvonne inhaled, and her bosom—always impressive—expanded. The eyes of the guy on the other side of the table, another scrawny youth with lank, brown hair and a scraggly goatee, glazed over.

"I'm going to have to ask you folks to leave," Yvonne said. "We don't hold with that kind of talk here."

The talker smirked and started to push his way out of the booth.

"*After* you pay your bill," Yvonne added, and he subsided back into the seat. I guess maybe he'd been hoping to make his escape without that. "I'll be right back."

She flounced off toward the front, and toward Maureen, who had the ticket ready to go. Yvonne snatched it from her fingers with a couple of words. Maureen nodded. Yvonne turned on her heel and stalked back to the table, where she slapped the bill down. "Pay and leave."

The kid on the other side of the booth made a production number out of pulling out his wallet—it was attached to his belt loop with a chain—and fishing out a couple of twenties, which he put down on top of the bill with the expression of someone who thought that having two twenties in his wallet made him an important person.

Yvonne snatched the bills and took them to the cash register to make change. Cletus followed her. They exchanged a few words, a conversation that ended with Yvonne patting Cletus on the arm, and then Cletus headed outside while Yvonne made her way back to the table. "I kept twenty percent for your waitress," she informed the two young men as she put the rest of the money down on the Formica. "Take the rest and go. And don't come back. Your kind isn't welcome here."

She went back to the hostess station. The two young men looked around, maybe hoping to see approval on someone's face, but if so they were disappointed. Everyone in Beulah's looked like they were on Cletus's side.

So the pair moved out of the booth and swaggered toward the door, making sure to bump into as many people as possible along the way. Nobody said anything, although every pair of eyes in the restaurant, from the kitchen staff to the waitresses to the guests, was on them as they made their way to the door in utter silence. In one final act of spite, the guy with the darker hair, not the one who had spoken to the little Johnson girl, reached out and knocked over a stack of menus sitting on the counter.

"Oops." He grinned offensively. Yvonne's eyes narrowed,

but she didn't say anything, just watched as they sauntered to the door and out.

The door shut behind them with a slam, but nobody moved or said anything. I think we were all waiting for the other shoe to drop. Outside in the parking lot, there was the roar of an engine, and then the sound of spitting gravel. Some of it hit the side of the building, and the windows. Charlotte flinched.

I leaned toward the window and peered out. It was no surprise to the see the truck we'd parked beside, the one with the Confederate flag sticker and steel balls hanging from the hitch, peel out of the parking lot and hit the blacktop with squealing tires. Of course it would belong to these two. They were just the types who'd need to hang a steel-plated scrotum from the back of their truck to compensate for the real balls they ought to have between their legs, but that they clearly lacked.

I squinted, but they were going too fast and kicking up too much dust for me to catch more than a couple of digits of the license plate. A number 4 and a K, followed by maybe a 3 or an 8.

And then they were gone, out of sight down the Columbia Highway in the direction of Sweetwater. "They've left," I said, and we all drew a collective breath of relief. The other conversations started up all around us.

"That was scary," Charlotte said, and I guess maybe it had been.

I mean, for a second or two, just after they walked out and before I heard the truck start up, the thought had crossed my mind that they might come back inside with an automatic weapon each, and would blow us all to kingdom come. It's the kind of thing you have to worry about these days.

But they hadn't, and other than that, I hadn't really been afraid at any point. Maybe all this time spent in Rafe's company, and all my encounters with rapists and murderers, had knocked most of the fear out of me. I'd been angry, but I hadn't been scared. At least not for myself.

"You OK?" I asked Darcy.

She nodded, but her lips were tight. "Nasty buggers."

They had been. "It makes you wonder about the kind of people who can look at a sweet little girl like that, and say something that ugly."

And then I wondered whether Darcy had ever been on the receiving end of comments like that. And whether Carrie would be. They were both lighter-skinned than Cletus's little girl, but they weren't white.

I didn't ask, though. Darcy was already upset, and having to answer that question would only upset her more.

"Where were we?" I said instead, trying to infuse some brightness into my voice. "Before this happened, how far had we gotten on discussing the Morris mess?"

"You're going to the courthouse tomorrow," Charlotte said promptly, "to look at the trial records." I got the feeling she was eager to put the whole event behind her as quickly as possible, too.

I nodded. "I don't know that it really matters whether he was guilty of the murder or not. As long as someone thought he was, and thought he got away with it, that would be reason enough to kill him. Although I guess I would like to know whether he actually did it and he was just let off on a technicality, or whether he was actually wrongfully arrested in the first place."

"Do you want me to come with you?" Charlotte asked.

I shook my head. "There's no need. If you want to read the transcript, we can get together afterwards. I'll stop by the office—" I glanced at Darcy, "so you can make a copy. In case you want to read it, too."

She nodded. "While you're in Columbia, do you think you might try to figure out whether Morris started the process to redeem the house, or whether we still own it?"

"He's dead," Charlotte said, looking from her to me and back. "Doesn't that mean we do?"

Darcy shook her head. "If he went ahead and filed a motion, his estate will get the house. The only way we keep it, is if he didn't do anything."

Then I'd definitely look into that, too. The sooner we knew one way or the other where we stood, the better.

"Ugly event at Beulah's earlier," I told Rafe that evening, after I had returned to the mansion from lunch and after he had brought Carrie back from their excursion to Dix's house after the game was over.

"How so?"

He was cooking tonight, which meant I was getting steak and baked potatoes done in the microwave. The only concession to healthy eating was a tossed salad I had put together so we'd have something green to eat along with the protein and starch. Rafe had curled his lip at it, but of course he didn't have to worry about his weight.

"Cletus Johnson was there," I said, from the island where I was sitting, watching him work, "with his mother and his kids."

He nodded.

"And as they were leaving, Cletus stopped at our table to say hello. He went on a date with Darcy once, did I tell you that?"

Rafe shook his head.

"It was soon after Marquita died. Darcy said he wasn't ready for another relationship, and she wasn't, either."

Rafe nodded.

"So Cletus was standing at our table, and one of the guys in the next booth said something to the little girl. Cletus's daughter. And the next second, Cletus transformed into the Incredible Hulk."

"No sh… kidding?"

I shook my head. "He didn't hurt anyone, but he looked like he wanted to. He got right in the guy's face, and you could tell the guy wasn't expecting that. He was young—probably just in his early twenties, so almost a decade younger than Cletus—and about half his size, too."

"What did he call the little girl?" Rafe asked.

I told him, and watched his eyes go flat.

I bit my lip. "Have you ever—"

He glanced at me, and I trailed off into, "Um…?"

"Oh, darlin'." His voice was light, but there was nothing happy about his expression. "I've been called every name in the book. I can't rightly recall every instance, but I'm sure that's one of'em."

No doubt. "Surely not when you were small, though? I mean, she can't be more than five…"

And she was beautiful. Just as he must have been. Just as Carrie was now, and I hated, with a passion, the idea that she would be exposed to that kind of ugliness.

He smiled, but there was no humor in it. "When I was little, folks called me a monkey. My grandpa called me a niglet."

"Old Jim was a bastard," I said, working hard to keep my voice even in spite of the flashes of hot and cold that threatened to make me howl in outrage.

Rafe shrugged. "I've been called a pickaninny. I've been called 'boy' more times than I can count. Long after I stopped being one."

"The sheriff calls everyone 'boy,'" I protested, since I'd certainly heard Bob refer to Rafe as a boy more than once. I'd even informed him that Rafe was no boy anymore, he was all grown up. Or growed up, as people say in these parts. "He calls Dix and Todd boys, too."

"But not in that same voice." His lips curved. "I ain't upset with the sheriff, darlin'. We've worked things out. But him calling his son and your brother 'boy,' is different from him calling me 'boy.'"

Maybe it was. I mean, he should know. And the way he said it, with that old-fashioned Southern drawl, certainly made it sound different.

"Well, these two called Cletus's little girl a jiggaboo. Yvonne came over and told them to leave, and they did. But you could tell they thought the whole thing was kind of funny. They were nervous, because Cletus is a big guy, and he was angry, and he looked like he wanted to hit someone..."

"I've been hit by Cletus," Rafe said, poking at the steaks. "I know what he looks like."

Of course he did. I remembered that black eye, and the memory made me wince. "Nothing happened, though. He didn't hit them. And they were still cocky when they swaggered out of there. One of them knocked over a stack of menus that was sitting on the hostess stand. On purpose."

Rafe nodded. "I know the type." After a second he smiled. "Hell, I used to be the type."

"You were never that type," I said. "These guys had a pair of steel balls in a sack hanging from their trailer hitch, probably because their own equipment is so insignificant that they have to compensate. That's not a problem you have."

And I meant that both physically and metaphorically. There's nothing wrong with the size of his equipment, but he also has metaphorical *cojones* to spare.

He grinned, but didn't take the bait. "You saw their truck?"

"We parked next to it when we got there," I said. "Then I

recognized it when they tore out of the parking lot, spitting gravel. They headed south."

Rafe nodded.

"Black truck, maybe a Chevy or a Dodge. Could have been a Ford. Not new, but not old, either. The license plate started with 4K, and then either a 3 or an 8."

"Some reason you're telling me this, darlin'?"

"I was just thinking," I said, "that two guys who would say something like that to Cletus's cute little girl, might know something about what you're working on."

He nodded. "Might, at that."

"There was a Confederate flag on the tailgate of the truck, next to an oval sticker with the number 88 inside it. Maybe it's a NASCAR number or something. They looked like the type who'd watch… No?"

He shook his head. "88 is a Nazi symbol."

Nazi? "It's a number," I said. "How can it be a Nazi symbol?"

"The eighth letter of the alphabet is H. 88 is HH. HH stands for—"

"Heil Hitler." I grimaced. "I can't believe I didn't know that."

"I didn't know it either," Rafe said, "till last week. I haven't spent much time dealing with Nazis."

No. Most of his career had been spent dealing with South American Theft Gangs, which aren't the same thing as Nazis at all, even if they're ruthless in their own way.

"You should talk to Cletus," I told him. "And get a description. I can give you the basics, but he looked at them more closely than I did. I mostly ignored them, to be honest, because they were staring at us when we walked in."

"Gimme what you can. I'll get Cletus to fill it in."

I gathered my impressions, obediently. "Two guys, early

twenties. One had light brown hair, the other dark brown. They were both white, obviously. The guy with the light brown hair looked like he might have had a bad case of acne as a kid, or maybe measles or something like that. His face was kind of pockmarked. They were both skinny, and average height. They paid with cash, so no credit card you can trace. The guy who paid kept his wallet on a chain attached to his belt loop. They both wore jeans. One of them had on a black hoodie and the other one a plaid shirt over a T-shirt."

Rafe nodded. "Might be enough to identify 'em. Starting with the truck."

"If you want to do that now," I offered, "I can finish dinner."

He smiled. "It's no hurry, darlin'. They ain't going nowhere. They've got World War III to prepare for."

"With that much at stake, you'd think they'd avoid drawing so much attention to themselves. Especially over something so stupid as calling a little girl a bad name."

"They can't help it," Rafe said, forking the steaks onto plates. "There she was, cute and little and brown, and scaring her, just 'cause they could, was too much of a temptation."

I uncurled the hands I'd curled into fists at his words, and examined the half-moon nail marks I'd inadvertently left in my own palms. "I really hope you get these guys."

"Oh," Rafe said, putting my plate in front on me, "we'll get 'em. It won't be tomorrow—we'll wanna follow 'em around for a while and see what they're up to—but we'll get them."

He took the seat next to me and cut into his steak. Blood oozed out. I averted my eyes and attacked my own steak, but not before a superstitious shudder had had time to make its way down my spine, like a slow trickle of ice.

Thirteen

I ran into Todd outside the courthouse again the next morning. We must be on the same Monday morning trajectory.

Or maybe this was always Todd's trajectory on Monday mornings, and I just happened to have been here for the past two weeks, intersecting with him.

After the usual pleasantries about Marley and Oliver, and Rafe and Carrie, he asked what I was doing, and I explained that I was on my way to the court house to see if I could get my hands on a set of old trial records. He wanted to know why, of course, and which trial, and when I told him, he made a face. "I heard about that."

"The murder?"

He nodded. "Your name didn't come up, though."

"No reason it would." Not for Todd's purposes, anyway. "You weren't here during the first trial, were you?"

"The mistrial?" He shook his head. "I was still in Atlanta."

"I guess you wouldn't know whether he was guilty or not, then."

"We don't tend to prosecute people unless we believe they're guilty," Todd said.

I smiled sweetly. "Of course you don't. It's OK. You weren't here, so it's no reflection on you. And I'm not suggesting that anyone did anything wrong. I'm just wondering whether he actually committed the murder or not, seeing as he was let go the second time."

"The first trial ended in a hung jury," Todd said. "But because he wasn't from around here, had no family and no ties to the community—"

"Other than his house."

Todd nodded. "—bail was set very high. High enough that he couldn't come up with the money. Even selling the house wouldn't have given him what he needed. So he stayed in jail waiting for a new trial."

"And that was last week?"

He nodded. "Between the first trial and this one, one of the witnesses died. A neighbor who testified that she'd heard Morris and the victim arguing a couple of days before the murder."

I felt a little buzz at the back of my brain. "Died?" That seemed very convenient, didn't it?

Although if Morris had been in jail, it wasn't like he could have killed her. And not like anyone else would have wanted to.

"She was old," Todd said. "There was nothing suspicious about it. But because she couldn't testify again, and because the defense dug up Morris's old girlfriend, who drove here and testified in his favor, he was acquitted."

"Were you involved in the second trial?"

"Only on the periphery," Todd said. "The DA sat first chair. The ADA from the first trial sat second chair. I wasn't involved beyond doing some research."

"Do you think the transcripts from the new trial are available, too?" Or was it too soon?

"We can find out," Todd said and gestured for me to precede him up the stairs and through the doors.

In the end, I ended up with transcripts from both trials, and took them both with me back to Sweetwater, where I presented them to Darcy like a prize. "You want to make copies?"

"I'm not sure how much time I'm going to have to read," Darcy said, "but I might as well."

She stuffed them into the copier and pushed the button. While the machine scanned and spit, I situated myself in front of the desk for a nice chat. "How are you?"

"About the same as yesterday," Darcy said. "Your husband showed up here an hour ago and wanted a description of the two guys from Beulah's yesterday."

"I told him about what happened. I think he thinks—and I think so, too—that they might be involved in that case he's working down in Laurel Hill. The guys yesterday had a Nazi sticker on the back of their truck."

Darcy's eyebrows winged up. "There are Nazi bumper-stickers?"

"Turns out there are." I explained about the number 8.

"I never knew that," Darcy said.

I shook my head. "Me, either. Rafe said he didn't, either, until last week. I guess they've all been getting crash courses in recognizing all things Nazi."

"Well, the guy sitting with his back to us had a swastika tattooed on his head," Darcy said.

My eyes widened. "Seriously? How did I not notice that?" I mean, it didn't seem like something you'd overlook.

"You had your back to him," Darcy said. "And it was under his hair. Only half visible. But I was staring at the back of his head the whole time we were sitting there, and I saw the outline of it."

"I don't doubt you," I said. "I just didn't notice. And I'm shocked that I didn't."

After a second I added, "Hard to believe that anyone would be that stupid. I mean, that's like tattooing 'loser' on your forehead, isn't it?"

"Or a serial number on your arm," Darcy said, which shut me up for a second.

"Yes, but they—the Jews—didn't do that to themselves. And anyway, what kind of moron grafts into his own skin—in permanent ink, no less—a symbol that shows he's a Nazi?"

"Someone who's proud of it," Darcy said.

Clearly. "If you want to sport an offensive symbol, why not put it somewhere you can cover it with clothes? Why flaunt it where everyone can see it and know what a jackass you are? That doesn't seem smart."

"I'm sure it's partly to shock," Darcy said. "And to make people uncomfortable. And probably because it makes them feel good about themselves when people look at them with fear and give them a wide berth. The people who do this kind of thing are the kind who confuse fear and loathing with respect."

Yes, indeed.

"Rafe will find them," I said. "He'll find them, and follow them, and figure out who their friends are, and eventually he—and Nolan, and Grimaldi, and Bob Satterfield, and the sheriffs of Lawrence and Lewis and Giles—will arrest them and put them behind bars."

"And it won't be any too soon," Darcy said.

I shook my head. No, it wouldn't. "In happier news, I checked at the county clerk's office, and it doesn't look like Morris had time to do anything about his statutory right of redemption. Nothing was filed on Friday afternoon, before or after he spoke to us. So the house is still ours. Yours."

"It's a shame that he had to die in order for us to keep the house," Darcy said, "but I'd rather have it than not."

So would I. But I agreed. "If we help Jarvis figure out who

killed him—so he doesn't arrest Charlotte for it—maybe it'll go a little way toward making up for the fact that we took the man's house."

"Maybe so," Darcy said and turned toward the printer.

Charlotte and I spent the rest of the day in the Victorian's parlor, reading court transcripts, in between feeding Carrie, taking care of Charlotte's two children, and fielding questions about what we were doing from Mrs. Albertson, who seemed worried. It was one of the more boring days I've ever spent, at least lately, and once we'd finished one, we switched transcripts and started over. By the end of it, we'd both struggled through the accounts of both trials, and looked as pale and wan as two people who hadn't seen sunlight or fresh air in a couple of weeks.

"Have you ever been called for jury duty?" I asked Charlotte as I gathered the paperwork preparatory to taking it home. I didn't expect Rafe to read it all, but I did plan to run a few sections past him.

She shook her head. "You?"

I hadn't. "I think, if I'd been on the jury for this trial—either of them—I would have found him not guilty."

"Really?"

I nodded. "Wouldn't you?"

"I don't know," Charlotte said. "He was there when she died. Nearby. He knew her. The neighbor said she'd heard them argue…"

She had. But she was old, so there was a chance she'd been wrong about what—or who—she'd heard. No one else had come forward to admit to arguing with Morris, and Morris hadn't named anyone else he'd had a conversation with on the day the neighbor said she'd heard the arguing, so maybe it had been another man and not Morris.

That man hadn't come forward either, of course, but that wasn't surprising, especially if he had killed Natalie Allen.

Or maybe the neighbor had been right, and she had heard Morris. At this point, there was no way to know for sure, and no way to find out, since she'd gone to be with her maker more than a year ago, in the time between the first and second trial.

The first had ended in a locked jury. The second had ended with acquittal. And the elderly neighbor not being there wasn't the only reason for the different verdict. While the first trial had included a police report filed in Florence, Alabama, when Steve Morris was seventeen, charging him with the statutory rape of a fourteen-year-old unnamed girl, in the second trial, that fourteen-year-old girl—all grown up now, and with a name and everything—had shown up to testify on his behalf, and had put the police report in context.

"Had you ever heard of a Romeo and Juliet defense before?" Charlotte asked.

I shook my head. "I wasn't sexually active in high school. I had no need to know."

She opened her mouth, and I raised my hand. "If you were sleeping with my brother back then, I'd just as soon not know."

Charlotte smirked, but didn't say anything. "Did you believe her?" she asked instead.

"Steve Morris's girlfriend? No reason not to. She was testifying under oath. She probably wasn't lying. And she drove a couple of hours to be here, to make sure the jury knew that the case was thrown out because they were both underage and dating."

And why would she go to all that trouble if it wasn't true?

There wasn't much to link Morris to the murder other than hearsay and innuendo. No DNA on the body, none of Natalie's DNA anywhere on Morris's person, in his car, or in his house. No motive anyone had come up with for why he'd want

Natalie Allen dead. So between the nosy neighbor not being there to testify about the quarrel, and the old girlfriend—now a happily married mother of three—testifying that Morris never had been a sexual predator, the jury found him not guilty of Natalie Allen's murder. And that's how he'd ended up on our doorstep.

"I feel better," Charlotte said. "At least he wasn't a sex offender."

He'd still been dead in our den, so I didn't feel much better, although I supposed I was happy that he'd been found not guilty in the end, since it sounded like he had, in fact, been not guilty.

None of this made a difference as to why he was killed, though. Just because I—and a jury of his peers—thought he'd been innocent, didn't mean someone else hadn't thought he was guilty—and had killed him because of it.

"We need to talk to Natalie's family," I said. "Her boyfriend, if she had one. Any girlfriends she might have had. Any of them might have killed Morris if they thought he'd gotten away with murder."

"We can't do that!" Charlotte said, shocked. "What will people think?"

"I suppose we could sit here and wait for Jarvis to figure it out on his own. Is that a chance you want to take?"

"He doesn't really think I did it!" Charlotte said. After a second she added, with a lot less certainty, "Right?"

"Of course he does. Or he might." He should. If I didn't know her, and it was my case to solve, I would. "You had motive, means, and opportunity. You were there, your fingerprints were all over the murder weapon, and you had a good reason to want Morris gone. I'm surprised he hasn't arrested you already."

From the other side of the wall came a sort of gasp, and I

deduced that Mrs. Albertson was out there in the kitchen, and could hear us. I waited a few seconds, to give her time to show up in the doorway and ask questions if she wanted to. When she didn't, I continued, "It makes more sense to build a case against you than look for someone else that may or may not be out there."

"What do you mean," Charlotte asked, outraged, "may not be out there? Of course he's out there! Or she. I didn't do it, so someone else must have!"

"Right." Of course. "I just meant that from the police's perspective, they've got a suspect with motive, means, and opportunity. Why bother to look for someone else?"

"Because I didn't do it!" Charlotte said.

"Yes, but from Jarvis's point of view..." I gave up. "Just work with me here. If we do a little sleuthing of our own, maybe we'll discover something we can share with him. While he focuses on looking for evidence to prove you did it," which he would probably be doing, since it was his job and made sense, "we'll look for evidence that someone else did. And when we tell him, he'll have to admit that someone else had motive, means, and opportunity, too."

And if that didn't work—and naturally I didn't mention this to Charlotte, certainly not while her mother was around the corner, listening—we'd have some information we could turn over to the defense for trial later. If Jarvis got as far as to charge Charlotte, at least we could make the prosecution's case hard to prove. And it wouldn't hurt to get a head start on that, since the case against Charlotte was pretty open and shut—a lot more open and shut than the case against Morris—and there was no reason why Jarvis would dilly-dally when it came to arresting her if he thought she did it.

"I suppose," Charlotte said reluctantly. "What do you want to do first?"

"I want to talk to Natalie's family. I can go on my own, or you can come with me. Your choice."

"You can go alone," Charlotte said.

I looked at her. Yes, of course I could. But I'd thought maybe she'd want to take a little more initiative to clear this up, since it was, after all, her criminal record on the line here, and not mine.

She stared back without budging, though, so I said, "If you prefer."

Charlotte nodded.

"I'll let you know what I find out," I said.

"Thank you," Charlotte answered.

I opened my mouth, and closed it again. And opened it again. "Is there some reason you can't be bothered to do a little legwork in your own best interest?"

"I'm not a detective," Charlotte said.

And I was? "Are you afraid to talk to these people?"

"I'm afraid to make Detective Jarvis angry," Charlotte said. Which I suppose was a somewhat valid concern.

"Fine. I'll go by myself and talk to the neighbors. I'll call you tonight."

"Thank you," Charlotte said again, and on that note, I scooped up the baby and headed out.

By now it was mid-afternoon, and I figured some of the neighbors might still be at work. Natalie Allen's parents probably wouldn't be at home. She'd be in her early twenties now; they were too young to be retired. But the old lady with the dog was probably home. I could start with her.

So I loaded Carrie back into the car and we headed from Sweetwater back to Fulton Street, and pulled to a stop in front of our house. Or Darcy's house.

Steve Morris's house.

I sat for a second and looked at it. It didn't look any

different than it had last week, the last time I'd been here. The dumpster was still full of the same junk, the door was securely closed—and hopefully locked. A string of yellow crime scene tape draped across the porch. There was still greenery growing in the gutter, because neither of us had ventured onto the ladder to rise that high yet.

I opened the door and swung my feet out. Carrie had fallen asleep on the way here, her long lashes dark against her cheeks and her pink lips pursed. I grabbed the car seat, hoping the change in temperature between the toasty car and the chilly February day wouldn't wake her, and hoofed it up the driveway and around to the rear of the house.

Another string of yellow tape ran from one side to the other of the French doors. And as Jarvis had promised, someone had taken the time to tape a piece of cardboard across the broken pane. I went all the way up to the glass and cupped my hands around my eyes, peering through.

Nothing looked any different than it had on Saturday morning. A little more gray and dusty, maybe. Fingerprint powder. I wondered whether they'd found any that belonged to anyone but us and Morris, and then I realized that if they had, it wouldn't mean anything. Fingerprints can last a while if they're not cleaned off, and no one had done any cleaning here for a very long time. Morris's prints, and Morris's guests' prints, could still be on the door jambs from four years ago.

With the crime scene tape still festooning the doors, the police clearly hadn't released the crime scene yet. I picked up my baby and headed back around the house, preparatory to talking to the neighbors.

I started with the lady with the dog.

She lived in a house that was pretty much a carbon copy of Morris's house—our house—but on the other side of the street. It was much better maintained, too, but perhaps I shouldn't hold that against Morris, since he'd had his hands full with other things these past few years.

It was painted a crisp white, with a watermelon-red door and black shutters: your most traditional American look. Unlike Morris's house, the front yard was immaculate, even before anything had started to bloom for the season. There were enough evergreens—small holly bushes with glossy leaves, and some spindly-looking fir-type things—to give brightness and color, and there were also several ornaments sitting around, that obviously stayed out all year. A concrete turtle sat next to an old-fashioned garden gnome, and in the other bed, some sort of brass ornament—maybe the kind you could hook up to a garden hose and turn into a sprinkler— gleamed in the late afternoon light.

There was a bell next to the door, with the name Oberlin in a small frame above it, and I put my finger on it. A conservative *ding-dong* rang through the house. The *dong* didn't even have time to fade before I heard the scrabbling of nails and furious barking coming closer.

Pearl does the same thing, so it didn't bother me. Besides, I'd seen Mrs. Oberlin's dog, and it was a lot smaller and less scary than Pearl.

It took half a minute, but then I heard human steps inside, too, and a voice telling Chester to be quiet. The peephole in the door darkened for a second—I put a non-threatening smile on my face, and gave it a wave—and then the lock tumbled. The door opened a crack. "Can I help you?"

"Hi," I said brightly. "Mrs. Oberlin, right? My name is Savannah Martin. Collier. My friend and I are working on the house across the street."

She gave me an up-and-down look before she opened the door wider. "I remember seeing you."

"I wondered if you had a couple of minutes to talk to me," I said. "If it isn't too much trouble."

"I've already spoken to the police."

I nodded. "So have I. I'm not expecting you to tell me anything you didn't tell them. I'm just trying to work things out in my own head. I mean, I didn't even know about Natalie Allen until after this happened…"

I trailed off invitingly. Mrs. Oberlin nibbled her bottom lip, looking unsure for a second, before she opened the door. "You better come on in."

Excellent. I stepped across the threshold and into the house.

It was set up in exactly the same way as our house across the street. The front door opened directly into a combination living/dining room, and I could see the kitchen beyond. It had been updated with oak cabinets in, at a guess, the nineteen-eighties or –nineties. If I continued, I'd surely find the same bathroom and two bedrooms as across the street.

Mrs. Oberlin's furniture was as traditional as the house. Dark wood with glass tops on the tables, chintz furniture. Beige wall-to-wall carpet on the floor.

"Have a seat." She gestured me toward the sofa.

"Would you mind if I put the baby on a dining room chair?" I didn't want to put her on the floor, or even the sofa, in case Chester the Shih-Tzu jumped on her and woke her up. If I could keep her asleep during my conversation with Mrs. Oberlin, that would probably be best.

She flapped a hand in that direction, which I took as permission. And gave Carrie a sharp look when I walked past. "Yours?"

I nodded. "She looks more like my husband. Although she has my eyes." Which you couldn't see now.

"I didn't realize any of you girls were married," Mrs. Oberlin said. "I haven't seen any men coming and going over there."

"Mine's come by once or twice. He has another job, though, so he isn't helping us with the renovations. Darcy's dating a guy who works for the police department, and Charlotte left her husband in North Carolina when she moved back here."

"Dear me," Mrs. Oberlin said, clicking her tongue. "Trouble in paradise?"

Trouble, certainly. I didn't think Charlotte's marriage to Doctor Dick had ever come close to being a paradise, and the more I learned about it, the surer I became about that assessment.

But it wasn't any of Mrs. Oberlin's business, so I just made a non-committal kind of noise and took a seat on the sofa.

"So what can I do for you?" Mrs. Oberlin wanted to know.

"I wanted to ask what you saw the night Steve Morris was stabbed. I know you saw Charlotte get here. My friend with the brown hair."

"She arrived when I was taking Chester out for his evening tinkle," Mrs. Oberlin nodded.

"And you didn't see her leave again?"

She shook her head.

"Did you see anyone else around the house? Before or after that?"

She didn't answer immediately, so I added, "We were working there all day. Around four o'clock, this guy knocked on the door and introduced himself as Steve Morris and said the house used to be his. I spoke to him for a few minutes, and then he left. Fifteen minutes later or so, Charlotte and I left, too."

"I saw Steve," Mrs. Oberlin said. "In the afternoon. I didn't recognize him at first."

"You knew him when he lived here?"

She nodded. "He'd changed a lot. Lost some weight, shaved his head…"

A couple of years in prison can do that to a man. Rafe had gone in with cornrows and come out shaved, too. Or so I assumed. I hadn't actually laid eyes on him until ten years later, so it could have happened anytime in that period, I guess. But the braids he'd had as a teenager were long gone when I saw him again at thirty.

"Were you friends? Before?"

"Friendly," Mrs. Oberlin said. "Neighborly. Not much in common other than that we lived on the same street. He worked at home. I'd see him come and go sometimes. Always had a friendly word for Chester."

She glanced at the small dog, that had settled in with a slobbery nylon bone on the carpet.

"You can tell a lot about someone from how they treat animals," I said. "And vice versa, too. We have a rescue dog, and she was kept chained under a trailer up in the hills by her owner."

"Poor thing." Mrs. Oberlin clicked her tongue again.

"It's a few months ago now. She's doing fine. Settling in. But I know, when she likes someone, they have to be a decent person. She knows when they're not."

"Chester liked Steve," Mrs. Oberlin said.

"I guess it must have been hard to believe that Steve would have done what they said he did, then."

A shadow crossed her face. "To Natalie? It was. Ida kept saying she'd heard arguing coming from Steve's place, but I told her she had to be wrong."

Ida Burns was the neighbor who had testified in the first trial and was dead by the second. I glanced out the window. "Where did Ida live?"

Mrs. Oberlin pointed across the street, to the house next to ours. "Been dead more than a year now, poor thing."

"I heard about that." I nodded sympathetically. "Were you

close?"

"Close enough that she talked to me about it. I kept telling her it couldn't have been Steve she heard that night, that Chester would have known if Steve had been capable of something like that."

Chester looked up at the sound of his name, slapped his tail once, and went back to gnawing the nylon.

"If not Steve," I asked, "who could it have been?"

She shrugged. "Ida probably heard the TV and thought it was a real conversation. She wasn't the brightest bulb in the chandelier."

Maybe so. Hard to imagine the defense wouldn't have brought that up at trial, though.

"I was starting to make some headway," Mrs. Oberlin added, with a shrug of skinny shoulders inside flowered polyester, "but then she died."

I felt a tingle go down my spine, the same way it had when Todd had mentioned Ida Burns's death this morning. He had dismissed my concerns, but— "Natural causes, right?"

She gave me a look. "Heart attack."

"No suspicious circumstances?"

"None I noticed." She sniffed. Not in an offended way, in a sort of sad one. "I was the one who found her. She was on the floor next to the bed, still in her nightgown. The police said it looked like she'd had a heart attack in the middle of the night."

The description reminded me of something, but it took a few seconds for me to place it. Then it came back to me: Beulah Odom had also died of a heart attack, and been found on the floor next to her bed in the morning. In that case, she'd been discovered by one of the employees at the restaurant, who came to check on her when she didn't show up to unlock the door in the morning.

In spite of the Otis Odoms doing everything they could to

turn it into murder, both the autopsies had been inconclusive. If Beulah had been murdered—as the Otis Odoms claimed—she'd been killed in a way that looked a lot like a heart attack.

"Which detective?" I asked Mrs. Oberlin.

She glanced across the street. "I ran and fetched Carl." Officer Enoch. "He called his friend. The same detective who investigated Natalie's murder. And now Steve's."

Paul Jarvis. "And he said he thought it was a heart attack?"

"Carl said it looked like one," Mrs. Oberlin said. "But I'm sure they investigated."

Hopefully they had. Given how assiduously Jarvis had investigated Beulah's murder, I guess it made sense that he'd give poor Mrs. Burns equal shrift.

"Who did you think killed Natalie?"

Mrs. Oberlin shook her head. "Probably some bum. Or maybe that no-good boyfriend of hers."

"She had a no-good boyfriend?" This was the first I'd heard of any no-good boyfriend. He hadn't featured in the transcript of the trial at all. The first or second.

"Name of Rodney," Mrs. Oberlin said, with a sniff. "Been dating since their junior year of high school. She even put off going to college so they could keep seeing each other."

"Why would he kill her?" Had she gotten tired of him, or something? It wouldn't be the first time some guy killed his girlfriend so he wouldn't have to watch her date someone else. Or maybe she'd decided to go to college after all, that waiting tables in a sports bar wasn't how she wanted to spend the rest of her life, and he hadn't wanted her to go?

Mrs. Oberlin shrugged. "Maybe he did something and she knew about it. So he killed her to shut her up."

And maybe Mrs. Oberlin had watched too many episodes of *True Crime*.

"I appreciate you talking to me," I said, and got to my feet.

"I should get going. Would you happen to know which house the Allens live in?"

She gave me a long look, but eventually she told me. "The yellow one. With the picket fence."

"I appreciate it." I gathered up my baby and car seat. "I'm sure I'll see you around again soon. The police will probably release the crime scene any moment now."

Mrs. Oberlin nodded and got to her feet to trail me to the door. Chester glanced up from the nylon bone, but didn't jump to his feet to follow. I guess now that I was inside the house, he had decided I was no threat and no problem. He didn't even bark when Mrs. Oberlin unlocked the door and held it open for me.

I stepped across the threshold and out on the stoop. "I don't suppose you'd have any idea why Morris came back here that night? Was he meeting someone? Maybe an old friend he was hoping to stay with?"

He couldn't expect to be able to stay in our house. He had to assume we'd be back the next day. For that matter, he couldn't really know that we wouldn't be there overnight. Not unless he kept an eye on the place.

"Any friends he used to have, stopped being his friends when he was arrested for killing Natalie," Mrs. Oberlin said. "No one on this street would have been happy to see him again."

"So why did he come back?"

"Maybe he wanted to clear his name," Mrs. Oberlin said. "If he didn't kill Natalie, someone else did."

She waited a second, and when I didn't say anything, added, "Good evening, Mrs. Collier."

She shut the door. I stared at it for a second before I walked down the steps to the grass and headed for the road.

Fourteen

At the yellow house behind the white picket fence, there was no response to my knock. I knocked again, and stood there for a second thinking about the possibility of wandering back behind the house in case there was a door back there I could knock on—or peer through.

It turned out to be a good thing that I didn't, because out of the blue, a voice behind me inquired, "What are you doing?"

I jumped about a foot and clapped a hand to my chest. And turned on my heel to see who had scared a couple of years off my life. "Oh. Officer Enoch. What are you doing here?"

"I live here," Enoch said.

"Here?" In this little yellow house that belonged to the Allens?

He shook his head. "I saw you when I pulled into my driveway. What are you doing?"

"Just seeing if anyone's home," I said.

Enoch arched his brows skeptically.

"Really. I just wanted to say hello. I haven't met many of the neighbors, and since I can't work on the house until Detective Jarvis releases it as a crime scene, I figured I might as well get to know people."

He looked like he didn't believe me, and who could blame

him?

"I knocked on Mrs. Oberlin's door, and spoke to her for a bit, and now I'm up here. I don't suppose there's any word on when I might get my sister's house back?" So I could stop doing what Enoch clearly didn't like—walking door to door, talking to the neighbors—and get back to doing something useful.

"You'd have to ask Paul," Enoch said.

"I would, but I haven't spoken to him for a couple of days. And I'm sure he's busy." I glanced around, and spotted the pickup truck from the other night parked in a driveway across the street. "Is that where you live?"

He nodded.

Across the street from the Allens and three doors up from us. "If you knew Steve Morris from before, you must have known Natalie Allen, too."

His face closed. "I knew who she was. Of course."

There was a very distinct 'but' at the end of that sentence. It was also a silent 'but,' but it was definitely there.

I tilted my head inquiringly, doing my best to look harmless and just like I was politely interested, not nosy.

"She was young," Enoch said grudgingly.

"Nineteen." He was around thirty, and had been younger back then. "Mrs. Oberlin told me she had a boyfriend."

"Rodney Clark," Enoch nodded. "Little pissant."

"Did anyone look at him for Natalie's murder?"

"I'm sure Paul did," Enoch said. "Like I told you before, it wasn't my case."

After a second he added, "Why do you care?"

"No particular reason." I smiled brightly. "Detective Jarvis seems suspicious of my friend Charlotte. I thought maybe I could come up with another suspect to give him."

"For Natalie's murder?"

Of course not. "For Steve Morris's. Maybe Rodney killed him because he thought Morris got away with Natalie's murder. Or maybe someone in Natalie's family did. Her parents, siblings if she had them…"

His expression turned stern. "Now, Mrs. Collier, I don't want you going to the Allens with nonsense like that. They lost their daughter, and had to deal with her murderer being set free last week. They don't need you knocking on the door accusing them of killing him."

"I wasn't going to accuse them," I said. I mean, I'm not stupid. You don't knock on someone's door and accuse them of murder. You smile and talk your way inside, and then you chatter around the subject and observe their reactions.

But Enoch shook his head. "Not on my watch. I want you to leave the Allens alone."

I sighed. "Fine. Nobody's home anyway."

And then what he'd said registered, a little belatedly, and I added, "So you still think Steve Morris killed her? Even if a jury found him innocent?"

"They acquitted him," Enoch corrected. "And only because Mrs. Burns wasn't there to give her testimony."

"I thought she was rethinking that," I said.

Enoch's brows lowered. "Where did you hear that?"

"From Mrs. Oberlin. She and Mrs. Burns were friendly. Mrs. Oberlin thought Mrs. Burns must have been mistaken. She didn't think Steve killed Natalie."

"There weren't any other suspects," Enoch said.

No, and that was a little strange, wasn't it? Why focus all the attention on Morris when Natalie had had a boyfriend, and surely other people around her, too, who might have made good suspects? Why the immediate focus on Morris?

"What about Rodney?" I suggested. "Maybe she was breaking up with him and he didn't want her to. Or maybe it was another boy she knew, who wanted her but she wasn't interested. Or just some random stranger who saw her walking home from work, and decided to approach her. And when she turned him down, he got upset. Or it could have been another girl. Maybe one who wanted Rodney but Natalie was in the way."

"No one else would have wanted Rodney," Enoch said tightly. "Rodney was a waste of oxygen. Still is. And anyway, Natalie was raped."

"That doesn't mean anything. There was no DNA on the body." And it wouldn't be the first time someone had tried to make a murder look like something it wasn't.

Hell—heck—maybe this hypothetical other girl wanted Rodney, but Rodney used Natalie as an excuse for why she couldn't have him, and she decided to get rid of Natalie and throw suspicion on Rodney, all at the same time.

Not that Rodney had fallen under suspicion. But he should have.

"How do you know that?" Enoch asked.

"What?"

He sounded long-suffering. "That there was no DNA on the body. That wouldn't have been in the papers."

No, probably not. "I read the court transcripts."

His brows lowered. "Where did you get those?"

"From the county clerk's office," I said. "They're public record."

He didn't say anything to that, but it didn't look like he was happy. "I don't know that you should get involved in this, Mrs. Collier."

"I'm not involved," I protested. "I'm just curious. He died in our house, after being acquitted of a murder he didn't commit. Or maybe didn't commit. And if he came back to clear himself..."

"Who told you he did?"

"Mrs. Oberlin suggested it," I said. "Anyway, it's natural that I should take an interest."

"It's rarely healthy for a civilian to take an interest in a murder investigation," Enoch told me darkly. "I'd hate to have to tell your husband that something happened to you, too."

Yeah, yeah. "What will happen to Natalie's case now? Will the police continue to investigate, or will it be closed?" With the understanding that Morris was guilty and now that he was dead, justice had been served?

"No idea," Enoch said, and he was starting to sound impatient. "Take your baby and go home, Mrs. Collier. This is none of your concern."

He was getting agitated, so I decided not to push my luck. "Sure thing." Hard to blame him, anyway. I wouldn't have wanted to tell Rafe that his wife was dead, either. "I have to go make dinner in any case. It was nice to see you again, Officer Enoch."

I hopped off the stoop and into the grass.

"You, too, Mrs. Collier." Enoch followed me down the driveway and onto the sidewalk. "You and your husband have a good evening."

He gave me a polite nod and sauntered across the street to his own driveway. I wandered down the street to the Volvo and got Carrie situated in the back seat. When I drove slowly up the street, Enoch was in the process of unlocking his front door.

"Darlin'," Rafe said about an hour later, when he came home from work and found me in the kitchen preparing dinner, "what've you been up to?"

"What do you mean?" There was that mixture of amusement and warning in his voice that made the question more than just a request for information.

"Enoch called me," Rafe said, and draped his leather jacket over the back of one of the stools. "He told me my wife's playing detective and putting herself in danger."

I scoffed. "I wasn't in any danger. I had a conversation with Mrs. Oberlin. The woman on Fulton Street who owns the Shih-Tzu. She saw Charlotte go into the house on Friday night, so I wanted to know what else she saw. But she's hardly dangerous. The dog isn't, either. And then I knocked on the Allens' door, to see if maybe I could get an idea of whether they'd wanted to kill Morris, but they weren't home. And then Enoch found me on the Allens doorstep and warned me off."

I gave the clam sauce in the pan an irritated swipe with the wooden spoon. "He actually called you?"

"Said he was worried my wife was meddling in things that didn't concern her," Rafe said, his lips twitching.

I sniffed. "If Jarvis is planning to arrest my best friend, it concerns me."

He smirked. "'Course it does."

I slanted a look at him. "All I'm doing is talking to some of the neighbors. I'm not doing anything dangerous. And I'm not meddling." At least not so far. Or very much.

"I ain't worried," Rafe said. "Just try to stay outta Enoch's way. He ain't used to you, the way Tammy and I are."

"I'm not in his way," I protested. "It's not even his case. What business is it of his if I'm asking questions?"

"It's his neighborhood," Rafe said.

Yes, of course it was. "So shouldn't he want to know what's going on?"

"I'm sure he wants to know what's going on. He just doesn't want you to figure it out."

I tapped the spoon against the edge of the pan to get the excess sauce off, and put it down. "Enoch already thinks he knows what's going on. He thinks Morris killed Natalie and got away with it. And he probably thinks one of the Allens killed Morris, and he doesn't want me to figure it out."

Rafe nodded pleasantly.

"Is Jarvis going to look at that possibility?"

"That'd be up to him," Rafe said. "It's his investigation."

Sure. "Any chance he'll look at the possibility that Morris didn't kill Natalie? Or will the police department proceed on the assumption that Morris killed her and then was killed by someone who thought he got away with murder?"

"At the moment," Rafe said blandly, "looks like Jarvis is going on the assumption that Charlotte killed Morris."

Ugh. I picked up the wooden spoon and gave the sauce another stir. "I understand that she's the obvious suspect. She was actually at the house that night. Her fingerprints are on the murder weapon. So it makes sense that Jarvis has to look at her."

Rafe nodded.

"But like when Natalie was killed, it's like he's picking a suspect and focusing all his energy on proving that that person did it, instead of looking for other people who might have had motive and opportunity."

Rafe didn't answer, and I added, "Morris was acquitted. Enoch still thinks he did it, but there was no physical evidence to tie him to Natalie's murder. No DNA. No witnesses. The neighbor who heard him argue with Natalie was reconsidering. She ended up dead anyway, so she wouldn't have been able to testify again in any case, but Mrs. Oberlin said that Mrs. Burns probably didn't hear Morris and Natalie, but someone else. Mrs. Oberlin never thought Steve Morris was guilty."

Rafe nodded.

"Meanwhile, Natalie had a boyfriend. The boyfriend is always a suspect, right?"

I didn't wait for him to tell me I was right. "Maybe she wanted to break up with him, and he didn't want her to. Maybe that's who Mrs. Burns heard argue. Why wasn't he a suspect?"

"Maybe he was," Rafe said. "Maybe he had an alibi."

Maybe so. The defense hadn't brought him up during the trial, not even to create reasonable doubt, so maybe he hadn't been even a remote possibility. "I just don't think Morris did it. The jury didn't think Morris did it, either. They deadlocked the first time and acquitted the second. He probably shouldn't have been charged at all, since there was very little evidence against him. I'm just worried that Jarvis will do the same thing to Charlotte. Get it in his head that she's guilty, and not consider anyone else."

I turned the burner off under the pot of spaghetti and carried it to the sink, where I dumped it. Water sloshed down the drain with a gurgle, and steam rose. Angel hair pasta slithered smoothly from the pot into the strainer.

"Smells good," Rafe said, and slipped another hand under the dish towel I had draped over the garlic bread to keep it warm for the couple of minutes it would take me to finish making dinner.

"You keep that up, there won't be enough left for later." I shook the strainer.

He grinned at me as he chomped into the piece of bread. "Don't much matter if I eat it now or later, does it?"

I guess it didn't. And I wasn't supposed to have garlic bread, anyway. Or pasta, for that matter. But one deprivation at a time.

"I'm just trying to come up with another suspect before Jarvis arrests Charlotte." I poured the pasta into the pot and began mixing angel hair and sauce. "At this point, I have to assume he's thinking about it. It's been almost three days, and we all know that cases are supposed to be wrapped up in seventy-two hours."

Rafe opened his mouth, and closed it again without speaking.

"There has to be someone," I said. "I mean, I know Charlotte didn't do it…"

Rafe didn't answer, and there was something in his silence that made me turn to look at him. He met my eyes, but didn't say anything.

"You can't be serious!" I said.

"I dunno that I am serious, darlin'. But hear me out for a second. Say Charlotte went back to the house on Friday night, to look for that earring she'd lost during the day."

"That's what she said she did."

"And say she walked inside and found Morris there."

"She can't have," I said. "Mrs. Oberlin would have seen him arrive."

"If he came through the backyard?"

Well, no. Maybe not then. "If she'd walked in and he was there, Charlotte would have run back out, screaming. Mrs. Oberlin would have noticed that."

Rafe ignored me. "And say Morris really did kill Natalie Allen three years ago. And say he attacked Charlotte. And she picked up the screwdriver and stabbed him with it so she could get away."

"Self defense," I said.

"If it happened something like that, you think she woulda called the cops? Or just left him there and acted like nothing happened the next morning?"

My hands had stilled on the pasta, and I realized it and started stirring again. "Hard to say. I mean… I'd like to think she would have called 911 and asked for an ambulance. I'd hope I would have, if it were me. But it's possible that she might have run out of there to get away from the whole thing.

Pretend it didn't happen."

It would explain why she'd been late getting to the house the next morning. Reluctance to go back to the crime scene. Unlike Darcy and me, she knew what we'd find once we walked inside.

"Something to think about," Rafe said.

"Don't you think Mrs. Oberlin would have noticed something amiss, though? I mean... you don't really think it happened that way, do you?" I put a plate full of angel hair and clam sauce in front of him.

He gave me a look at he picked up his fork. "It mighta happened that way. On the evidence, it's as likely as anything else. She was there. Nobody else had a reason to be."

No. And that included Morris.

"What do you think he was doing there?" It wasn't his house anymore. And all his belongings were gone.

"Looking for a dry place to sleep?" Rafe said, winding angel hair around his fork.

Maybe so. I wound spaghetti around my own fork and tried to picture the scenario. Morris inside the dark house, and Charlotte pulling up to look for her earring. She would have opened the front door with her key, and turned on the light. She had no reason to hide.

So why hadn't Morris, if he was there, just scooted out the back until she was gone? He must have known she wasn't going to stay. There was nothing there to sleep on. Why confront her, when he could have just faded into the dark in the yard and waited for her to leave again?

But maybe he hadn't heard her coming. Maybe he'd conked out, and she had walked in on him sleeping, and he hadn't had time to get out. And then he had attacked her?

It was possible, but if all he was doing was sleeping, surely it was also—pardon my pun—overkill?

On the other hand, he had just been released from prison. He might have had powerful incentive not to want to go back there. Maybe he had tried to talk to Charlotte, and she had refused to listen to reason…

But in that case, wouldn't it have been Charlotte dead on the floor, and not Morris?

"Eat." Rafe's voice cut through the thoughts looping through my brain. "Your food's getting cold."

I glanced at him, and he added, with a wink, "You gotta keep your strength up. I got plans for later."

Good to know. "I'm just worried," I said, lifting my fork and picking at the pasta. "Prison wouldn't agree with Charlotte."

"Prison don't agree with most of us," Rafe agreed. "That's the point of it."

I slanted a look his way. "You did all right, didn't you?"

"I managed to keep outta Big Ned's bunk, if that's what you mean." He looked at my face and grinned. "Yeah, darlin'. I did all right. But I was eighteen, and acted like I was tough…"

He'd done more than act like it. Even at eighteen, he had been tough. He hadn't looked like someone you wanted to take on. He was bigger now, more muscular, but he'd never been small or weak. And he'd been at Riverbend for assault and battery with intent, after putting his mother's boyfriend in the hospital, so it was understandable that even Big Ned—had he existed, which he hadn't—would have given Rafe a wide berth.

"Charlotte wouldn't end up where I was, though," he added.

No. If she were convicted of murder, she'd end up at Southern Belle Hell, the Tennessee Women's Prison, out in West Nashville. Not the same as Riverbend, but no picnic, either. There'd be no Big Ned, although possibly a Big Bertha. And there'd definitely be Denise Seaver, who hated me for putting her there, twice, and who wouldn't be above taking revenge on someone I cared about.

"Charlotte ain't gonna end up at Southern Belle Hell, darlin'," Rafe said. "You and I wouldn't let that happen. And Satterfield wouldn't prosecute her, anyway."

Possibly not. "So you don't think there's anything to worry about?"

"Till I find out otherwise," Rafe said, "I'm gonna give Jarvis the benefit of the doubt. And if it looks like he's gonna come close to wanting to arrest Charlotte, I'll talk to him."

"Will he appreciate that?"

"No," Rafe said, "but I'd do it anyway. And if he don't listen to me, I'll talk to Tammy. He'll have to listen to her."

I nodded.

"But Jarvis is a reasonable guy. I don't think he's gonna arrest Charlotte without making damn sure she's guilty."

I opened my mouth, and closed it again when he continued. "And if she ain't, then you got nothing to worry about."

Right.

"Now eat your food." He devoted himself to his own.

"Any luck on tracking down the two guys from Beulah's?"

He swallowed. "The guy who owns the truck, yeah. Name of Kyle Scoggins. Lives in an apartment complex north of Columbia. I spent part of the day in the parking lot, waiting for him to show up."

"Did you see him?"

"The truck pulled in just before I had to leave for the day. I guess he was coming home from work. I left Lupe Vasquez to keep an eye on him."

"Is that safe?" Lupe is young, female, and Hispanic, all of which sounded like a bad idea when it came to keeping an eye on a guy we suspected was a white supremacist.

"It's the job," Rafe said. "But yeah, she'll be fine for a couple hours. And I'm working on something more permanent for tomorrow."

Good to know. "So you'll be keeping an eye on this guy for a few days, to see what he's up to?"

"And who he meets with. We still gotta identify the other guy." He bit into a piece of garlic bread and took his time chewing and swallowing. "I'll have to leave early tomorrow. I'm picking up the surveillance at six. Hopefully he'll head out to work, and that'll give me his place of employment."

"Maybe the other guy will be there. Maybe they work together."

Rafe nodded. "We'll be keeping these guys under observation for a while. Pulling in people from Lawrence and Lewis and Giles as needed. Less chance they'll recognize any of 'em that way, too."

There was. "You'll be careful, right?"

"Always," Rafe said, and gave me a grin.

I rolled my eyes but didn't say anything.

Fifteen

Detective Jarvis released the house to Darcy on Tuesday morning. Darcy called and told me we could go back to work. I called Charlotte and told her to meet me there at ten. For the first few seconds I thought she was going to refuse, but then she sighed. "OK."

"I know it's unpleasant," I said. "But it's still our house. We can still sell it and make some money."

"Even after someone was murdered there?"

"Yes," I said firmly. "We'll be able to sell it and make money. We'll get you out from under Richard's thumb. I promise."

She sighed. "It might not matter. Not if I end up in prison."

"Do you have reason to think you'll end up in prison?"

"No," Charlotte said.

"Then let's not worry about it for now. I'll see you at ten." I hung up before she could say anything else, or change her mind, if she were planning to.

She was there at ten, though. Waiting outside the house, like she was afraid of going inside on her own. But dressed in old jeans and sneakers, looking like she was ready to work.

I parked the Volvo at the curb and pulled the baby seat out, and headed over to her. "Problem?"

She shook her head. "I just don't want to go in on my own."

The body was long gone, and there was nothing inside to worry about. I thought about saying so, but then I bit my tongue. Just because I was blasé about dead bodies now, didn't mean I'd always been. For quite a while after I moved in with Rafe, into Mrs. Jenkins's house, the site of Brenda Puckett's murder, I'd given the library sidelong looks when I walked down the hallway, just in case I should happen to catch some kind of echo of what had happened there. I don't believe in ghosts, not really, but Dix had scared the crap out of me all through our formative years, and I guess some of the old superstitions still hung on.

I'd never seen anything out of the ordinary, though, and eventually I'd stopped being afraid of the library, but it still wasn't my favorite room in the house. You wouldn't find me in there by myself after dark, snuggled up with a good book, for instance.

"It'll be fine," I told Charlotte. "You don't have to go in the den. We'll work in the kitchen today."

"There's nothing left to do in the kitchen," Charlotte said.

"Living room, then. Or bathroom."

"There's nothing left to do there, either."

Of course there were things left to do, everywhere in the house. It looked like a bomb had gone off inside, with all our tearing out and down.

The problem was that we weren't really ready to start building up again. I had planned to spend the weekend prepping for that, and instead, I had spent it worrying about Steve Morris's murder and the possibility that Charlotte might be arrested.

But we were going to make a start on it today. "The cabinet guy from Leiper's Fork is coming this afternoon, to give us a quote on the kitchen cabinet doors. After that, we can start taking them off."

Charlotte nodded.

"We also have to figure out how much wood we need for the den, to get the floor up to the same level as the rest of the house. But I'll do that. You don't have to come in there with me."

"You'll need someone to hold the other end of the measuring tape," Charlotte said. She was pale, but looked determined.

It was probably good for her to push through her feelings, anyway. If she hadn't killed Morris, there was no reason to be afraid of the den.

So we measured, and the cabinet guy showed up, and was kind of cute with dark curly hair and bright green eyes. He flirted with Charlotte—she flirted back, sort of half-heartedly, but maybe she was out of practice—and then he left, after telling me he'd be back in a week with the doors.

"Nice guy," I said to Charlotte.

She looked at me for a moment, blankly, before she nodded. "Sure."

"He flirted with you."

"I'm married," Charlotte said.

"You're not wearing a ring."

She glanced down at her empty ring finger, still sporting a paler line where her wedding band must have been. "That doesn't mean I'm not still married."

I tilted my head. "You're not still hoping to work things out with Richard, are you?"

"No," Charlotte said, flushing. "After what he did? No, I'm not going back to him. I don't care if he cuts off all the money and sues for custody of the children. I'm not going back to him. But I'm not ready to get involved with anyone else yet, either."

And small wonder. By the time I met Rafe, it had been two

years since Bradley and I broke up. I sometimes wonder whether things would have worked out differently if I'd met him—Rafe—sooner. Whether, if I had, I would have been ready for him.

When you lose a spouse in the usual way, there's a mourning period, and it's the same thing when you lose a spouse to divorce. Maybe even more of one. When you love someone and they die, all you have to do is deal with the loss. And while that's enormous, there's not the same self-doubt and self-examination as when your spouse leaves you for someone else. When that happens, you question everything about yourself and the relationship, what you might have done differently, whether you're unlovable, if it was your fault... in a way you certainly don't when your spouse up and dies.

"Anyway," Charlotte said, "even if I were ready, he wouldn't be my type."

Maybe not. An honest carpenter—assuming he was honest, and I guess we'd find out when he presented us with the bill for the cabinet doors—wasn't what either of us had been brought up to look for.

"There's a lot to be said for a man who's good with his hands," I responded, and had to laugh when she flushed delicately. "Sorry to be blunt, but it has to be said. Maybe you got lucky and Richard was great in bed. Bradley wasn't. He was a lousy lover, and on top of it, he told me it was my fault. And because I didn't know any better, I believed him. It wasn't until I met Rafe—" who's very good with his hands, and various other body parts, as well, "that I realized that there wasn't anything wrong with me. It was all Bradley. And if I'd stayed with him, I would have spent the next fifty years faking orgasms and thinking it was my fault that I couldn't get off."

By now Charlotte was beet red and looked like she was having problems breathing. I shrugged. "I know we weren't brought up to talk like this. Not ladylike. But there's more to a happy marriage than money and social status. And you could do worse than a carpenter who loves you."

"Aren't you jumping the gun a little?" Charlotte wanted to know. "It was ten minutes. And he probably flirts with everyone."

He might. He'd looked like the type who would. Handsome and charming and with that twinkle in his eye that said he knew it.

"I wasn't talking about him specifically," I said. "Just don't let the failure with Doctor Dick keep you from trying again with someone else. When you're ready. There are lots of fish in the sea. And having you find someone else and be happy would go a long way toward sticking it to him."

"I don't think Richard would be impressed if I took up with a carpenter," Charlotte said.

Maybe not. Bradley hadn't been impressed when I took up with Rafe, either. More shocked and appalled, and—to his credit—worried about me. Like everyone else I'd known. Although no man likes it when his ex-wife takes up with someone younger and hotter who looks like he'd be better in the sack.

I didn't bother saying so. Charlotte would only be shocked again. "Looks like we'll be able to save some money on the cabinets, anyway," I noted instead. "Now we can start taking off the old doors and sanding and painting the boxes. When he comes back next week with the new doors, we'll paint and hang them."

Charlotte nodded, looking relieved that the conversation had turned.

"And we'll have to make decisions about the backsplash and countertop. The tile we can probably just pick up at the store—there's a Home Depot out by the interstate, near the

Cracker Barrel, and we don't need much of it; it's a small kitchen—but we'll have to order the counters and wait for them to be delivered."

Another nod.

"Why don't we drive out there now, and see what's available? We can grab some lunch on the way, too. My treat."

"Sure," Charlotte said.

"We'll just measure the area that needs to be tiled..." I grabbed the nearest measuring tape and stretched it. "Grab the other end... what's that say? And by how tall? Tile all the way up to the ceiling, don't you think? It'll cost a few dollars more..." Or more like a couple hundred dollars more, maybe, depending on the tile, "but it looks so elegant and custom. And we'll have to make this place look special to sell it."

Charlotte nodded and wrote down the measurements I dictated. After that, we braved the den for long enough to measure how much wood it would take to raise the floor, in the way of two-by-fours and plywood, and then we took Carrie and our coats and piled into the Volvo for the trip to the home improvement store.

"I spoke to a couple of the neighbors yesterday," I said, once we were in the car and on our way. "Mrs. Oberlin—the lady across the street, who walks Chester the Shih-Tzu—said that Natalie Allen had a boyfriend named Rodney Clark. I'm wondering whether it would be worth talking to him."

"About what?" Charlotte said.

I gave her a look—was that just an insane amount on non-interest, or was it just me? "He might have killed Natalie. It seems like Morris didn't, so someone else must have. Might have been the boyfriend. And if it wasn't, maybe he killed Morris, because he thought Morris killed Natalie—even if a jury acquitted him—and he didn't want Morris to get away with it."

"I'm starting to feel really sorry for Steve Morris," Charlotte said. "Poor guy. First he was accused of a murder he didn't commit, and spent a couple of years in jail before he was acquitted. And when he finally got out, he'd lost his house. And then someone killed him."

And on top of that, his reputation had been shot when everyone thought he was a rapist.

I nodded. I was feeling sorry for Morris, too. Sorry enough that I would like to figure out who killed him, and who killed Natalie, so at least people could stop thinking he'd done it. It might not be much good to him now, but I felt like I wanted to do something.

"Mrs. Oberlin said that Rodney and Natalie started dating in high school. We could probably figure out who he was based on that."

"We could just ask her parents," Charlotte said.

"I knocked on their door yesterday. They weren't home, and then Officer Enoch showed up and told me to leave them alone."

"Maybe he thinks they killed Morris," Charlotte said.

"If he thinks they killed Morris, shouldn't he want to arrest them? Not protect them from me?"

"Maybe he sympathizes with them," Charlotte said with a shrug.

Maybe he did. "Maybe Mrs. Oberlin knows where to find Rodney. Or who his parents are. Where he lives." I should have asked yesterday, I guess. But that was when I thought I'd be able to talk to the Allens and get some information from them.

"We can knock on her door when we get back," Charlotte said. "If we're coming back here today."

"It's only eleven." And I didn't intend to spend more than an hour at the home improvement store. Even if we added lunch, we'd have plenty of time to work in the afternoon.

"Besides, your car is parked on Fulton. We'll have to come back."

She didn't respond to that, but she didn't protest either. We kept driving in silence.

At the home improvement store, we settled on white subway tile for the backsplash— "Classic, but this bit of irregularity in the glaze makes it look handmade,"—and a marble-looking slab for the counters.

"Marble makes everything look better," I said. And also more expensive, even when it wasn't.

"Gold finish for the handles?" Charlotte wanted to know, fondling one she liked.

I shrugged. "Sure." Gold has made a comeback after years of brushed nickel and polished bronze, so we might as well take advantage of it to look hip and up-to-date. It's an easy thing to change out later. "Ten cabinet doors and…" I counted rapidly in my head, "seven drawer pulls."

Charlotte gathered gold handles into the basket.

"Add a few more for the bathroom," I told her. "Two doors, one drawer for the hall bath, and probably four doors, three or four drawers for the master." We hadn't chosen the vanities for either yet, but it sounded reasonable.

Charlotte scooped more handles into the basket, and we moved on to floor tile.

"I'd like to restore the wood floors in the kitchen," I said, "to make them flow from the living room and dining room all the way through the kitchen, down the hallway and into the two smaller bedrooms. But we'll need tile for the bathrooms. What do you think?"

We chose tile—concrete look with a stylized design; very elegant with the white subway tile—ordered what we needed to order, and paid for everything. I'm sure I turned pale when I saw the damage to the bottom line. "Darcy's going to have a fit."

"I'm sure she understands that it costs money," Charlotte said placidly. Which was easy for her, since it wasn't her money, or her sister. But shrieking about it wasn't going to make any difference, and we did need everything we'd bought, so I put it out of my mind and headed back to the car.

We were halfway across the parking lot when I stopped dead—pardon the pun—and turned around. "Marley!"

Charlotte stopped, too, of course, and so did the woman I thought was Marley. Who turned out, on a second look, to be Marley. If a pale and puny-looking Marley. Markedly better-looking than the first time I'd seen her, when she'd been smoking and drinking herself into an early grave worrying about her missing son and her impending murder trial. But not as bright-eyed as she'd been the last time I'd seen her, which had been sometime in the fall, when she and Todd and Bob Satterfield had caught Darcy, Dix, and me crossing Marley's backyard with a box of medical files we'd liberated from Denise Seaver's house on the next street over.

"Savannah." She gave me a wan smile.

"It's good to see you!" I reached out and gave her a hug. She felt brittle in my arms. "I haven't congratulated you on the engagement yet. And Todd told me you're pregnant!"

She nodded, with a sideways glance at Charlotte.

"Oh," I said, "I'm sorry. This is Charlotte Albertson. We grew up together. She's been living in North Carolina for a few years, but she's back now."

Marley nodded.

"Charlotte," I added, "Marley Cartwright. She's engaged to marry Todd."

"Todd Satterfield?" Charlotte sounded shocked.

"I don't think we know any other Todds, do we?"

She had no answer for that, and I wasn't surprised.

"I saw Todd the other day," I told Marley. "He said you're really sick."

She grimaced. "I don't remember it being this bad with Oliver. But it's been a few years, so I could have forgotten, I guess."

Maybe. I'd had a fair bit of morning sickness with Carrie, but I know it's different from pregnancy to pregnancy and woman to woman. "Not that long until you're through the first trimester, though?"

She didn't look pregnant yet. Or if she did, it was enough that she was able to hide it under the plaid coat she had on.

"A few more weeks," she told me.

"We should get together. Once you're interested in eating again."

"Oh, I'm interested in eating now," Marley said. "I just can't keep anything down. But lunch in a few weeks would be nice."

"I'll call you. Have you set a date for the wedding?"

If they had, my invitation must have gotten lost in the mail. Not that that was surprising, perhaps. Marley and I were friendly, but given the fact that Todd had taken up with her on the rebound from me, she might not want me to attend the ceremony. Or maybe it was Todd who didn't want me there.

Or maybe neither of them cared.

She shook her head. "It won't be until after the baby's born. I'm not walking down the aisle looking like a white whale."

I'd walked down the aisle looking like a white whale, but I didn't point it out. And anyway, Charlotte got in ahead of me, not even attempting to hide her shock. "You don't care if your baby is born out of wedlock?"

"I care more about the wedding," Marley said. "When I'm walking down the aisle to marry Todd, I want him to look at me like I'm the most beautiful woman he's ever seen. Not like he's afraid my water's going to break at any moment."

Charlotte looked, if possible, even more shocked. "Good for you," I told Marley.

She shrugged. "What are you doing here?"

"Picking out finishes for a house we're renovating. You?"

"Looking at colors for the nursery," Marley said. "I'm not allowed to do any painting. I'm not even allowed to lift the paint brush. But I get to pick the color."

She smiled. I smiled back. "Doctor's orders?"

She shook her head. "Todd's. I've never seen a man so worried about anything bad happening."

He'd been there in the hospital two hours after I'd had my miscarriage a year and a half ago. Mother had invited him, in the mistaken belief that if I was pregnant, I must have slept with Todd. Needless to say, Todd knew it wasn't his baby, but maybe the occasion had had an impact anyway.

Naturally I didn't say so. "That's a good thing, surely."

"I'm not complaining," Marley said, and in spite of the pallor and tired eyes, her grin was bright and infectious. I smiled back.

"Happy?"

"So happy." She beamed. "I'm not in prison. I have my son back, and another baby on the way. And I'm engaged to be married to the greatest guy in the world, who loves me. Why wouldn't I be happy?"

No reason at all, and I told her so. And then we watched her make her way toward the front of the store while we loaded up the trunk of the Volvo with our purchases, and got back in the car.

"Prison?" Charlotte said when we were on our way out of the parking lot.

I glanced at her. "Haven't you heard the story? Her son disappeared when he was just a baby. From the baby carriage in her backyard. It was a similar situation to the Natalie Allen case, actually, in that someone made it sound like Marley was slightly unhinged after the birth. Postpartum depression or something. The police thought she had killed Oliver and disposed of the body, and the DA's office—and Todd—were prosecuting her. And it turned out that the baby had been kidnapped and sold to a couple who couldn't have their own. Sheila figured it out before she died. Dix's wife. And Marley got Oliver back."

"And now she's marrying Todd?"

I nodded. "Isn't it great?"

Charlotte muttered something.

"Just goes to show," I said, "that life isn't over just because someone thinks you committed a crime."

Charlotte looked at me. "You aren't helping, Savannah."

Maybe not. Although I was trying. And I was still smiling as I turned the car toward Fulton Street and Steve Morris's house. I may not have solved any murders this week, but if nothing else, I could stop worrying about Marley and Todd, because they seemed to be doing just fine.

Sixteen

By the time we got back to Fulton, Carrie was in full hunger mode. Charlotte and I had grabbed a quick bite—very quick, and very cheap—to eat along the way, but I hadn't been able to feed her and drive at the same time, so she had been cheated of her afternoon meal. When I pulled up to the curb outside the house, she was starting to whimper. I knew from experience that the next thing would be a full-blown wail.

"I'm just going to stay here in the car and feed her," I told Charlotte. "There's nothing to sit on inside, other than the floor, so I might as well just stay here, where it's comfortable."

She nodded.

"Would you mind getting the baby out of the seat and giving her to me?" I was already scooting the driver's seat back and unbuttoning my coat. "If you want, you can walk across the street and see if Mrs. Oberlin is home, and ask her if she knows where to find Rodney Clark, while I do this. I'll help you carry the tile and wood inside afterwards."

"Sure," Charlotte said. She unbuckled Carrie from the seat and hauled her around the car, and put her in my arms.

I turned her and helped her find what she was looking for. When she was latched on and making noises like a hungry piglet, I told Charlotte, "If Mrs. Oberlin doesn't know where

Rodney lives, ask about his parents' names or where he used to live. He's probably not in the phone book," most young people these days aren't, "but his parents may be."

Charlotte nodded. "You going to be all right?"

"I'm going to be fine," I said. It was broad daylight, and I was sitting in my own car. I'd just shut the door again once she walked away, and nobody would realize I was here, let alone what I was doing.

So Charlotte wandered across the street toward Mrs. Oberlin's house. After a couple of minutes, she came back down the driveway and across the street again. I rolled the window down. "Nobody home?"

"The dog's there," Charlotte said. "I can hear it barking. But nobody's answering."

"She probably went to the store or the library." Or to lunch with a friend or wherever older ladies go to spend their time. Mother does all those things, in addition to trips to the spa and time with Catherine or Dix or me. "We'll try again later. Maybe, by the time we're done for the day, she'll be back. Would you mind starting to carry in the things we bought while I finish up with Carrie? I'll help you when I'm done."

Charlotte nodded and went around to the trunk. I popped the button, and she started carrying in boxes and bags while I finished tending to Carrie.

We spent the rest of the afternoon figuring out how to tile the backsplash in the kitchen. It wasn't a big area, and I'm sure someone who knew what he was doing could have had it done in an hour or so. It took us four, but by then it was done, all the way up to the ceiling around the window.

"That doesn't look too bad," I told Charlotte at the end of it, as we were standing side by side in the middle of the kitchen floor looking at our handiwork. "Maybe it would look more professional if a professional had done it. But once we grout it—tomorrow—that'll help. And seeing as it's our first time, I think we did all right."

Charlotte nodded. "It's pretty tile. That helps."

It did. And once the new cabinets doors—with the sparkly gold handles—were in, that would help, too. Not to mention the expensive-looking countertops.

"This is going to look great when it's done." I could see it in my mind's eye, all clean and white and new.

"So we're done?" Charlotte asked.

I nodded. "For now. Tomorrow, we'll grout. But for now, let's go home. After we knock on Mrs. Oberlin's door again."

"Like this?" Charlotte looked at me and down at herself. If she was anything to go by, we both looked a bit worse for wear. Not quite as bad as we had Friday night, maybe, but bad enough that paying visits on people was questionable.

"We won't go inside," I told her. "Looking like this, she probably wouldn't invite us in anyway. Her place was pristine yesterday. Old-fashioned, you know—all dark wood and flowery furniture—but spotless."

Charlotte nodded.

"But it won't hurt to knock on the door and see if she's back. I'd like to talk to Rodney Clark. Just in case he killed Natalie. Or Steve Morris."

Charlotte shivered. "I don't want to talk to him."

"That's all right. You don't have to." If it had been my head on the chopping block, I'd talk to anyone I had to, to get the suspicion off myself. But to each their own. "Just come across the street with me, and then we'll go home."

Charlotte agreed, grudgingly, and kept in step with me as we crossed the road.

The light beside the front door was on now—or maybe it had been on earlier, too, and I just hadn't noticed in the bright light of day. By now it was going on five, and getting darker.

"She turned it on yesterday afternoon around this time, when she let me out. I remember that. And she probably shut it off again this morning, when the sun rose. So maybe she's back home."

I put my finger on the doorbell and listened to the sonorous *ding-dong* from inside. A few seconds passed, and then came the barking and scrabbling from Chester.

"Hi, Chester," I told him through the door. It didn't calm him down at all. In fact, it sounded like it made things worse. Chester was throwing himself at the door, yipping hysterically.

Other than that, there were no sounds from within. No sign that Mrs. Oberlin was making her way toward the door. I applied my knuckles to the wood—just in case she hadn't heard the bell—and raised my voice. "Mrs. Oberlin? Are you there? It's Savannah from across the street."

We waited a bit longer. Once I stopped talking and knocking, Chester calmed down, although I could still hear him growling on the other side of the door.

"I don't like this," I told Charlotte.

She looked around. "She's probably just out with a friend, like you said earlier. It isn't that late."

It wasn't. And there wasn't any reason, or at least none I could put my finger on, why I was feeling uneasy. I just felt like Mrs. Oberlin should be there, that Chester shouldn't be alone. That if she wasn't answering the door, it was because she couldn't.

Charlotte's eyes popped when I reached for the door handle. "Savannah, you can't…!"

I could, and if the door had been open I would have. It wasn't, though. The knob turned, and the dog went crazy, but the door was locked.

"Stay here with Carrie for a minute," I told Charlotte, and let go of the knob as I put the baby carrier down. "I want to go around the back and check the kitchen door."

Charlotte opened her mouth and then closed it again.

"I'm sure it's nothing to worry about. I just want to make sure."

She nodded. I gave her a bracing pat on the shoulder, and then I left her there and headed around the corner of the house to the backyard.

Mrs. Oberlin's backyard looked pretty much as I had expected it to look. Very green, just like the front. Lots of plants and bushes, and spindly sticks that would turn into vegetation again as soon as spring sprang. She clearly enjoyed gardening. There was even a small garden shed, with the same cheerful red door as the main house, and the kitchen window had one of those bump-out greenhouse windows you see, that look like it belongs on a submarine. It was full of green plants.

I wandered over to the back door and put the tip of my nose to the glass. "Mrs. Oberlin? Hello?"

There was no answer, but Chester must have realized I was here, because I heard him bark as he came closer, skidding through the house to get to me.

"It's just me," I told him through the door. It didn't make any difference. He lunged at the door, yapping hysterically. I could see his dog bowls from here, tucked in the corner by the fridge—a matching pair of ceramic with paw prints along the rim—and they were both bone dry.

I tried the knob, but like the front, the door was locked.

"I can't get in," I told Charlotte after I'd trudged back around the house to the front step. "The door's locked and there's no answer."

Charlotte nodded. I could see her gearing up to suggest that we just head home, because Mrs. Oberlin was probably just visiting a friend somewhere. And I didn't want to hear it, so I looked away before she had time to say anything. "Chester's bowls are dry. He has no food and no water. I wonder whether there's a hide-a-key somewhere."

"We can't just go in..." Charlotte said, but she didn't say anything else. And when I went up on my toes to feel along the top of the door, she didn't tell me to stop, either.

It wasn't on top of the door. It wasn't under the mat, either. Or under the flower pot on the stoop. I looked around. No fake rock or convenient pile of fake doggie doo-doo in the grass next to the porch. Mrs. Oberlin probably wouldn't stand for something like that in her yard anyway, and no one who knew her would think, for a moment, that she'd allow something like that to stay around for more than a moment.

I headed for the flower bed and the concrete turtle. It was heavy, and had no hidden compartments that I could see. The head didn't come off, and there was no convenient panel on the underside. I turned to the gnome, and then to the metal dragonfly in the other bed. And that's where it was, glued to a small magnet that attached to the underside of one of the dragonfly wings.

I lifted it triumphantly. "Got it!"

Charlotte smiled, but looked acutely uncomfortable. "Are you sure we should be doing this?"

"If she's not home, there's no harm done," I told her, as I stepped back onto the stoop and pointed the key at the lock. "If she's not here, we'll just lock the door behind us and pretend we never opened it. After we feed the dog."

Charlotte looked unconvinced, but she didn't turn tail and run when I inserted the key in the lock and twisted it. "Mrs. Oberlin?"

There was no answer, although Chester came scrambling around the corner from the kitchen again, yipping. I braced myself, but instead of launching himself at me, snarling, he aimed for the space between my legs and Charlotte's, and ran, full-bore, past us and into the grass, where he lifted his leg with a relief I could practically feel.

I turned back to the open door. "Mrs. Oberlin? Are you here? It's Savannah Martin. Collier."

One of these days I was going to get that out without the period first, but today was obviously not that day.

Mrs. Oberlin didn't answer. Behind me on the grass, Chester moved a few feet, and squatted to do the rest of his business.

"Doesn't look like he's been out today," I told Charlotte.

She shook her head, her lips clamped shut.

I turned back to the door. "I'm going in."

"I'll stay here with the dog," Charlotte said. "We don't want him to run into the street."

No, we didn't. Not that I thought that was really the reason she didn't want to go inside.

But there was no sense in pushing it. I pulled my coat closer around myself—a sort of instinctual need not to brush against anything—and stepped across the threshold.

The living room and dining room were empty, and looked just as they had when I'd been here yesterday. The kitchen was empty, too. The counters were pristine, and there were no dirty dishes in the sink. I continued down the hallway toward the two bedrooms, my heart knocking harder against my ribs now.

The bathroom was empty. I stuck my head into the door of the smaller bedroom on the back of the house. It had a pristine bed with an old-fashioned chenille throw, unwrinkled.

I backed out again and turned in the other direction.

The door to the bigger bedroom on the front of the house was closed. I drew some air into my lungs and knocked on it. "Mrs. Oberlin?"

There was no answer, and at this point, I think I would have freaked out if there had been.

I reached for the doorknob and pushed the door open. And let out the breath I didn't realize I'd been holding. "Mrs. Oberlin?"

I guess a part of me was still hoping, even though I knew better, that she was just a heavy sleeper. Maybe she'd been taken ill and that's why she was still in bed. But it was no surprise at all to stop at the side of the bed and see that there was no movement of the chest underneath the blankets.

I backed away, and then turned and headed out. By the time I reached the stoop and Charlotte, I already had my phone in my hand.

"Everything all right?" Charlotte asked.

I shook my head. "She's dead. Flat on her back in bed. I have to call it in. And get somebody out here."

Charlotte nodded. "What do you want me to do?"

She sounded worried but composed. I guess not seeing the body made a difference, because she hadn't been this calm across the street last Saturday.

I started to dial 911 and then reconsidered. The phone rang once or twice on the other end, and then a voice came on. "Grimaldi."

"Detec…" I began, and then caught myself. "Tamara."

"Savannah." Her voice was dry.

"I found a dead body," I said.

She went from dry to crisp in a heartbeat. "Where?"

"On Fulton. Across the street from the house we're renovating, where Steve Morris was murdered."

"Do you know the victim?"

I thought I could hear the scratching of her pen as she took notes, although it was probably just my imagination. I mean, I'm sure she was taking them. I just didn't think it was likely that I'd be able to hear it.

"It's Mrs. Oberlin, the woman who lives here. She's dead in bed. No sign of anything wrong, or none that I could see, but she's definitely dead. I thought you might want to send somebody out."

"Did you have someone in mind?" Some of that dryness was back in her voice.

"I wanted you to have a chance to consider it," I said, "or I would have called 911. Like I said, nothing here looks like a crime. She's an elderly woman in a nightgown lying in bed with the blankets up to her chin. But it is the fourth death on this street in four years. And the third in the past year. The second in a week. She lived across the street from where Steve Morris was stabbed. She might have seen something she didn't realize she saw."

"What other deaths are you talking about?" Grimaldi wanted to know.

"Natalie Allen. Raped and murdered between three and four years ago. Another neighbor, Ida Burns, last year. She testified in the first trial that she'd heard Morris argue with Natalie before she was killed. Then Morris ended up stabbed on Friday night. And now Mrs. Oberlin is dead. She told me just yesterday that she never thought Morris killed Natalie."

Grimaldi didn't say anything, but that imaginary scratching of notes was getting louder.

"If there's a chance it's related to Morris's murder," I said, "I thought you might want to put Jarvis on it. Or alternatively, not put Jarvis on it."

"You have a problem with the way Jarvis is doing his job?"

I hesitated. "I wouldn't say I have a problem. I mean, he seems to be pretty focused on Charlotte. Which makes sense, since she was there and had motive and all that..."

Charlotte stared at me, wide-eyed. Grimaldi didn't speak. "But she didn't do it, and I'm not getting the impression that

Jarvis is working awfully hard to come up with anyone else. He did the same thing when Natalie Allen died. Zeroed in on Morris, to the exclusion of everyone else, and arrested him."

"He wouldn't have been arrested if there hadn't been a case against him," Grimaldi said.

"I know that. But Morris didn't do it. Or at least the jury acquitted him. And if they're right, the real killer must still be out here somewhere."

Grimaldi didn't respond to that. "Stay where you are," she said instead. "I'll let Jarvis know what's going on."

I opened my mouth, and she added, before I could get anything out, "The Morris murder is his case. The Allen murder was his case. If I keep him out of the loop on this, he's going to wonder why."

True. "I guess we'll just deal with Jarvis."

"I'll deal with Jarvis. You just stay where you are and wait." She hung up.

I dropped the phone back in my pocket. "She said to stay here. Jarvis is coming."

Charlotte made a face. "Do you think he'll try to pin this on me, too?"

"I don't see how he can," I said. "You didn't go inside the house, so none of your fingerprints or DNA will be there. And it didn't look like murder, anyway. It's probably just a natural death that happened at a weird time."

Charlotte nodded. "What do you want to do?"

"You can leave." She hadn't gone inside with me, so it wasn't as if she'd have anything to contribute. We'd been together all day, except for the minute or two I'd sat in the car with Carrie while Charlotte walked up to Mrs. Oberlin's door and knocked on it. She'd been in sight the whole time, though, so it wasn't like she'd had the opportunity to kill Mrs. Oberlin then. And unless I missed my guess, Mrs. Oberlin had been dead since sometime overnight, anyway. Poor Chester clearly hadn't been outside yet today.

Speaking of Chester…

I looked around and saw him nosing his way down the driveway. "Come here, Chester. Don't go in the street."

He lifted his head and turned to look at me. After a moment, he came trotting back.

"What should we do with him?" Charlotte asked. She wasn't making any moves toward her car, or toward leaving before Jarvis got here.

"I guess we could let him back inside. He's been in there all day, so if he was going to destroy any kind of evidence, he's probably already done it."

"It seems kind of mean, though, to shut him inside with his dead owner."

Maybe it did. I flashed back to Pearl, tied under an old trailer while her owner lay dead on the grass twenty feet away.

"Feel free to pick him up," I said, "if he'll let you. We can go sit in the car while we wait for Jarvis to arrive."

Or we could go inside and wait in the living room. If there was a crime scene inside the house, it would be in the bedroom.

Chester took the decision out of our hands when he trotted up the two steps to the stoop and then through the door. I stretched my head around the door jamb to watch as he grabbed his nylon bone and settled into the middle of the carpet to chew on it.

"I think I'd better stay out here," Charlotte said. "That way I don't have to worry about there being anything of mine in the house."

Good point. "Feel free to go sit in the car. Really. We don't both have to stand here."

"I don't mind," Charlotte said, and turned toward the road as there came the sound of a car approaching. "Surely that can't be him already?"

It didn't seem likely. And in fact wasn't likely. It was Carl Enoch's truck that came rolling up the street and came to a stop outside his house. Enoch got out and stood for a second looking around. And must have noticed us standing here, because after another second he crossed the street and headed across the grass toward us. "Something wrong?"

"It's under control," I told him, politely. It wasn't his case, after all, and Jarvis might not want him trampling all over the crime scene. Again.

He looked from me to Charlotte to the open door, and back to me.

I sighed. "Mrs. Oberlin passed away. We're waiting for the police to get here."

"I am the police," Enoch said.

Of course he was. "Jarvis is on his way. In case this has something to do with the Morris case."

Enoch arched his brows, but didn't say anything. He also didn't listen to me, but pushed the door open and stepped across the threshold. Chester looked up and started growling, but when Enoch headed for him, he scurried out of the way. Enoch strode past and into the kitchen. We heard his footsteps disappear down the hall toward the bedrooms.

Charlotte looked at me, raising her brows. I shrugged. Not my business to keep him out. He and Jarvis could duke it out if they wanted to, once Jarvis got here.

Seventeen

Enoch came back out after a minute or two. "She's dead, all right. Would you like me to wait with you?"

"No," I said, "that's OK. We've got this."

He gave me a sort of narrow look, but then he nodded. "Tell Paul to stop by when he's done."

I told him I'd pass the message on to Jarvis, and then we watched him make the trek back across Mrs. Oberlin's lawn, across the street, and inside his house.

Two minutes later, Paul Jarvis's unmarked sedan pulled to a stop in the driveway.

The detective climbed out, adjusted his trench coat, and scowled at us. However, after he'd stomped up the driveway and across the grass to the front door, the first words out of his mouth were, "You OK?"

It wasn't what I'd expected, so it took me a second to hike my jaw up. Charlotte, meanwhile, nodded. "Yes, thank you. I didn't go inside. Savannah did."

Jarvis eyed me.

"She's in bed," I said, having found my voice again. "Looks like she's sleeping." Except the dead never look like they sleep. "No sign of trauma. She's just lying there."

"How did you get in?"

"We've been knocking on the door all day," I explained. That was a slight exaggeration, I guess, but we'd been trying to raise Mrs. Oberlin for a while now. "By the end of the day, we started to get worried. She usually walked Chester a few times a day, and we hadn't seen either of them. So before we went home, we knocked on the door. When she didn't answer, but the dog was going crazy inside, I looked around for a hide-a-key and found one."

"And went in."

"It's a good thing I did," I said. "Another day, and Chester might have gotten hungry."

Jarvis winced and Charlotte turned pale. And then pale green. I shrugged. It isn't a pretty picture, but it happens.

"Stay here," Jarvis commanded. He moved across the threshold into the living room. Chester looked up at him, but didn't even bother to growl before he went back to his nylon bone. Maybe he was getting used to all the people traipsing through his house. Or maybe he'd realized that something had happened. Dogs understand more than we think.

"Hungry?" Charlotte said, eyeing him with revulsion.

"He's an animal. If he didn't get anything else to eat, he might have gotten desperate."

Charlotte looked like she was about to lose her lunch, so I added, "Although she's mostly covered by the blankets, and his legs are very short, so he might not be able to make it onto the bed."

Charlotte shuddered, and turned back to the door as Jarvis's footsteps came back the hallway and into the living room. A few seconds later, he appeared in the doorway.

"You went inside." He looked at me, and then turned to Charlotte, "You didn't?"

We both nodded.

"You can go," he told Charlotte. "You—" This was me,

"had better stay a few more minutes."

"Of course." I waved to Charlotte, who didn't waste any time hoofing it off the stoop and across the driveway. Away from the body and the dog as quickly as her feet could carry her.

"Just for your information," I added once she was out of range, "Officer Enoch went inside, too."

Jarvis's eyebrows arched.

"He saw us standing here and came over to see what was going on. I told him not to go inside, that there was nothing he could do, but he did anyway."

Jarvis nodded. "Tell me again what happened. Don't leave anything out this time."

I hadn't left anything out last time—unless he was talking about the fact that Enoch had been here—but I went over the story one more time anyway. "Mrs. Oberlin and I spoke yesterday," I added. "She mentioned Rodney Clark, Natalie Allen's boyfriend. I didn't think about it then—I was going to ask Natalie's parents where to find him—but I never had a chance to talk to them. Enoch saw me knocking on the door and told me to leave them alone, that they've been through enough and don't need me sticking my nose in where it isn't wanted. So I thought I'd knock on Mrs. Oberlin's door again, and see if she knew where he lived. But she didn't answer."

"What do you want to talk to Clark about?"

"I thought there was a chance he might have killed Steve Morris," I said. "And I thought you could use another suspect, since Charlotte seems to be your only one."

His eyebrows lowered. "I don't need your help doing my job, Mrs. Collier."

"That's not what you said last month," I pointed out. When his scowl deepened, I added, "I'm not trying to do your job, Detective. I'm just concerned that, like with Natalie's murder, you're going to arrest the obvious suspect—Charlotte, in this case—and not consider anyone else."

"I'm considering everyone," Jarvis said stiffly. "As for Natalie Allen's murder, there were no other suspects."

"There had to be. The jury acquitted Morris. They obviously thought someone else did it."

"There wasn't anyone else!"

I put my hands on my hips. "What about Rodney?"

"Rodney Clark had an alibi," Jarvis said, his teeth gritted, "and no motive."

"He was the boyfriend. The boyfriend always has a motive."

"Not this time," Jarvis said. "They weren't breaking up. He wasn't cheating. She wasn't, either. Everyone we spoke to said they were doing fine. And he was with his best friend when she died."

"And you don't think his best friend would lie for him?"

"I'm sure he would," Jarvis said, with patience that was starting to fray around the edges, "but Clark and Scoggins were also surrounded by a lot of other people in a movie theatre—"

"Movie theatres are dark! They could have left, and nobody would have noticed!"

And then I stopped. "Wait a second. Did you say Scoggins?"

Jarvis nodded.

"Kyle Scoggins?"

"Yes," Jarvis said.

"Well, there's your motive, right there. Kyle Scoggins is a neo-Nazi. He's part of the case my husband's working, down in Laurel Hill."

Jarvis looked blank.

"Surely you know about that. There's a group of neo-Nazis meeting in Laurel Hill for target practice. Kyle Scoggins might be one of them." We didn't actually know that yet, but it was likely. Either way, he was a nasty specimen who wouldn't be above murder.

Jarvis didn't say anything, and I added, "If Kyle Scoggins is a Nazi, maybe Rodney Clark is one, too." Maybe Rodney was the other guy from Beulah's. "And maybe Natalie found out and they killed her."

"We're getting off the subject, Mrs. Collier," Jarvis told me. "If Clark and Scoggins killed Natalie, they wouldn't have killed Morris. And I thought you were trying to come up with another suspect for Morris's murder so I'd leave your friend alone."

He was right. I was. While it was interesting to speculate, it didn't actually matter who had killed Natalie. What mattered was that Charlotte not go to prison for murdering Steve Morris. "Did you happen to check Rodney's alibi for this Friday night?" Just in case he hadn't killed Natalie, and thought Morris had.

"Yes," Jarvis said. "He and Scoggins were at the movies."

"Again?"

Jarvis didn't respond to that. Maybe it didn't sound as far-fetched to him as it did to me.

"Fine," I said. "What about Natalie's family? Any chance one of them killed Morris?"

"No," Jarvis said, and I could tell by the set of his jaw that he dearly wanted me to stop asking him these questions.

"Were they somewhere else? Halfway across the state so they couldn't have done it?"

"They were here," Jarvis said. "In their house. Together."

"So just a few yards away. And you can't tell me Natalie's parents wouldn't alibi each other for the murder of the man who killed her."

Jarvis didn't respond. After a few seconds he pried his jaws apart, though, to tell me, "Feel free to leave now, Mrs. Collier.

I've got this under control."

"I'm sure you do, Detective," I said politely. "Officer Enoch said to tell you to walk over there after you're done here. I guess he wants to know what's going on."

Jarvis eyed Enoch's house.

"Any objection to me telling Rafe that Kyle Scoggins is BFFs with Rodney Clark? It would probably help with his case."

"Go ahead," Jarvis said. "Have him call me if he has any questions."

I told him I would, and then I picked up Carrie and the car seat and walked away from Mrs. Oberlin's house toward my car.

"I feel like somebody dropped the ball on the Natalie Allen thing," I told Rafe a couple hours later.

We were sitting on the peach velvet love-seat in the parlor, while Carrie was enjoying tummy-time on the floor, and Pearl was watching from her pillow in the corner. The fireplace had a flicker going, I had my feet in Rafe's lap, and the whole situation was lovely, warm and comforting. The only part that wasn't, was the conversation. But then we were used to that. "They were so gung-ho to arrest Steve Morris that I feel like they didn't spend enough time eliminating any other suspects."

"How d'you know how much time they spent?" Rafe wanted to know. "You ain't seen the case file."

I had to admit that I hadn't. "But Jarvis told me that Rodney Clark, Natalie's boyfriend, was off the hook because he had no motive and an alibi. And then it turned out his alibi was his best friend, who you know would probably lie for him, and the other part of the alibi was being at the movies, which isn't worth the paper it's written on. The movies are dark. One or both of them could have walked out at any time, and chances are no one around them would have noticed."

Rafe nodded, running his thumbs up the sole of my foot. I had told him about the Natalie Allen/Rodney Clark/Kyle Scoggins connection as soon as he'd walked in the door earlier, so we were already past that point. Dinner had been spent talking about that. Now we were onto my concerns for Charlotte. Again.

"And then there's the motive," I continued. "Jarvis said Rodney Clark didn't have one. That he and Natalie were doing fine, weren't breaking up, nobody was cheating, etcetera, etcetera. And that might have been true. But if Rodney's best friend is a white supremacist, isn't it likely that Rodney's one, too? And that they were, even back then?"

Rafe shrugged, but nodded.

"Maybe Natalie didn't like that about Rodney," I said. "Or maybe—if he wasn't a Nazi—she just didn't like that he was hanging out with one."

Rafe dug his fingers into the arch of my foot, and I squeaked and tensed before I forced myself to calm down and keep going with the conversation. "That sounds like motive to me. Or at least like it might be a motive. If she wanted to break up with Rodney, maybe Rodney killed her. Or if she wanted Rodney to break up with Kyle, maybe Kyle killed her. Or maybe she threatened to tell someone they were Nazis, and they both killed her."

"No evidence of any of that," Rafe said.

"But it makes sense. Doesn't it?"

I waited for him to shrug again, and then I went on. "But Jarvis didn't consider any of it. He just took Rodney's word for it that he and Kyle were together and couldn't have killed Natalie, and then he arrested Morris instead."

"Where were Clark and Scoggins when Morris was killed?"

I made a face. "Believe it or not, they were at the movies again."

"Folks do go to the movies every couple years," Rafe said. "Not like they can say they were practicing goose stepping and *Sieg Heil* at Laurel Hill, after all."

No, I supposed not. "I'm not saying they did it. I have no idea whether they killed Natalie or not. Or killed Morris or not. I'm just saying that they might have, that there are other suspects in this case in addition to Charlotte—or in addition to Morris—and it would be nice to see Jarvis do something about investigating them."

"How d'you know he don't?"

He abandoned my right foot and moved to my left.

"I guess I don't," I admitted, crossing my legs the other way to give him better access. "He arrested Morris for Natalie's murder without doing a particularly good job of eliminating the other suspects. I'm afraid he's going to do the same thing to Charlotte."

"He mighta gotten away with that under Carter," Rafe said. "Carter wanted to solve cases. Tammy won't let nobody get arrested without evidence."

"I'm sure she wants to solve cases, too."

Rafe nodded. "'Course. But part of the reason she's here— the reason *we're* here—is to look into this kinda thing. Corruption, or malfeasance, or just general cutting of corners that Carter allowed 'cause he was trying to make himself and his department look good."

He dug his thumbs into the arch of my other foot, and I squeaked and twitched. He grinned and eased up. "Paul Jarvis ain't a bad detective. He kept on going on the Mason investigation last month, when a lotta other cops woulda let it go. There wasn't much evidence to go on. Just gut feeling. But he kept scraping away at it 'cause he thought there was something there."

And he'd ended up solving—or helping to solve—two cold

cases, in addition to the fresh murder that had kicked the whole thing off.

"I just want him to arrest someone other than Charlotte," I said, as, down on the blanket, Carrie gurgled and pushed herself up on her chubby little arms, kicking her feet. "Charlotte didn't do it. That means someone else did. And that means that there has to be another suspect out there. Rodney Clark, or Natalie's family. Someone with a reason to kill Morris. If Rodney's part of your group of white supremacists, he isn't above murder."

"He ain't above talking about it," Rafe said, "but that don't mean he'd actually kill anybody."

No, I guess it didn't. A lot of people talk big until they're faced with doing whatever it is they say they want to do, and then they can't go through with it.

"He has an alibi for Friday night," I said, "but it's Kyle Scoggins again, and I don't know how far I'd trust him. And Mr. and Mrs. Allen alibi each other…"

Rafe nodded. "Not exactly iron-clad, either."

No. Even if it seemed to be good enough for Jarvis.

We sat in silence a moment. Down on the blanket, Carrie was still doing pushups.

"Here's another theory," Rafe said eventually, his eyes on the baby. "Say Morris didn't kill Natalie. That don't mean that somebody couldn't have killed Morris because they thought he'd gotten away with it. But say he didn't. Say someone else did."

"If Morris didn't, then someone else would have had to. Someone did."

Rafe nodded. "And say that someone thought he'd gotten away with it. It'd been a couple of years, and the first trial ended in a hung jury. Another trial was coming up, and there was no reason to think that'd go any differently."

"But then Ida Burns died," I said, "and the defense dug up Morris's old girlfriend."

"And Morris was released. And came back home. How d'you think Natalie's killer would feel about that?"

"I don't imagine he'd be happy," I said slowly. "Not only had Morris been acquitted, so there was the chance that the police would open the case again and look for someone else. But Morris might have wanted to look for someone else, too. Mrs. Oberlin suggested that. That he came back to clear his name."

"He spent three years in prison," Rafe said, "and he woulda had a lot of time to think. If he thought he knew who mighta been responsible, he coulda made life difficult for that person."

We sat in silence a moment.

"I wrote off Ida Burns," I said. "I mean, I got this little tingle down my spine, you know, when I heard that she'd been a witness in the first trial and had died before she could testify in the second. But Morris was in prison when that happened, and couldn't have killed her, so I kind of wrote that possibility off…"

He arched a brow.

"But then Mrs. Oberlin said that Mrs. Burns might be rethinking what she'd heard. Which would only help Morris, right? If she stayed alive to testify that she wasn't sure it was him she'd heard after all?"

Rafe nodded. "That'd give somebody else reason to want to shut her up, though. If she was changing her tune."

Exactly what I'd been thinking. "Jarvis handled that case, too. Mrs. Oberlin found Mrs. Burns. She called Enoch—makes sense, right?—and Enoch called Jarvis."

"And Jarvis determined natural causes?"

"I think the ME did," I said. "Or at least there didn't seem to have been any question about it being anything but natural causes."

He thought for a moment. "Lotsa deaths on Fulton."

Indeed. "I don't suppose you'd be willing to double-check the results from Mrs. Oberlin's autopsy, if there is one? Or whatever the ME decides to do in her case?"

"Any evidence it was something more than a natural death?"

I shook my head. I hadn't noticed anything like that. "But the timing is interesting. She might have seen something on Friday, and not even realized it."

He nodded. "I'll talk to the ME tomorrow. And to Jarvis, too. I'll have to anyway, to discuss the way his case—again—touches on mine."

That made sense.

He added, pensively, "I'd like to have a chat with Clark and Scoggins without letting'em know that we know about the Laurel Hill connection, too. Maybe Jarvis'll agree to take me along on an interview, so I can size'em up without them realizing I'm doing it. That way, I can take a look at the way Jarvis handles the Morris case at the same time."

"Thank you," I said.

He gave me a look. "I'm not just doing it for you, darlin'. Part of the reason I'm here is to help Tammy flush out bad cops. Jarvis came up from Alabama with Carter. I gotta give him a close look."

I nodded. "I still appreciate it. Is there anything I can do to help?"

"We can spend some time doing something that isn't work," Rafe said.

We could, although with the baby on the floor and the dog watching us, what we could do right this moment was quite limited.

And then I realized he wasn't reaching for me, he was

reaching for the remote. "Basketball OK?"

"Fine," I said, as down on the floor, Caroline flopped over on her back with a surprised squawk.

Pearl gave a yip and startled Carrie into a howl. I moved to pick her up, but Rafe beat me there.

"Hush, baby." He cradled her against his chest, one big hand on her fuzzy, pink butt, and sat back down on the loveseat with a grin at me. "D'you see that? She turned over. First time, right?"

It was the first time I'd seen her flip from her front to her back. And judging from her startled reaction, it was new to Carrie, too. "She's growing up."

"Not so much that you'd notice," Rafe said, and reached out an arm to pull me close. We snuggled together, all in a huddle, while Pearl grinned a doggie grin from over in the corner.

Eighteen

When I got to Fulton Street the next morning, Charlotte wasn't there yet. I brought Carrie inside, put her on the kitchen floor, and got busy grouting the tile we'd hung yesterday afternoon. There wasn't a lot of it, so it only took an hour or so, including the time I spent figuring out how to grout tile. I'd looked up the process on YouTube yesterday, and asked Rafe—who had done some grouting in Mrs. Jenkins's house in the past—but this was my first time actually attempting the work myself. It turned out to be messy, but strangely satisfying. A little bit like playing with mud, something I hadn't been allowed to do much as a girl. Not lady-like.

By the time I was finished, Charlotte still hadn't shown up, though, and I was starting to get worried. Had Jarvis arrested her, and no one had told me? Or had she had a car accident on the way over, or something like that? If something was wrong and she couldn't make it, why didn't she call?

I tried to call her, but she didn't answer. And when I called the Albertsons' house, the phone just rang and rang, which wasn't encouraging.

I had to wait for the grout to dry anyway—or so I told myself. It wasn't entirely true, because there were lots of other things I could be doing, that had nothing to do with the grout.

But they were things that would be easier with four hands instead of two, and anyway, Charlotte was *supposed* to be here. So in the end, I ended up bundling Carrie back into the car, and climbing behind the wheel, and rolling off down the road.

Only to roll to a stop two seconds later, when I saw a guy get into a car in the Allens driveway.

It wasn't any of the Allens. Or at least I was pretty sure it wasn't. He was too young to be Natalie's father, and anyway, I recognized him. Or thought I did. I hadn't gotten a particularly good look at him the other day—when I walked into Beulah's he'd had his back to me, and when I'd sat down, I'd had my back to him—but I was pretty sure I was looking at Rodney Clark.

So I stopped down the street—blocking Carl Enoch's driveway, as it happened, although Enoch's truck was gone, so he was probably at work—and waved Rodney down as he backed his car off the Allens property.

He rolled down the window. "Help you?"

It didn't look like he recognized me. I was wearing a different coat today than I'd worn at Beulah's for Sunday brunch, and I had my hair up in a ponytail and minimal makeup on, so maybe it wasn't surprising. It was a good thing, anyway, so the adage about gift horses came to mind.

"I'm sorry," I said, giving him my sweetest smile, "but aren't you Rodney Clark?"

He squinted at me. "Who wants to know?"

"I'm Savannah Martin," I said, and then wondered if maybe I shouldn't have given him my name. It was too late for that, of course, but I could leave Rafe's name off, though, so I did. "My sister and I bought Steve Morris's house two weeks ago. We're fixing it up. Or we were, until he came back and got killed in what was supposed to be the master suite."

I watched for his reaction. If he'd killed Morris, would he

preen? He probably wouldn't admit it, but would I be able to see some sort of pride on his face or in his eyes?

What he did, was smirk. "That's too bad."

It didn't look like pride. More like amusement, but that didn't necessarily mean anything one way or the other. If he had killed Morris, he might feel amusement about the fact that Morris's death had inconvenienced me.

"You were Natalie Allen's boyfriend, right?"

He nodded. "How d'you know that?"

"One of the neighbors told me," I said. "Mrs. Oberlin. She lives—lived over there." I waved a hand in the direction of her house.

Rodney glanced at it. "Old lady with a dog?"

I nodded. He nodded too. "What about it?"

If he'd killed Mrs. Oberlin, there was certainly no sign of it. "I was just wondering what you thought happened. Steve Morris was arrested for Natalie's murder, but they couldn't convict him, and then he was acquitted. I was wondering whether you thought he did it, or if not, who did."

He stared at me through the window of the car. "You some kind of detective or something?"

I shook my head. "Not at all. Just curious. There have been a lot of deaths on Fulton Street in the past three or four years."

Rodney eyed me. Up and down a few times, where I stood in the open door of my Volvo. "You look like somebody I should know," he said eventually.

"I don't see why," I answered lightly, even as I felt a prickle of alarm. "I don't think we've ever met."

"How d'you know who I was?"

Oh. Um… "Good guess?"

His eyes narrowed.

"Fine," I said, scrambling for a believable lie. "I saw a picture. I talked to the Allens the other day, and Mrs. Allen showed me a picture of you and Natalie."

He glanced at the house. "She didn't mention that."

"No reason she would, right?" I smiled sunnily. "Who do they think killed Steve Morris?"

But I'd lost him. He'd caught on that something wasn't quite right, and wasn't willing to say anything else. "If you talked to them the other day, didn't they tell you?"

It made sense that they would have, so when I opened my mouth, nothing came out. Rodney snorted and put his car in gear. "See you around," he told me, and shot off in a cloud of exhaust. I stood where I was and waited for it to dissipate before I got back into the car.

And pulled out my phone. And called Rafe. "Rodney Clark was just here. Do you want me to try to follow him?"

If I could. If he wouldn't notice me at the first red light.

"Did he see you?"

"I talked to him," I said, as—in the rearview mirror—Rodney's car disappeared around the corner.

"Then no. Don't follow him. I don't suppose you happened to catch the license plate?"

I had, as a matter of fact. That was why I'd stood there, breathing exhaust, instead of getting into the Volvo immediately. I rattled it off. "Some kind of muscle car. A Charger or something."

"Thanks, darlin'. I'll get on the phone to the DMV."

"Happy to help," I said. "Um... You haven't heard anything about Charlotte, have you?"

His voice got more alert. "Like what?"

"Like, Jarvis arrested her."

"Ain't she there?"

She wasn't. "And she isn't answering her phone. Her parents don't, either. I'm worried."

"I think Tammy woulda let me know if that was gonna

happen," Rafe said judiciously, "but I can make a couple calls and see what I can find out."

I told him I'd appreciate it. "I was on my way back to Sweetwater when I saw Rodney." After a second I added, "Where are you?"

"Sitting outside Kyle Scoggins's place of employment," Rafe said.

"Where does he work?"

"Body shop on Lewisburg Pike. Just a couple minutes from where you are."

"Do you want company?"

"No," Rafe said. And softened the blow by adding, "Run on back to Sweetwater, darlin', and look for Charlotte. You won't breathe easy till you figure out what's going on."

That was probably correct.

"So you'll check with Grimaldi and let me know whether she's been arrested?"

"As soon as I get off the phone with you." A second passed, and then he added, his voice different, "Or not. What kinda car did you say Rodney was driving?"

"Some kind of beefy-looking thing with a lot of horsepower. Maybe a Dodger? Or Charger? Or whatever it's called?"

"Dodge Charger," Rafe said. "Navy blue?"

It had been navy blue. "Is he there?"

"Looks like he could be. There's a blue Challenger coming into the lot."

"It might have been a Challenger." I would have no idea of the difference, to be honest. I can tell a Dodge from a Ford most of the time, and that's pretty much all I can do.

"Yep," Rafe said, with satisfaction in his voice, "that's him."

"Is he there to talk to Kyle?"

"Must be. I gotta go, darlin'. Go look for Charlotte. I'll

contact Tammy and call you back when I can."

He hung up before I had time to say anything, even goodbye. "Fine," I told the phone. "Be that way."

Carrie made an inquiring gurgle from the back seat, and I turned the key in the ignition. "No worries, baby. Here we go."

We went, down the street and around the corner and back through Columbia toward Sweetwater.

It's roughly a thirty-minute drive from Fulton Street past Beulah's and the mansion, all the way into downtown Sweetwater where the Albertsons live. We pulled up across the street from the house and I sat for a second looking at it.

It's a big, white, Queen Anne style Victorian with a white picket fence enclosing the yard. Charlotte's minivan was parked at the curb, and Mrs. Albertson's little Subaru was in the driveway. Charlotte's dad drove an old truck, and I couldn't see it anywhere, so maybe he was out. He still worked part-time, as far as I knew.

There was a spiffy BMW parked in front of me, though, one I hadn't seen around here before. It had Davidson County plates—Nashville plates, like my car—and a small sticker on the back window. The kind of thing they put on rental cars to scan them in and out.

No sooner had the thought gone through my mind, than the front door of the Victorian opened, and Charlotte came out. She had little JR on her arm, and held her daughter by the hand, and even from across the street, I could see the tension in her body. She was holding herself stiffly, her face was pale, and as they stopped on the edge of the porch, a pale ray of sun snuck under the porch roof and reflected on something wet on her cheeks.

My heart skipped for a second. Something was very wrong here.

And then I noticed that behind her, someone else had come

out, and was closing the door to the house.

I sharpened my eyes.

I'd only met Richard once, and it was a long time ago. He and Charlotte had been dating, so six years, at least. And he'd been standoffish. Coldly polite, but making it very clear that he wanted me to go away and leave them alone. And since I'd had Bradley to occupy me at that time, I'd obliged.

He was older now. Had a touch of gray at the temples. Maybe a little middle-aged spread around the middle. But this was Richard. He must have flown in to the Nashville airport, rented a car—a BMW—and driven down here.

And he had brought his gun. I saw the sunlight glint on that, too, for a second, as he followed Charlotte and the kids down the stairs.

I watched from across the street, biting my knuckles, afraid to blink, as Charlotte instructed the little girl to open the gate. She did it with her free hand, while still clutching Charlotte tightly with the other. She looked just as pale and shell-shocked as her mother. Maybe she was old enough to realize what the gun was and what it could do, or maybe she was just picking up on Charlotte's tension. Even from here, I could tell that Charlotte looked brittle enough to snap in two at the least provocation. Even the little boy on her hip looked tense and worried. His eyes were huge, and he was sucking his thumb.

Richard passed through the gate after them, and looked up and down the street. His eyes lit on the Volvo for a second, and I saw his eyes narrow.

The windows are tinted, so I didn't think he could see me sitting here. But if he was feeling desperate enough, he might put a bullet through the window anyway, just to be safe. If he was kidnapping his family at gunpoint, he'd clearly passed the point of no return.

Charlotte must have realized the same thing, because a hot

wave of color flooded her cheeks, and she turned and said something to him. It took a second, but then he dragged his attention off the Volvo—off me—and onto her. His lips tightened, and he made a move with the gun hand as if he was going to hit her.

The little girl squealed in fear and threw her arms around Charlotte's hips. Richard subsided.

I fumbled my phone out of my purse with shaking hands, and took my eyes off the action across the street just long enough to make sure I called the right person.

"Yeah?" my husband's voice said in my ear, and I opened my mouth. And had to try a couple of time before I could force the words out.

"I need help."

"Savannah?" I imagined him straightening in the seat of the unmarked police Chevy. "What's wrong?"

"Richard's here," I said, my teeth knocking together. "He's taking Charlotte and the kids away at gunpoint."

"Where are you?"

I told him I was outside the Albertsons' house in Sweetwater. "I'm sorry. I shouldn't have called you. You're in Columbia, and on a stake-out. There's nothing you can do. I should have called the sheriff." Rafe has no jurisdiction in Sweetwater. I needed Bob Satterfield or Cletus Johnson.

"Hang on, darlin'."

A moment passed, and then I heard his voice in the background. "32 to dispatch."

"32, this is dispatch," an even fainter voice said. I thought it belonged to Officer Robinson, and my eyes narrowed. When it continued, "Go ahead, Rafe," I was sure of it.

"Got a report of a 10-68 in progress on Green Street in Sweetwater," my husband said, and there was nothing but business in his voice. "Contact the sheriff down there and get a car out ASAP. 32 out."

He came back on the line. "Tell me what's going on."

"I was on my way to talk to Charlotte," I said, doing my best to keep my voice even when it wanted to jitter and shake. "I pulled up across the street, behind a rental car with Nashville plates."

I knew I didn't have to explain the connection to Rafe. He'd figure it out quicker than I had.

"Her minivan was parked across the street, and her mother's car is in the driveway. Before I could get out—" *Thank you, God,* "the door to the house opened and Charlotte came out on the porch with both the kids, and then Richard followed. He had a gun in his hand."

"Has he seen you?" Rafe asked, his voice tight.

"He saw the car. Charlotte distracted him. Or maybe he's afraid to cause any kind of disturbance. So far, it looks like I'm the only one seeing what's going on."

"What's going on?"

I heard the squeal of tires, faintly, through the phone. He had clearly left his post outside Kyle Scoggins's place of employment to come to my rescue.

I gave myself a sharp mental kick. *Stupid, Savannah!* I should have thought for a second longer before I called him. This wasn't his fight. He had another job to do. But now that he knew what was going on, it was clearly too late to stop him from coming, so I answered the question.

"They're getting into the minivan. Or Charlotte's strapping the kids into the car seats in the back. Richard's behind her with the gun. Looks like he's putting her in the passenger seat. No, wait… he's making her slide across and into the driver's seat. He's getting in beside her."

"It's hard to juggle a gun and the steering wheel at the same time," Rafe said, like he'd know. And he probably did.

"Making Charlotte drive is safer. He can keep the gun on her, and she ain't gonna do nothing dangerous. Not with both the kids in the car."

No, she wouldn't.

"They're driving away," I said, reaching for the key.

"Wait." It was almost like he knew what I was doing. I waited for him to tell me to stay where I was, but he added, "Give it a couple seconds. See which way they're going at the corner."

I watched in the rearview mirror as the minivan rolled slowly up the street, drawing no attention to itself. "They're stopping at the first stop sign. No signal." Charlotte wasn't taking any chances, but coming to a complete and utter stop. "They're going straight for another block. Can I start the car?"

"Are you sure you don't wanna stay there and see if Mrs. Albertson's OK?"

I hesitated. Now that he mentioned it, I guess I was worried about Charlotte's mother, too. Richard might have shot her dead. Or she might be bound and gagged and stuck to a chair inside, so she couldn't call for help for her daughter and grandchildren. Or she might be bleeding out on the floor right now. I probably should check on her.

On the other hand, Charlotte was driving away at gunpoint. And if I didn't see where they were going, nobody would know where they were.

"Tell the sheriff to send somebody to check on Mrs. Albertson." If she was alive, two minutes to or from weren't likely to make much of a difference. And if she was dead... well, two minutes wouldn't matter then either. "I'm going after Charlotte."

I cranked the key over in the ignition.

"Be careful," Rafe said as I executed a tight U-turn between sidewalks and zoomed off down the street after the minivan. I came to a rolling stop at the first stop sign in time to see the Town & Country take a right at the next stop up at Oak Street.

"They're going north on Oak. Probably headed for the interstate."

They'd be passing the mansion in a minute or two, and Beulah's a few minutes after that. And with luck, they'd run into Rafe and the Chevy before they could turn off the Columbia Highway onto the Damascus Road and I-65.

"I'm on my way," Rafe said calmly. I was sure he was going eighty, zigzagging between the other cars on the road, making his way through Columbia to the south side, but you'd never be able to hear it in his voice. "Be careful, darlin'. You got the baby in the backseat, right?"

I glanced in the rearview mirror. I did indeed have the baby in the backseat. She was asleep, her little rosebud mouth pursed, and had been so quiet that for a minute or two, I'd almost forgotten that she was there. And that could be dangerous. I nodded, not that he could see me. "I've got her. And I'll be careful. I promise."

"Put the phone in the cradle. Keep it on speaker. Both hands on the wheel. Talk to me about what you see."

I dumped the phone into the cradle. It took two tries to get it in because I was shaking. "I'm turning the corner now," I announced. "I can see them up ahead, but there are two cars between us."

"Any of those belong to the sheriff?"

Not as far as I could see. "Not unless they're unmarked. Does the sheriff have unmarked vehicles?"

"They all have private cars," Rafe said. "The sheriff has a truck. Cletus drives a minivan because of the kids."

"These are both sedans." So probably nobody from the sheriff's office had caught up yet.

We chugged past the Oak Street cemetery on the right.

"They're getting close to the mansion," I said.

"You wanna stop?"

I did want to stop. My hands were shaking and I had a sour feeling in my stomach from the fear and adrenaline. But— "No. I'll keep going. At least until someone from the sheriff's office catches up. Somebody has to make sure we don't lose sight of them."

Up ahead, the minivan rolled past the mansion. Half a minute later, so did I, at the end of the little procession of cars.

It was kind of crazy. Charlotte was driving at such a sedate pace, probably afraid to do anything to draw attention to their car, that it was like a car chase in slow motion on screen. Creeping down the road in thirty-five, practically like a funeral procession, only increasing the speed to forty-five once we were past the mansion and outside the Sweetwater city limits. Hardly the pace of a desperate criminal trying to get away with three hostages, yet that was pretty much what I was looking at up ahead.

Was he taking them back to the airport in Nashville? Or did he plan to drive at gunpoint all the way back to North Carolina?

"Did you have any clue this was gonna happen?" Rafe wanted to know.

I shook my head at the phone, even though I knew he couldn't see me. "None. Maybe I should have. I knew he wasn't giving her any money. That's why we picked up this house to flip, so that Charlotte could make some quick cash."

Or relatively quick. None of us had anticipated the problems we had run into. Just as I hadn't anticipated this.

"She told me he was doing it to try to force them to come back to him," I added. "I didn't think that meant he was willing to take them back at gunpoint. Maybe I should have."

"Any indications he's been violent before?"

Charlotte hadn't mentioned anything like that. "I know he's been controlling. Back in the spring, during our high school reunion, I got the impression that he wasn't treating her as well as he should. She didn't seem happy. I thought he was making her feel bad about herself, you know? Two kids, not twenty-two anymore. But no. She never said anything about him hitting or anything like that. If I thought about abuse at all," and I wasn't sure I had, not in those terms, "I guess I would have suspected emotional or verbal abuse, but nothing physical."

"That can be bad enough," Rafe said, and again, he would know. Old Jim, Rafe's grandfather, hadn't stopped at verbal and emotional, though, he's sailed right into physical, too. But yes, verbal and emotional abuse can do just as much damage over time as physical abuse. In much more insidious ways.

"How close are you?" I asked.

"I'm getting to the south side of Columbia. You?"

"They're just coming up on Beulah's. Still going at a funeral pace. I'm still two car lengths behind. No, wait—one of the cars between us is turning into the parking lot."

"Anyone behind you?"

I glanced in the mirror. "No. Just the three of us on the road now."

"A couple of sheriff's vehicles should be catching up soon," Rafe said.

"Good." Or maybe it wasn't good. "Are they going to pull the minivan over? What will Richard do if they do that? Once he knows that he won't get away with this?"

"Hard to say," Rafe said, as the Volvo rolled past Beulah's Meat'n Three. "Depends on how crazy he is. And what he's already done."

"Meaning?"

"So far, he's kidnapped his wife and kids at gunpoint.

That's a big deal, but not as big as if he shot Charlotte's mama."

Understood. "Any news on her?"

"A car's on its way," Rafe said. "Ambulance too, just in case."

Good. "So what you're saying is, if he's already shot somebody—maybe already killed somebody—he'll be more likely to do it again."

"It gets easier with practice," Rafe said. "But yeah, less and less to lose the farther he's already gone."

That wasn't encouraging. "How close are you to the Damascus Road?"

"Couple minutes. You?"

"About the same." Although he was surely driving like a bat out of hell. He does that even when he's not in a hurry, and at the moment, he was probably flying. Meanwhile, Charlotte was carefully obeying the speed limit and rules of the road. But if she increased her speed just a little, she'd get to the turnoff before him. While he probably couldn't go any faster than he already was unless he wanted to risk an accident.

"Any sign of the sheriff?"

I glanced up in the rearview mirror again. "Yes! They're coming. I see flashing lights."

I didn't hear any sirens, but maybe they weren't close enough yet. Or maybe they were coming in silently, so as not to give Richard advance warning.

"See the intersection yet?"

"I can see the traffic lights," I said. "The minivan's signaling to go into the right lane. They're definitely turning toward the interstate."

"I see them coming." His voice was calm. "Turn off to the side, darlin'. Get outta the way of the sheriff."

"I don't see you," I said, trying to look around for him while at the same time preparing to do as he said. The sheriff's vehicles were coming up on my rear now, flashing their lights. I scooted off to the right, onto the shoulder of the road, and crept forward while they zoomed past me.

Up ahead, the light changed from red to green.

I'd been here before, at this same intersection in much this same situation. Then, it had been Dix, Darcy, and me, with Dix behind the wheel and a different baby in the backseat, trying to catch up to Denise Seaver in Darcy's Honda. And as she'd turned the corner—at a much faster clip than Charlotte was going now—a three-ton pickup with the Virgin Mary on the back window, with my husband behind the wheel and José Garcia next to him, had blasted across the intersection and knocked her clear across four lanes of traffic and into the ditch.

That didn't happen this time. Charlotte slowed to a crawl, and took the corner at a sedate fifteen miles an hour. One of the sheriff's vehicles put on a burst of speed, skidded into the next lane, and wrenched the wheel hard to the right, to come to a quivering stop diagonally in front of the minivan.

The other sheriff's car, meanwhile, fell in behind, also at an angle, so the minivan couldn't go backward. And the shoulder of the road dropped off to a deep ditch, so no way to drive around.

I stayed on my side of the corner, where I had a good view of the proceedings, but where I probably wouldn't get caught up in anything bad, assuming anything bad was going to happen.

By now, the two sheriff's deputies—or actually, it was Sheriff Satterfield himself getting out of one car, and Cletus Johnson out of the other—had both pulled their guns and were pointing them at the minivan. They were both bracing their hands on the tops of the door frames of their respective cars to keep the guns steady.

What that meant, of course, was that poor Charlotte, in the

driver's seat, had three guns pointed at her. Richard's, and the two of them. She was probably hysterical, and the kids, too.

I was so busy watching that I didn't even notice Rafe's tan Chevy zooming across the intersection and making a squealing U-turn before coming to a stop behind me.

He wrenched open the door and ran toward me, crouching to keep out of the line of fire. I unlocked my door and let him pull it open.

He squatted in the space between the open door and the rest of the car to peer in at me. "You all right?"

"Fine," I said. "We're both fine. And I'm staying out of the way." *So don't tell me to leave.*

He nodded. "Not far enough back if bullets start to fly, but I don't imagine it'd do much good to tell you to go home and leave it to the professionals."

"Not until I know if Charlotte's going to be all right."

Richard still had her at gunpoint, as far as I was able to tell from over here. And so, of course, did Bob and Cletus. Not that they'd shoot her on purpose—Richard might—but you never know what can happen once bullets—as Rafe had said—start to fly.

"Besides," I added, "my husband just showed up, and is about to get himself involved, and I want to make sure he comes out of this in one piece, too."

He smiled "Always, darlin'."

Not always. He'd been shot before. And stabbed before. And had other bad things happen to him before, too. He wasn't indestructible. Hard to kill, maybe, but one well-placed bullet could do a lot of damage.

"I'm staying," I told him.

He nodded. "Stay back, then. And down. Don't get outta the car until you know it's safe."

I promised I wouldn't. "What are you going to do?"

"My job," Rafe said. He put his hand on mine for a second—not long enough for me to turn mine over and latch on—and then he was gone. Around the open door and around the front of the Volvo and into the ditch bordering the road.

I held my breath as he moved, still in a crouch, toward the corner, and then around the corner and toward the minivan, still following the ditch. I could see his head bobbing, but nothing more of him now.

Richard would be able to see him coming, though. All he had to do was turn his head and he'd be able to see Rafe moving toward him. And all he'd have to do then, was open his door and shoot. He could get Rafe square in the chest—because of course my husband hadn't taken the time to put on tactical gear—while Rafe wouldn't have a clear shot at all, at Richard inside the minivan.

Is it any wonder I was holding my breath, and turning purple with the effort, until I couldn't hold my breath any longer, and gulped a mouthful of air into my lungs?

Richard's attention was focused in the other direction, though, at Charlotte in the driver's seat, and at the two law enforcement officers keeping him at gunpoint from the road. Rafe made it to the back corner of the minivan and up onto the pavement with no shots being fired.

When he popped out of the ditch, Cletus noticed him. I guess he and Bob had been too focused on Richard so far, to realize that Rafe was approaching from the other direction. Or maybe Bob knew, but Cletus certainly didn't. His attention flickered to Rafe for a second, and as a result, Richard became aware of him, too.

It all happened quickly after that. Too quickly for me to really see the progression. There was a shot, and another shot, so close together that they sounded almost like the same shot. Rafe dropped to the ground behind the minivan—my breath stopped, and not because I was holding it this time. Blood spatter hit the inside of the minivan's window, where Richard was sitting. And then there was a lot of noise and movement both inside and outside the minivan.

Rafe popped back up again—my heart went back to beating, a little unevenly until it caught back up to normal—and ran to Richard's door. He wrenched it open—someone must have popped the button from the other side, I guess; probably Charlotte—and Richard half fell out of the car. Rafe grabbed him, and skidded a little on the gravel shoulder of the road as he tried to hold on.

Then Bob skirted the front of the car and was there to help, and Cletus ran around the back, and I saw Charlotte open her door and pretty much fall to her knees on the pavement. And at that point I figured the danger was over, so I left my own car—although I made sure to lock it behind me on the run, so nobody would be able to get at Carrie—as I hustled up the shoulder of the road and down the other side to see what, if anything, I could do to help.

Nineteen

Charlotte was on her hands and knees on the road, retching, so I took it upon myself to open the back door of the minivan and look in on the kids. They were both screaming, with tears coursing down their cheeks. The little girl was sobbing so hard she was hiccupping. "Mommy! Daddy!"

"Shhh," I told her. "It's OK." It wasn't, but what else could I say? "Your mom's coming."

She wasn't listening to me. "Daddy!" she screamed. "Daddy!"

I glanced over the back of the seat, into the front of the car and out the door. "Daddy's OK, too."

He was, actually. Or if not OK, at least he was alive and kicking. He was down on the side of the road, bellowing in rage, loud enough that whatever gunshot wound he'd contracted couldn't have been that big a deal. I've been shot once, and it does tend to take all your attention when it happens. Richard wasn't unduly put out by his, it seemed. His voice worked just fine, and so did his lungs. He was cursing and weeping—tears of rage, no doubt—and fighting as Rafe and Cletus together wrestled him to the ground and fastened handcuffs around his wrists. It took both of them to do it, which should tell you something about just how angry he was.

They're both bigger and considerably more muscular than Richard, and it still took their combined effort to get the job done.

"Richard Whitaker," the sheriff intoned, "you're under arrest for kidnapping—"

I squatted next to Charlotte as the guys hauled Richard to his feet and began moving him toward one of the sheriff's vehicles. He was kicking and bucking, trying to throw them off, and I didn't doubt for a second that if he could have gotten free, he would have taken off down the road. When he saw Charlotte on her knees on the pavement, he spat at her, and then let loose with a string of invective. "You ungrateful bitch, I should have…"

Charlotte raised her head to look at him, her cheeks pale and tear-stained and her lips quivering.

Rafe and Cletus paid him no mind, just kept wrestling him toward the squad car, where the sheriff was holding the door open. They maneuvered him inside, still cursing and bellowing—Cletus put his hand on Richard's head and shoved it down—and then the door shut behind him, and it was blessedly silent. Or more silent. He was still carrying on inside the car, but distantly, muted, like a bumblebee in a jar. Hopefully, once he realized that nobody out here could hear him, he'd stop doing that, too, although I didn't envy whoever would have to drive him back to the sheriff's office for lockup.

He kept kicking and throwing himself around, too, like a five-year-old having a temper tantrum, making the whole car bounce and jerk.

"Better get him outta here," the sheriff told Cletus. "I'll follow you in a couple minutes."

Cletus grimaced, but nodded. He and Rafe exchanged a wary sort of nod, like two tomcats circling one another in an alley, and then Cletus skirted the back of the squad car and headed for the front seat. Richard's curses got louder for the few seconds it took Cletus to get himself seated behind the wheel, and then they were cut off again when Cletus shut the door. We watched as he made a U-turn across all the lanes of traffic—all the other cars moved out of the way of the flashing blue lights—and then he took the turn back down the Columbia Highway—or Pulaski Highway—toward Sweetwater.

Charlotte watched the car until it disappeared, her eyes wide, before she blinked and seemed to come back to herself. She looked around, from Sheriff Satterfield to Rafe to me.

Her brows lowered. "What are you doing here?"

Her voice was hoarse, either from the crying or the throwing up.

"I followed you," I said, "after Richard loaded you into the minivan. You saw me, parked across the street."

Or so I assumed, seeing as she'd taken Richard's attention off me when it looked like he might be inclined to investigate my car.

"Oh." She ran the tip of her tongue over her lips. "Right."

Maybe she'd forgotten I was there, in the terror. It wouldn't be surprising.

"I called Rafe from the car," I said. "He called the sheriff. And then we all caught up to you here."

She nodded, sort of vaguely. And looked around. And finally seemed to realize that her children were in the back seat of the minivan, screaming their heads off. "Oh, my God!" She scrambled to her feet. "Michaela! JR!"

Rafe put an arm around me and pulled me out of the way so I wouldn't get mowed down. As Charlotte flew, head-first, into the back of the van to console her kids, I turned to Bob Satterfield. "Hi, Sheriff. Any news on Charlotte's mother?"

The sheriff nodded a greeting and filled me—us—in. "Shook up, but all right. Whitaker gagged her and tied her to a chair so she couldn't call for help when he took his family and left. She's not a young woman, so the shock and rough handling didn't do her any good, but the paramedics are staying with her until her husband gets there, and knowing that Charlotte and the kids are all right will go a long way toward making everything right again."

A beat passed, and then he added, "Let me go do that."

He headed for the remaining squad car. Rafe tightened his arm around me and leaned down to drop a kiss on my cheek. I turned my head at the last second so it landed on my mouth instead.

"You OK?" I asked against his lips.

They curved up. "Yeah. A couple bruises, but nothing worse."

"What about Richard? He got shot, obviously." I'd seen the blood spray on the inside of the window. "But he was in good enough condition to put up a fight."

"Just a scratch," Rafe said. His just-a-scratches tend to be a bit worse than... well, scratches, but I believed him when he added, "He'll need a couple stitches and some padding. But he'll survive to stand trial. And live for a long time afterwards."

Good to know.

"I should get back," he added, with a glance over his shoulder. "I got work of my own to do."

I nodded. "I'm sorry to take you away from it."

"I'm not." He dropped another kiss, this time right on my mouth, and lingered. "But now that everything's in hand here," he added once he'd raised his head, "I should get back to it."

"I'm going to stay for a few minutes, and then follow Charlotte home. Make sure she and the kids get there OK. Check on Carrie on your way past the car, would you? She's probably still asleep—"

It had only been a few minutes since I stumbled out of the

Volvo, but they'd been a couple of minutes that had gone on for what had seemed like a long time. "If not, I'll take her out of the car while I wait."

He nodded. "I'll see you at home later."

Count on it. I unclenched my hands from his sleeves and watched him saunter away, along the side of the road, down to the corner, and from there, over to the Volvo. He peered through the back window for a second, and turned to give me a thumbs up. I lifted a hand in acknowledgement, and then I watched him get into the Chevy and drive away, merging with traffic headed toward the center of Columbia.

"He going back to work?" the sheriff asked. I hadn't even noticed him come back out of the car and toward me, but now he was standing next to me watching the Chevy disappear up the road.

I nodded. "He's following Kyle Scoggins and Rodney Clark around. Rodney was the other guy from Beulah's the other day. I saw him on Fulton Street earlier, and recognized him. And Rafe said he showed up at Kyle Scoggins's place of employment just before this whole—" I waved my hand at Charlotte, at the minivan, and at the two screaming kids, "— mess happened."

"Things are coming together," Bob said, sounding pleased. I guess he was talking about the Laurel Hill case, and not this... mess. Although with Richard being caught red-handed the way he'd been, this was pretty open and shut too, if you asked me.

I cleared my throat. "What are the chances, in your opinion, that Rodney and/or Kyle killed Natalie Allen because she knew they were Nazi sympathizers and she was threatening to rat them out?"

"Rat them out to who?"

Whom. "I don't know," I said. "Somebody."

He shook his head. "Here's the thing, darlin'. There's no

law against being a Nazi. It makes people look at you sideways, especially when you go in a clump to a place like Laurel Hill for target practice. But we can't arrest somebody for that. It's no crime to think a certain way. It's only a crime if you act on it."

I nodded. "What if they were planning to do more? And what if Natalie knew about it?"

"More than three years ago?" The sheriff made a skeptical face. "Don't you think they woulda done it by now? Especially if they killed somebody so nobody'd figure out what they planned to do?"

Maybe. I mean... that did make sense. "So not Kyle or Rodney."

"It mighta been Kyle or Rodney," the sheriff said. "I don't recall the case. It wasn't one of mine. But if it was Kyle or Rodney, it probably wasn't for that reason."

No. "I appreciate it."

He nodded. And turned back to the minivan and Charlotte. "Think she's gonna be all right driving home?"

"I think she'll have to be," I said. "Although I suppose I could pile them all into my car and drive them back if she can't manage. You wouldn't pull us over and give us a ticket if she held one of the kids on her lap on the way home, would you? I've got Carrie in the back seat, so there's only room for one more car seat."

"I don't think that'd be a problem today," Bob said. "We're all pretty busy right now."

No doubt. "What'll happen to Richard?"

"We'll get him patched up," Bob said, "and then we'll talk to him. But before that I'll call Todd, and give the DA's office a heads up. He'll get out on bail, of course. He has plenty of money." Unlike Steve Morris. And unlike his wife. "But eventually we'll convict him and put him in prison. And then Charlotte won't have to worry about him again."

He sent a fatherly glance her way.

"Feel free to head out," I told him. "I'll get her either back behind the wheel of her own car, or into mine. You'll want to talk to her, right?"

He nodded. "But it can wait an hour or two. Let her get the kids back home and settled first. Tell her I'll stop by the house later."

I said I would, and then I watched him walk to his car and drive away. By then, little Michaela and JR had calmed down enough that Charlotte was coming back up for air again, too.

"The sheriff said we could leave," I told her. "You can drive home if you want to, or we can all pile into my car and I'll drive. Bob said nobody would give us a ticket for not having all the kids strapped into booster seats today. Your choice."

Charlotte glanced at the blood spatter on the inside of her car windows and shuddered. "We'll go with you, if you don't mind."

I didn't mind at all, and told her so. "Carrie's in the car, so we'll have to squeeze both the kids in next to her. If we take JR's car seat out of the minivan, we can probably wedge Michaela in the middle without a seat. Or you can keep her on your lap."

"I don't care," Charlotte said. "I just want to get away from here."

Then that's what we'd do. I helped her unhook Michaela from the booster seat, and then stood and held Michaela's hand while Charlotte crawled into the minivan and released JR. She hauled the car seat out and shut the minivan door while I walked the kids around the corner and down to the Volvo. We got them both situated in the back—waking Carrie up in the process; although the upshot was that Michaela was fascinated by the baby, which went a long way toward taking her mind off what had happened earlier. I put her in charge of making sure that Carrie didn't lose her pacifier, and she sat there patiently while I drove us back toward Sweetwater, sticking the pacifier back into Carrie's mouth every time the baby spat it out. And because Michaela was calmer, JR quieted down, too.

"You holding up all right?" I asked Charlotte under my breath as we rolled past Beulah's in the opposite direction.

She blew out a breath and shoved her hand through her hair. "Not sure. I had no idea he'd…"

She trailed off.

No, I'd had no idea my first husband would break the law, either. It hadn't been to get me back—he had Shelby and a baby on the way by then, and didn't want me—but I'd totally underestimated who he was and what he was willing to do to hang on to what he wanted.

"Thank God I got worried and got to your house in time to see him leave with you." A couple minutes later, and they'd be gone. "Otherwise, he could have kept going, and until your father came home and found your mother, nobody would have known what had happened."

"Oh, God!" Charlotte said. "My mother!"

"She's fine." Or mostly fine. "The sheriff sent a car over there. The paramedics were going to stay with her until your father could make it home. She was shaken up and afraid, but I'm sure, once Bob called and let her know that you and the kids are safe, it went a long way toward calming her down."

Charlotte's eyes filled with tears. "I can't believe I bought that down on my parents. I had no idea Richard was capable of something like that."

I'd had no idea, either, or I would have been concerned as soon as she didn't show up on Fulton Street this morning. "You never told me he was abusive," I said.

"He wasn't!"

After a second she changed it to, "I mean… not like that. He didn't get physical. He just liked things a certain way, you know? And if they weren't that way, then he wouldn't talk to me until I changed them. For days, sometimes. One time, he didn't talk to me for two weeks after I cut my hair shorter than he liked."

"What would you call that," I wanted to know, as we passed the driveway to the mansion and kept going, "if not abuse?"

I didn't wait for her answer. "That's controlling behavior, at the very least. Emotional abuse. Probably verbal abuse. The man's a menace!"

Charlotte shushed me, with a glance into the back seat. Poor little JR had fallen asleep, probably from crying so hard, but Michaela was still poking at Carrie. Neither of them were paying attention to us. Nonetheless, I lowered my voice. "You should have said something."

"What could you have done?" Charlotte wanted to know. "I was ten hours away."

Back then? Not a lot. But since she came home… "It would have helped to know this might be coming."

"I had no idea this was coming!" Charlotte exclaimed, and then shot another guilty glance into the back seat.

We rode in silence a few seconds.

"I know you told me these antics with the money— canceling your credit cards, shutting you out of the accounts— were a way to try to force you to come back to him." A statement I obviously hadn't taken to its logical conclusion back then. "But did you realize he wanted you back this badly?"

Charlotte shook her head, and shoved another shaking hand through her hair. That alone would have told me how upset she was. We Southern Belles never, ever touch our hair after it's styled in the morning. "God, no. I thought, with this new woman and a baby on the way, he'd be focused on them, and maybe wouldn't care that we left and didn't come back. I mean... I didn't think he'd seriously expect me to stay married to him while he had a baby with someone else on the side."

"But he did?"

She shrugged. "He must have. He was taking us back at gunpoint. Because—" Her tone changed to mimic his, "nobody leaves him until he says they can."

Outside the window, the Oak Street Cemetery rolled by.

"The earring..." I said, and didn't need to say any more.

Charlotte sighed. "Richard called. I didn't want to scream at him in front of my parents and the kids, so I went for a drive. But after a while it got hard to drive and scream, so I stopped at the house so I could scream without worrying about keeping the car on the road."

Perfectly understandable.

"He said..." She swallowed, and her voice got stronger. "He said a lot of really unforgivable things. And touched on the jewelry he'd given me. He said he wanted his engagement ring back. I assumed so he could give it to the floozy."

That would have been my assumption, too.

"I stopped wearing that, and my wedding band, after I left him. But I had the earrings on. And I took one out and threw it. As hard as I could. At the wall."

She grimaced. "And then I realized that I was throwing away money. Money I could use to feed my kids. So I looked for it. But it was late, and I was tired, and it's a big room..."

"You couldn't find it."

She shook her head. "Morris wasn't there. I swear. It was just me. I gave up, and drove home, and figured I'd just look again in the morning, when the sun was out and I could see better."

I nodded. "But by morning..."

"I overslept. Because I'd lain awake half the night, fuming

and fretting. And when I got there..."

Morris was dead on the floor. On top of her earring.

"Thanks for telling me," I said, since the story about the earring had bothered me a little. "Do you want me to call Catherine?" I'm not sure where the two of you are in the divorce proceedings, whether he's been served or not—"

"Yesterday," Charlotte said with a grimace.

So that was what had set this off. Her taking actual steps to separate herself from him was what had set Richard off on this path.

"Well, she probably needs to know what's going on. Do you want me to call her so she can meet us at your house, or would you rather do it yourself later?"

"Later," Charlotte said. "I want to see my mom first."

That made sense. However— "I wouldn't wait too long, if I were you."

We reached Green Street, and I made the left turn. And drove down a block and half and parked in the same spot I'd been parked earlier, behind Richard's rental. "Someone will have to drive that back to Nashville, I guess. Or maybe the company can send someone out to pick it up." After the sheriff had gone through it for anything Richard might have left. There probably wasn't anything there—he had abandoned the rental in favor of the minivan, and probably didn't plan to come back to it—but someone had to take a look.

Charlotte nodded, but her attention was across the street, on the house. An ambulance was still parked at the curb, and now her father's truck had joined her mother's little compact in the driveway.

"Go," I told her. "I'll get the kids."

She gave me an agonized look, but then she nodded. And opened the door and sprinted across the street. Good thing it's a quiet area without many cars.

"Mommy!" Michaela shrieked, terror in her voice. JR jerked upright and, after a stunned second, began screaming, too.

Definitely time to go. I opened my own door, and then JR's. "Come on." I leaned in and unhooked the straps holding him to the seat, and wrestled him out. This would be what I'd be doing with Carrie in a couple of years, I realized, so it was probably good practice. Hopefully she wouldn't be screaming in my ear when I lifted her, though. Although sometimes, I'm sure she would.

Michaela scrambled across the car seat and out, no doubt terrified to be left behind. I put JR down and looked back and forth, left and right, up and down the street. There were no cars in sight. "Go."

They took off across the street together. JR slowed down in time to carefully negotiate the step-up to the sidewalk, and then they were both running through the gate and up the walkway to the house. I shut the door and walked around to the other side of the car to grab Carrie and the car seat.

By the time I got inside, both the kids had flung themselves at Mrs. Albertson, who was sitting on the sofa with Charlotte's father clutching her hand. Charlotte was on the other side of her, streaming tears, while the two paramedics were hovering, seemingly unsure what to do. When I came through the door, as the only person in sight who wasn't visibly crying, they turned to me with what looked like relief.

"Everything good here?" I asked.

They nodded. "Yes, ma'am," one of them said. "We've checked out Mrs. Albertson. Her daughter says she and the kids weren't hurt."

Not physically. Mentally was another story, but unless we wanted to dope them all to the gills, there wasn't much the paramedics could do about that. The kids might need therapy, and Charlotte might too, but we could worry about that later.

"You can probably go," I told them. There might be other people needing the ambulance today, after all. "Everyone's OK. The bad guy's in jail, and the sheriff's coming to take statements and update everyone. I don't think we need you anymore."

They both nodded—a man and a woman, around my age. "If anything changes, just let us know."

I promised I would, and saw them out. By the time I got back into the living room, the kids had stopped screaming and Charlotte was wiping her face. "You all right?" I asked Mrs. Albertson, who was pale and looked shell-shocked, but otherwise didn't seem to have anything wrong with her.

She nodded. And cleared her throat. "Charlotte tells me I have you to thank for calling the police."

"I was worried when Charlotte didn't show up this morning," I said, "and nobody answered the phone. So I drove over here. I was parked across the street when I saw them all come out and get into the minivan. I called Rafe. He called the sheriff. And then we all converged on the car up at the intersection of the Columbia Highway and the Damascus Road." Before they'd made it to the interstate, thankfully. If they had, it would have been much harder to catch up, and much more dangerous to pull them over. Charlotte wouldn't have had a choice but to speed up once they were on the interstate.

"Well, thank your husband for us," Mrs. Albertson said. A little stiffly, but she said it. Which was nice, since I'd gotten the impression that she wasn't entirely reconciled to my marriage.

Not that it matters to me what Charlotte's mother thinks of my husband. Not really. But I want all of Sweetwater to realize that he isn't the hoodlum they all saw growing up—or isn't just that kid—so I'll take any little victory I can get.

The doorbell rang at that moment, and I got to my feet. "I'll get it." It was probably Sheriff Satterfield, coming to update them all and take official statements. Maybe he'd brought Mother. She and Mrs. Albertson were friendly.

I pulled the door open with a smile on my face. "Hello, Sh... Oh."

It wasn't the sheriff. Nor my mother. Instead, it was Detective Paul Jarvis staring at me over the fuzzy head of Chester the Shih-Tzu.

Twenty

I blinked. He blinked back.

Jarvis, not the dog. The dog was panting.

"Detective," I said eventually.

"Mrs. Collier." He nodded. And looked a little uncomfortable.

I lowered my voice. "You aren't here to arrest anyone, are you?"

With the dog riding on his arm, that was perhaps a little unlikely, but I thought it was safer to ask.

Jarvis shook his head. "I heard about what happened. I wanted to make sure everything was all right."

Nice. If a little inexplicable.

I nodded to the Shih-Tzu. "What's with Chester?"

Jarvis glanced down at him, and if I hadn't known better, I would have said his cheeks got a little pink. "I took him home with me last night. Didn't want to bother the folks at the shelter. Thought he could use the company."

My eyebrows went up, all on their own. "That was nice of you." Surprisingly so.

"I'm nice," Jarvis said. And added, "Sometimes."

When I didn't say anything, he continued, "I thought he might take the kids' minds off things. And he'd enjoy the attention."

He probably would. I took a step back. "Come on in."

Jarvis stepped across the threshold, and I closed the door behind him. "Can I take your trench coat, Detective?"

He gave me a look, as if suspecting that I was being snarky. "I won't stay long."

Fine. "This way." I gestured him through the foyer and into the living room. And raised my voice. "Detective Jarvis stopped by."

Charlotte's eyes widened. So did her mother's. They both looked frightened.

"He took Chester home with him yesterday," I continued, brightly, as the kids eyes zoomed in on the dog like homing beacons. "He thought Chester might like some company."

"OK if I put him down?" Jarvis inquired gruffly. He waited for Mrs. Albertson's nod before lowering Chester carefully to the floor. Michaela gazed at him with wonder, while JR looked a little apprehensive. Chester began to sniff the rug and the leg of the coffee table.

"I hope you emptied him out before you brought him in here," I told Jarvis out of the corner of my mouth.

He gave me a look and turned to Charlotte. "I heard about what happened. Everyone OK?"

She nodded. And got her voice to cooperate. "Thank you, Detective."

"My pleasure," Jarvis said, and sounded like he meant it.

Mrs. Albertson also found speech, finally. "Won't you have a seat, Detective Jarvis?"

Jarvis perched on the edge of one of the wingback chairs across from the sofa. I took the other one, and leaned back, crossing one leg over the other. Jarvis leaned forward, hands between his knees. "I won't stay long. I just wanted to make sure that everything was OK."

"Making sure you'll still be able to arrest me later?" Charlotte asked tartly, and then looked horrified at her own forwardness. Her mother gave her a shocked look.

"Charlotte!"

Jarvis's lips twitched, but he didn't say anything. Not about that. "When we spoke this weekend," he said instead, directed at Charlotte, "you didn't tell me that your husband was a threat."

"I didn't know!" She glanced at her mother and father, and then back. "I knew he was upset that I left and took the kids. I explained about the money…"

Jarvis nodded.

"But I didn't think he'd come here. I thought, now that he has a new girlfriend and a baby on the way, he'd focus on them and let us go. Eventually."

Michaela's hand stilled on Chester's fur, and she looked up and over at her mother. Maybe Charlotte hadn't told the kids about Richard's mistress and the baby yet.

"The gun…?" Jarvis said.

Charlotte sighed. "He kept it in the bedside table drawer."

"Did he ever threaten you with it?"

"No." Charlotte shook her head. "At least…"

I rolled my eyes. "Goodness, Charlotte." If he'd threatened to shoot her, why hadn't she gotten the hell—heck—out of there before now? And why didn't she have a restraining order in place against him?

She turned to me. Or on me, more accurately. "You don't know what it's like, Savannah!"

Well, no. I didn't. Bradley had been a jerk, but he hadn't been violent. Not until I had the evidence to put him in prison for conspiracy to murder, and by then we'd been divorced for years. And while Rafe keeps a gun in the house, I don't have to worry about him threatening me with it. There are no circumstances whatsoever where I'd ever have to worry about Rafe hurting me, or threatening to hurt me, in any way.

Which makes me just about the luckiest woman in the world.

But Charlotte had never had that. So I lifted my hands, palms out, signaling peace, and turned to Jarvis. "Now that I have you here, Detective…"

He nodded, looking wary.

"Rafe told me that you came up here from Alabama with Chief Carter when he took the job."

"That's right," Jarvis said.

"So you must have known Steve Morris already, when Natalie Allen died?"

"I didn't know him," Jarvis said. "I never met him. Not until I interviewed him after the murder. I never worked special victims cases in Florence, so I had no idea the report existed until Carter told me."

"So it was Carter who told you to arrest Morris?"

"He told me that Morris might be involved," Jarvis said. "And that I should see what other evidence I could find that might implicate him."

"And that's what you did."

He nodded. "It's not my job to convince the jury. That's the prosecution's job. I investigate the crime and arrest the most likely suspect based on the available evidence. This case wasn't any different than any other in that respect."

"Except that he didn't do it."

"The evidence pointed to him," Jarvis said. "More than it pointed to anyone else."

That was probably true. At any rate, it didn't sound as if Jarvis had gone after Morris with any sort of malice. His boss had told him to focus on Morris, and he had. If anyone was at fault here, it was Carter, who must have known that the previous police report was bogus. And who had been concerned enough about making an arrest and making himself look good that he'd ignored it.

"Any news on Mrs. Oberlin?" I asked.

"She's still dead," Jarvis answered. He glanced at Charlotte's kids, now fully invested in rubbing Chester's belly and ears. "I should get back to work. But I can leave him here for a while. Give them something to distract them."

Charlotte hesitated and glanced at her mom. Mrs. Albertson shrugged.

"Thank you," Charlotte said politely, "that would be helpful."

Jarvis pushed to his feet. "I'll be back for him later, then."

He nodded to Mr. and Mrs. Allen, spared me a look, and spared a longer one for Charlotte. It might be just because she'd been through an ordeal and he wanted to make sure she was all right, but it made me wonder. Then he excused himself, and headed for the hallway.

"I should probably go, too," I said after we'd heard the sound of the front door open and close. "The sheriff should be here soon to take your statements and give you an update, but you don't need me for that. Unless there's anything I can do?"

Mrs. Albertson shook her head. "Thank you, Savannah."

"My pleasure," I said. "Charlotte? OK if I go?"

She nodded, her eyes on the kids and on Chester. "That was nice of Detective Jarvis."

"I'm sure he'll let you keep the dog permanently if you want to." Otherwise, Chester might end up at the shelter. Unless Jarvis planned to keep the dog himself, I guess. But even if he did, he might give Chester up to Charlotte if she asked. "You can ask him when he comes back later."

"You don't think he's coming to arrest me, do you?"

I shook my head. "I didn't get the impression that he was

thinking about that at all." Quite the opposite, in fact. "I'll check back with you later, OK? Let me know if anything happens."

She promised she would, and I gathered up my baby and left them there, to watch JR and Michaela and Chester bond.

"I think Jarvis is sweet on Charlotte," I told Rafe five minutes later, in the car on my way back to the mansion for lunch. "He showed up with Chester the Shih-Tzu—the dog that belonged to Mrs. Oberlin across the street from our house on Fulton; it was really nice of him to keep the dog rather than give him to the pound, I think…"

Rafe made an encouraging noise, and I derailed my train of thought and went back to where I'd been before the question of Jarvis's kindness to small animals entered my head.

"I guess someone must have told him what happened this morning, or maybe he listens to a police scanner, or something—" He was the type who might. "—because he and the dog showed up at the Albertsons' house not long after we got there. Charlotte and her mother were afraid he was going to arrest her, of course. But the kids were charmed. Chester gave them something else to focus on besides what had happened. They were both pretty devastated earlier. But Jarvis asked if he should leave Chester there for a while, and Charlotte agreed."

"Prob'ly looking for another home for him," Rafe said, which might be true. If cynical.

"I thought it was interesting that he showed up at all. What happened had nothing to do with his case."

"And so you think he's sweet on Charlotte." My husband's voice was amused.

"It would explain it. There's no other reason I can think of why he'd drive all the way from Columbia to Sweetwater to see how she is." And in the middle of the workday, too.

"Maybe he's just trying to get rid of the dog," Rafe said.

Maybe. "If that's it, I think he may have succeeded. I don't see any way that Charlotte, or even Mr. or Mrs. Albertson, can refuse to let those kids keep him if they ask. Not today."

And if Jarvis left Chester there all day, the kids would be fully attached to him by nightfall, and would probably scream bloody murder if anyone tried to take him away.

"I asked him about Natalie Allen's murder," I changed the subject. "He told me that Chief Carter told him about Steve Morris's police report for statutory rape, and that it was Carter's suggestion, more or less, that he should focus on Morris."

"Any particular reason you thought to ask him about that?"

"I've been thinking," I said, and ignored Rafe's murmurs about the dangers—to him—of such an activity. "Is it possible that Carter killed Natalie? That the Skinners wasn't the first time he committed murder so he could solve the crime and make himself—and his police department—look good?"

There was a pause. "I don't guess it's impossible," Rafe said eventually. "Somebody should maybe take a look at some of the closed cases to rule that out."

Including the Natalie Allen case. "More work for you."

"More likely Tammy. I keep getting hung up on new cases."

He did. And speaking of... "Are you back in front of the body shop? Is Rodney still there?"

"He was gone by the time I got back," Rafe said.

Oh. *Ouch.* "Sorry."

"Don't worry about it. What you had going on was more imminent."

Nice of him to say so.

"Now that I have a name for him," he added, "I can track him down. And there's no hurry on any of this. This case'll take time to set up."

"Are you sure they aren't planning something you'll have to prevent?"

"Nothing imminent," Rafe said. "Not from what I can see. Scoggins is wandering around here like he has nothing on his mind except the next car to come through the door and the beer he's gonna drink after work. If they're planning to start a war in the next few days, he's being very laid back about it."

Good to know. Both that we didn't have to worry about World War III erupting in quiet Middle Tennessee in the next week or two, and that the diversion of Charlotte's rescue hadn't cost Rafe the case.

"You on your way home?" he added.

"Unless you're free for lunch. Or want me to bring you something."

He sounded regretful. "Better not, darlin'. I don't want nothing drawing attention to me sitting here. Getting a delivery prob'ly would."

No question. "What do you do if you have to pee?"

"Didn't we have this conversation before?" He didn't wait for me to answer. "I have an empty soda bottle behind the seat."

Lovely. "I'm going home," I said. "I'm going to eat something, and feed Carrie in the privacy of our own home—or Mother's home—our home now..."

I couldn't see him, but I could feel the smile. "—and then I'll probably run back over to the house on Fulton Street for a bit, to make sure I did the grouting right. I just want to make sure that it's set and looks the way it should. And that the tile hasn't fallen off the wall. I'll probably check in on Charlotte again, too. Either by phone or in person. I'm sure they'll all be just fine, but I want to know what's going to happen to Richard."

"I'll be home by seven," Rafe said.

"That's a long day. Didn't you start following Kyle Scoggins at six this morning?"

"Time and a half salary," Rafe said lightly. And added, "there's another SWAT meeting at five I gotta be at. I'll be home after that."

"I'll be there," I said. "So you'll talk to Grimaldi about the possibility that Carter might have killed Natalie Allen?" And maybe even Ida Burns, if she was reconsidering her testimony about the argument she'd overheard.

He said he would. "That don't explain who killed Morris, though, darlin'."

It didn't. Carter had been long gone when Morris was killed. Nor did it explain who had killed Mrs. Oberlin, if Mrs. Oberlin had been killed and hadn't just died of old age.

But Grimaldi would figure it out, if there was something to figure out. She'd spent years solving homicides for Metro Nashville. If anyone could pick through the evidence and get to the bottom of this, Grimaldi could.

So I hung up with Rafe in time to turn the Volvo up the driveway to the mansion, and resolved to focus entirely on my dog, and my daughter, and my lunch—in that order—for the next hour.

It was easier said than done, naturally. I let Pearl out, and let her run and pee. When she came back inside, I sat down with Carrie on the peach velvet loveseat, while Pearl curled up on her pillow with a biscuit. And in the stillness of the early afternoon, with no sounds except the low humming of the electronics and Pearl's crunching, my mind went back to the case.

The fact that Natalie had been raped bothered me.

On general terms, obviously, but also while trying to fit ex-Chief Carter into the role of murderer.

He's killed the Skinners, yes. In cold blood and with malice aforethought. But the Skinners had been criminals, too. Maybe not on the scale of murder, but they'd run illegal dog-fighting rings. They'd grown pot on a commercial scale. They'd distributed said pot. I didn't know the details of how—that had been someone else's problem to figure out; Rafe had only been responsible for the murders—but there had been several greenhouses up on the Devil's Backbone filled with plants, so their crop had been well beyond personal consumption. And then there had been Darrell's womanizing—which wasn't illegal, but made him a jerk—and Robbie's spousal abuse...

So yes, while there was no excuse for killing them all, at least I could see the justification in Chief Carter's eyes, even if it wasn't justification in anyone else's. He was ridding the county of a family of hardened criminals.

But Natalie... What could nineteen-year-old Natalie Allen have been involved in, to deserve to die?

And especially to die in such a way. The Skinners had been shot. All seven of them, in a matter of just a quarter of an hour or so.

Natalie had been raped first, and then strangled. And it was hard to reconcile ex-Chief Carter with that. Not only because it was way over the line if the point was to solve the crime and make himself and his department look good, but because it takes a certain type of person to rape and murder. Carter might have had a blatant disregard for human life, but he didn't— hadn't—come across as the type to do that.

I decided that Carrie had spent enough time on one side, and shifted her to my other arm. Down on the pillow, Pearl crunched the last of her biscuit and settled down with a contented sigh, her chin on her paws. I went back to cogitating.

So if not Carter, then who?

There was Jarvis. He had come up from Alabama with

Carter, and although he'd told me he hadn't known about Morris's past until Carter told him, he might have been lying.

He was male, so he had the necessary equipment. There'd been no DNA on Natalie's body, so no way to tie Jarvis, or anyone else, to the rape. But he was physically capable, so one checkmark in his column.

He knew Enoch, and Enoch lived on Fulton, so Jarvis might have had the opportunity to see, or meet, Natalie that way. That was another checkmark.

He had built the case against Morris, and had arrested him. That was a big checkmark right there. If he was the killer, he had every reason to want Morris to be arrested and go to prison. With Morris behind bars, there was no need to look at anyone else for the crime. And no reason for anyone to look at Jarvis.

And when Morris was acquitted, Jarvis would have been the first to know. If he hadn't been in the courtroom, someone would have told him. As the arresting officer, that was probably standard procedure. And since he would have had no idea that Darcy had bought Morris's house, and that Morris no longer owned it, he would probably expect Morris to show up at home that night.

As Morris had, in fact, done. And where he had ended up dead.

Jarvis was single, as far as I knew. Nobody would be able to alibi him for Friday night. Not that anyone would ask him for an alibi. He was the investigating officer. Asking for alibis was his job.

Carrie finished eating—or drinking. I lifted her to my shoulder and patted her back so she'd burp while my thoughts kept churning.

If Jarvis was guilty, then it was imperative that he find someone else to arrest for Morris's murder, the same way he'd arrested Morris for the crimes against Natalie back then.

Hell—heck—even if Jarvis wasn't guilty, he had to arrest someone for Morris's murder.

Charlotte was probably safe for the time being. I would defy even Jarvis to slap handcuffs on her after the morning she'd just had.

That left Rodney Clark—whose alibi was flimsy, to say the least—and the Allens, who alibied each other, and had every reason to lie when it came to the murder of the man they believed had killed their daughter.

Or maybe Morris really had killed Natalie. There'd been enough evidence to result in a hung jury the first time. At least some of the members must have believed he did it, or he would have been acquitted then. Maybe Ida Burns was right, and she had heard Morris and Natalie argue. Maybe he really did get away with murder when he was acquitted.

And maybe someone who cared about Natalie—her mother or father or old boyfriend—had killed him for it.

Just because Rodney was a despicable human being didn't mean he hadn't sincerely loved Natalie and hated the man he thought had taken her away from him. The fact that Morris was black would only make Rodney hate him more.

In fact, Natalie's rape and murder by Morris might be the reason Rodney had turned toward the white supremacy group in the first place. He wouldn't be the first one, after something like that.

He obviously still frequented this area. I'd seen him leave the Allens house just this morning, and nobody would have thought anything of it, if they'd seen him cruise by on Friday. Like Jarvis, Rodney would have expected Morris to go back to his house after the acquittal. If he'd wanted a showdown with Morris, that's where he would have gone to look for him. And Kyle Scoggins would certainly have alibied him, and probably even helped him in other ways, if Rodney wanted to kill the man—the black man—who had raped and murdered Natalie.

Twenty-One

I put Carrie down for her nap and went back to thinking.

What I wanted to do, was track down the Allens, but from experience I knew that they weren't home at this time of day, and I had no idea where they might work, so it would be better to wait until early evening and knock on the door then. Enoch wouldn't be around, not with the SWAT meeting going until six-thirty or seven, so he'd never know I'd ignored his request to leave the Allens alone.

Instead, I spent the time while Carrie slept trying to dig up any information I didn't already have about Natalie Allen's murder.

I'd done this search once already, several days ago, and there was surprisingly little to be found. Unlike the long and drawn out Katie Graves case, that had kept all of Maury County in thrall for weeks the year I was twelve, the story of Natalie Allen was short and poignant.

She'd been working the last shift at the sports bar where she waited tables the night she was murdered. A few patrons lingering in the parking lot had watched her walk down the street around 11:15 or so. One of them had offered her a ride, and she'd said no, that it was just a few minutes to walk. (He'd been investigated and cleared.) And she had been found a couple of blocks away, not quite on the route she'd have to walk between the bar and Fulton Street, but not too far off, either, early the next morning.

An update the next day said that the police had eliminated Natalie's boyfriend as a suspect, and were looking for anyone who might have seen her walking between the bar and the place she was found. The article was accompanied by a picture—high school senior portrait, at a guess—of a pretty girl with dimples and lots of fluffy, fair hair.

Two days later, the paper reported that the police had arrested a suspect in the Natalie Allen murder. They named Steve Morris, said a neighbor had heard him argue with the deceased a few days before the murder, and revealed that he had a history of sexual misconduct. And his grainy black and white picture, in juxtaposition to Natalie's blonde prettiness, probably did its own job of playing on the stereotypes of the old Southern racial relations.

That was the end of the coverage until the first trial had ended in a hung jury the following year. The paper had reported it, and done a quick recap of the story—with no information I didn't already know, with the same picture of Natalie, and one of Morris from the trial, in an orange jumpsuit and with his hands cuffed. That image probably hadn't done anything to help his case in the public opinion, either.

After that, it had been quiet again until last week, when Morris was acquitted in the second trial. The paper had reported that fact, with another recap—still just the same old stuff—and then had reported Morris's murder after he was found. The police were investigating the possibility that his murder was related to the murder of Natalie Allen, the article said. And ended with a little note saying that while the reporter had attempted to reach out to Natalie's family for comment, the Allens had not responded to the inquiry.

Did that mean anything? Had they been afraid they were going to be asked whether they'd been involved in the murder? Or asked who they thought might be responsible?

Or maybe they just didn't want to have to go on record with their glee that the man responsible for their daughter's death was no more. Nothing wrong with that.

I was spinning my wheels, I realized. Mentally trying to solve a crime that better brains than mine had been noodling over for four years. Who did I think I was?

Besides, I was married to a cop. Another cop was my best friend. I trusted the police. If they said Steve Morris had done it, maybe he'd done it. And Tamara Grimaldi was in charge of the police department now. If Morris hadn't done it, she'd figure that out, too. And then figure out who had done Morris. It was out of my hands and none of my business. I was a real estate agent, and I had a house to renovate and sell.

I turned to YouTube and started searching for videos on how to sand and finish hardwood floors.

The tile on the kitchen backsplash turned out pretty good.

OK, so maybe it wasn't the most professional job I'd ever seen, but I'd done all right for my first time. The fact that we'd picked slightly irregular tile helped, too, because any little imperfections I may have left—and I'm not saying I'd left any, but for the sake of argument—were less noticeable.

I stepped back from it and tilted my head one way and then the other. Yes, this would do nicely. When the new cabinet doors arrived next week, and we put the new handles on, and added the new stainless steel appliances, it would look like a brand new kitchen.

Outside on the road, there was the sound of a car going by, and I scurried down the hall and into the front bedroom to peer through the window.

No, false alarm. The car—a dark sedan—continued on down the street and out of sight. I went back to the kitchen.

The second time, I was luckier. The car, a burgundy SUV of the ladylike, smaller type, slowed down as it passed the house, and then flicked on its turn signal. A few seconds later it turned into the Allens' driveway and up toward the house. The garage door rose slowly—remote in the car, probably—and I saw a glimpse of another car in the next bay before the burgundy SUV disappeared inside and the door lowered again. I threw on my coat, grabbed the baby carrier, and hurried outside and across the street. As I walked past the picket fence and up the driveway to the yellow house, a light flicked on inside the living room. I climbed up on the stoop and applied my knuckles to the door.

A few seconds later it opened, and I found myself face to face with Mrs. Allen.

She was in her early forties, at a guess, and had her daughter's curly fair hair—cropped shorter than in the picture of Natalie I'd seen in the paper—and round cheeks. "Yes?" Wary blue eyes moved from my face to Carrie and back. "Can I help you?"

I smiled politely. "Mrs. Allen? My name is Savannah Martin. Collier. I own the house where Steve Morris used to live."

Or my sister did, but now didn't seem like the time to go into the details.

"I thought you might have a couple of minutes to talk to me," I added.

"About what?"

"Your daughter. Steve Morris. What happened."

"Go read the paper." She made to shut the door.

I got my foot into the gap just in time. "I've already read the paper. I had a couple of questions that weren't answered in the paper."

She looked from my foot up at me, but at least she stopped pushing on the door. "Why?"

Why? "I'm curious, I guess. Mr. Morris died in our house. My husband's a cop. My best friend is the new chief of police. And I've lost a few people to murder. My sister-in-law was killed a couple of years ago. A good friend a couple of months before that." In a situation similar to Natalie's. "A couple of coworkers…"

And a lot more than that, actually, now that I started counting. A handful of classmates. Several other school-friends, or at least school-acquaintances. People I knew a little, and people I knew well. Some people I didn't know at all. Friends of friends. Sometimes it seemed like my life since I'd hooked up with Rafe had been one long line of dead bodies, of friends and enemies alike.

But Mrs. Allen's eyes were widening, so it was probably better if I didn't go into any more detail. I was already starting to sound like the homicide equivalent of Typhoid Mary, and if I wasn't careful, she'd shut the door on me in self-defense, because anyone found talking to me would surely be next in line.

So I pasted another friendly smile on my face and backtracked. "I just wanted to talk for a couple of minutes."

She hesitated. And then she sighed and stepped back. "I guess it couldn't hurt. We're neighbors, after all. And your husband's a cop, you said?"

"Yes, ma'am." I carried the baby carrier across the threshold. "For the Columbia PD. He came down from Nashville with Chief Grimaldi at the beginning of the new year."

Not entirely accurate, but there was no point in going into the details of Rafe losing his job with the TBI and then getting it back and all the associated intricacies. As far as Mrs. Allen went, the fact that he'd come down with Grimaldi was good enough. It was true, if not entirely accurate.

"Is he investigating Steve Morris's murder?" She waved me to a seat on the sofa. I kept my coat on, since she hadn't offered to take it. She had her own coat on, if it came to that. Maybe that's why she'd come into the living room, to hang it in the coat closet by the door, and then I had interrupted her.

But in any case, I deduced she wasn't entirely sold on having me here, and I'd better talk fast, or she'd change her mind.

"Detective Jarvis is doing that," I said. "He was the detective who investigated your daughter's case. Since Morris's death is likely to be related, he's investigating that, too."

"We've spoken to him," Mrs. Allen said. "So what can I do for you, Mrs.…. Martin, was it?"

"Collier." When I'm asked point blank like this, I remember who I'm supposed to be. I may not always remember the rest of the time, but in these situations I do.

She opened her mouth, almost like she was going to say something. Then she must have thought better of it, because she closed it again. Maybe she remembered Rafe. Everyone in Sweetwater knew who he was back when he was a teenager, but he wasn't as well-known—or notorious—in Columbia. Still, she might have known his name.

If she did, she didn't say anything about it. Just nodded for me to go on.

"I found Steve Morris's body," I said. "Or my sister and I did, when we walked into the house on Saturday morning. He'd been stabbed with a screwdriver we'd left lying around."

She nodded.

"Did you think he killed your daughter?"

She blinked. I guess maybe that had been a bit too abrupt.

But I was afraid that if I didn't get to the point, she'd show me out.

So I waited, and eventually she said, "Not at first. We knew Steve. He'd lived down the street for a few years by then. He'd always seemed like a nice man. Quiet and polite. And we didn't think anyone we knew would be capable of something like… like what happened to Natalie."

"When did you start to suspect him?"

"We didn't," Mrs. Allen said. "The police investigated Natalie's boyfriend—"

"Rodney."

"—and that friend of his, Kyle."

"They always investigate the boyfriend," I said.

She nodded. "But they were together at the movies when Natalie…" She swallowed, and went on as if there's been no pause, "and the police said it couldn't be him."

"Did you think it might be him?"

"We thought it was a stranger," Mrs. Allen said. "We didn't think it could be anyone Natalie knew. Who would kill our beautiful daughter? She wouldn't harm a fly!"

Her voice had risen, and I gave her a few seconds to calm down and get her breathing under control before I asked my next question. "Did you like Rodney?"

She made a face. "I thought she could do better. Not that there was anything wrong with him, that I knew of. He didn't do drugs or anything like that. And he treated her well. He just didn't seem like he'd be a good bet for the future. Not enough drive."

"But you didn't think he could have killed her?"

"Why would he?" Mrs. Allen said. "They were getting along fine. She'd stayed home instead of going to college so they could be together. He had no reason to kill her."

"What about Kyle?"

"Rodney's friend?" She shrugged. "I only met him once or twice. He was another Rodney, I thought. No ambition. He's working on cars now, I think."

"What's Rodney doing?"

"Some kind of retail. Maybe a pawn shop?"

Maybe. It was a little tidbit I could share with Rafe, anyway. "So you didn't think Rodney had anything to do with happened to your daughter. And you didn't think Steve Morris did. What did you think when the police arrested him?"

"That they'd made a mistake," Mrs. Allen said.

"What about the argument Mrs. Burns said she overheard? Between Morris and Natalie?"

"It wasn't Natalie," Mrs. Allen said. And added, "Or if it was, it wasn't Morris. She had no reason to argue with Steve Morris. They barely knew each other. And he wasn't the type to get into an argument where the neighbors could hear, anyway. He was a quiet man, not the type to get involved in other people's business."

And then she seemed to think she'd said too much, because she shut her lips with a snap, her cheeks turning pink.

"Was someone else the type to get involved in other people's business?"

But she shook her head. "I don't know anything about an argument. The cop would get on Natalie and Rodney sometimes, for sitting in the car and steaming up the windows, but I'm sure that wasn't what poor Mrs. Burns was talking about."

"The cop?"

"Carl," Mrs. Allen said. "Across the street."

Enoch? There was someone I hadn't considered. "What was his relationship with Natalie?"

She gave me a sort of weird look. "He didn't have one."

"They knew each other, obviously."

"Of course," Mrs. Allen said. "Carl has lived here five or six years. Since a few years before Natalie…" She swallowed.

"Were they friends?"

"Friendly," Mrs. Allen said. "Neighborly. The same way she was with Steve and with old Mr. Ferguson in number 113."

"You said Enoch would get on Natalie and Rodney sometimes. Why?"

"I guess he didn't like to watch them sit in front of his house and make out." She shrugged.

That was a little weird. Not like it was any of his business, after all. But strange that he'd care.

Unless… "Did the police investigate him?"

She gave me a weird look. "You'd have to ask them."

"Did you tell them—tell Detective Jarvis—that maybe it was Enoch Mrs. Burns had heard arguing with Natalie?"

"I'm sure we did," Mrs. Allen said. "When he came to tell us our daughter was dead, we told him everything we could think of. Anything that might help him figure out what happened to our Natalie."

She glanced at the kitchen and beyond it, to the hallway to the bedrooms. "We didn't even know she hadn't come home the night before. We thought she was just sleeping late. She often did when she'd worked the night before."

I nodded.

"So we told him about Rodney, that they'd been dating for a few years. And about the job she took to be home with Rodney instead of going to college. He came back the next day and said that Rodney had an alibi. That he'd been at the movies with a friend when Natalie died. And he also said that they'd talked to everyone at the bar where Natalie worked, and no one there seemed to be involved. He said one of the neighbors had mentioned overhearing an argument a couple of days before, and he wanted to know if she'd had any altercations with anyone over anything…"

"And did you tell him about Enoch? About Carl?"

"I'm sure I mentioned it," Mrs. Allen said. "I mean, there wasn't anyone else. She and Rodney didn't even argue. She was a sunny girl. Almost always in a good mood."

"But then they arrested Steve Morris."

She nodded.

"What did you think about that?"

"At first I couldn't believe it. But then Carl told us that he'd raped a girl in Alabama before he came here." A shadow crossed her face. "And they arrested him… I figured they knew what they were doing, and it was because he'd done it."

I would have figured the same thing, I guess. It's the police's job to catch the bad guys. When they arrest someone, we tend to believe it's because that person's guilty.

"But then he was acquitted," I said. "Were you angry?"

"No," Mrs. Allen said, shaking her head. "I never believed he'd done it. Not in my heart. I tried to convince myself, after he was arrested, that maybe I was wrong, and I didn't really know him. But when the jury believed he hadn't done it, either, I knew I'd been right all along."

"So you wouldn't have minded if he came back to Fulton Street?"

"He did come back," Mrs. Allen said, and then flushed.

"You saw him?"

"In the afternoon." She sounded reluctant to admit it, but she did. "He was leaving your house—the house you're renovating—and getting in his car."

"You didn't talk to him?"

She shook her head. "I waved. But he didn't stop. I figured he didn't want to talk to me. He probably thought I was going to yell at him. That we all believed he was guilty."

"Did your husband agree with you? That Morris was

innocent?"

She gave me a quick look. "He wasn't as sure as me. You have to understand, she was our baby. Our only daughter. Gary wanted someone to pay."

I had no problem understanding that. If anything happened to Carrie, Rafe would want someone to pay, too. And would probably take care of arranging that payment himself.

Just as Gary Allen might have done.

I decided to just come out and ask, point blank. If nothing else, I could watch her reaction if I did. "Did your husband kill Steve Morris, Mrs. Allen?"

"No," Mrs. Allen said, and didn't seem to get upset that I suggested it. Or if she did, she hid it well. "The police asked. We were together that night. All night. Besides, Gary wouldn't kill anyone. And he wasn't sure Morris was guilty, either. Not after the jury acquitted him. Not after the girlfriend explained about that other police record..."

They'd been there in the courtroom for Sarah's testimony. Of course they had. It was their daughter who died; of course they'd have been there. "You believed her?"

"She had no reason to lie," Mrs. Allen said. "And I spoke to her afterwards. She swore it was true. That she wouldn't have lied for him if it wasn't. I believed her."

I'd believed her, too. Even if all I'd done, was read the trial transcript.

"Who do you think killed him?" I asked.

"The same person who killed Natalie," Mrs. Allen answered, without even a second's pause.

"And who was that?"

But there she faltered. "If I knew, don't you think I would have told someone? I guess in the end it must have been just some random person, someone who saw her walking home and..."

Maybe so. But then, who killed Morris?

It didn't sound as if she knew anything more, though, so I thanked her for talking to me and apologized for bringing up her daughter's murder.

She gave me a smile. "It's been long enough that we can talk about it. At first it was almost more than we could bear. But it's been long enough now, that we can be grateful for having had her for nineteen years, more than be angry because we lost her."

That was big of her, and I said so. "Do you think the police are going to look into Natalie's case again, now that Steve Morris has been acquitted?" And killed.

"If they are, no one's told us," Mrs. Allen said, walking me to the door. "That detective from before—Jarvits, did you say?"

"Jarvis," I said.

"He came by on Saturday to ask us about the night before. To make sure we hadn't had anything to do with Steve's murder. But we haven't heard anything since then."

"Rodney was here this morning," I said. "I saw him leave."

She nodded. "He stops by once in a while. Less now than he used to. We're all moving on. Even Carl's a little less devoted than he used to be."

Devoted? Enoch?

"He found Natalie," Mrs. Allen said. "He was out jogging before work, and saw her from the sidewalk."

"That wasn't in the paper." Or even in the trial transcript, as far as I could recall.

She shrugged. "It's what happened."

"I can see why it would be personal for him, then."

Although it did make me wonder whether Jarvis had ever considered Enoch for the murder. All the things I had attributed to Jarvis applied equally to Enoch. He knew Natalie. If he'd killed her, he had incentive to want someone else—like

Morris—to go down for the murder. The person who discovers the body is always suspect, of course, and now that I thought about it, Enoch had been Johnny-on-the-spot when Morris died, too. Darcy and I had found him, but Enoch had shown up before we could call for help. And he'd come to check on Charlotte and me when we were standing on Mrs. Oberlin's stoop waiting for Jarvis to show up the other day. Enoch had even walked into Mrs. Oberlin's bedroom to ascertain for himself that she was really dead.

If it came to that, he had walked in on Rafe and me, gun drawn, the night before the auction, as well. And I suddenly considered, with a trickle of cold down my spine, what might have happened if I'd been there alone that night.

I shook it off, and turned to Mrs. Allen with a bland smile. No need to let her know what I was thinking. Not until I got it straight in my head, at any rate. "Thank you so much for your time. It's been interesting."

"Thank you for stopping by," Mrs. Allen said politely, and turned the knob on the front door. "I hope to see you again."

It sounded like she meant it. I smiled at her as she pulled the front door open, and that's why I didn't notice the figure standing on the doorstep.

Twenty-Two

"Oh." I blinked at Enoch, and for a second or two, I can't swear that some of what I'd been thinking didn't flicker across my face. Something certainly flickered across his before it was gone, leaving me to wonder whether I'd actually seen it, or whether it was just my own suspicions that had put it there.

"Carl!" Mrs. Allen said, sounding pleased.

He glanced at her, and mustered something that could almost pass for a smile. "Nancy."

Or maybe that was just in my mind, too. Maybe it had been a perfectly acceptable smile. Mrs. Allen didn't seem to have found any issues with it. She looked just as welcoming as before. "Won't you come in?"

"Actually—" He turned his attention to me, "I saw your vehicle outside. I thought you might have a minute. I'd like to talk to you."

His tone hinted at dire things to come.

The most logical explanation was that he was going to yell at me for not leaving the Allens alone, the way he'd told me. That's probably what he wanted me to believe. And maybe that's all it was. Hopefully that was all it was.

But just in case I was right, and those suspicions that had started to blossom while Mrs. Allen had been talking were on the money, I should take a little thought for what to do next.

If I refused to go with him, he'd know that I suspected him.

On the other hand, I didn't want to put Mrs. Allen in danger by insisting on staying here. Enoch was still wearing his work clothes, with his weapon's belt strapped around his hips. If I refused to go with him, would he take us both into the house at gunpoint?

But no. Probably not. He wouldn't want Mrs. Allen to know what was going on.

Would he?

And then there was the third hand, which was Carrie in her car seat. My first responsibility was to my baby. What scenario had the best potential for getting her through this alive?

I turned to Mrs. Allen. "Would you mind holding onto the baby for a minute? I'm sure this won't take long."

She looked flabbergasted, and out of the corner of my eye, I could see Enoch's face change. There went any doubt he might have had that I suspected him. If I was trying to keep my baby from him, it was because I knew she was in danger.

"On second thought," he said, drawing his gun smoothly, "let's just go inside."

He pointed it at my stomach. I backed up. Mrs. Allen squeaked and turned pale. "Carl...!"

He turned to her—gun, too—and I took her arm in my free hand and tugged her back inside the living room. "Let's just do as he says. That way, maybe nobody'll get hurt."

Enoch smiled, but it didn't reach his eyes. They were small and beady and flat as pebbles. "That's right. We don't want anyone to get hurt."

Mrs. Allen gulped, but she backed up right next to me.

Enoch stepped across the threshold and shut the door. And gestured with the gun. "On the sofa."

I moved to the sofa and sat down, and put Carrie's car seat

on the floor next to me. If bullets started flying, at least she'd be a little bit protected by the coffee table.

Mrs. Allen sat down next to me and wound her hands together in her lap. "What's this about, Carl?" Her voice shook, and so did the rest of her body, too.

"I didn't want it to come to this," Enoch said, sounding aggrieved, like we had seriously inconvenienced him by figuring out that he'd killed at least a couple of people, and maybe more.

Or maybe I was the only one who had figured it out. Mrs. Allen looked clueless. Like she had no idea that the man standing in front of her, waving his gun, had taken her daughter from her.

Would it help or hurt for me to point that out? Would it be better to keep that out of the conversation for as long as possible, or would our chances of survival be better if I said something?

For the time being, since I didn't know the answer, I decided that for now, it was best if I didn't go there. "You killed Steve Morris," I said instead.

Enoch glanced at me, but didn't confirm or deny it. Mrs. Allen gasped, though, and put a shaking hand to her mouth, staring at him over it.

"I should have thought of you," I added. "You were right there when Darcy and I found him. We didn't even have time to yell for help. It was almost like you were waiting for him to be found, so you could swoop in and save the day."

Or maybe more so he could swoop in and any DNA that might be found on or around Morris would be explained away.

He'd done the same thing with Mrs. Oberlin: gone inside the house to look at her, even after I told him she was dead, that there was nothing anyone could do, and that we had called it in and were waiting for the police to show up.

"I had no choice," Enoch said. He was still standing, shifting from foot to foot, with the gun pointed in our direction. Mostly at me, probably because he didn't think Mrs. Allen was as much of a threat.

"How do you figure that?"

His eyes flickered from me, to Mrs. Allen, out the window to the street, and back to me in a continual loop. "He came back. He was supposed to stay in prison. He was supposed to be convicted!"

"Oh, Carl," Mrs. Allen said, sadly. "I know you cared about Natalie. You worked hard to get justice for her, and for us. But we didn't want him to be convicted if he didn't do it!"

She sounded absolutely sincere, and so sad to have to explain this undeniable fact to Enoch, that I felt almost bad about having to burst her bubble. "It has nothing to do with justice," I told her. "You're misunderstanding what he's saying. He killed Natalie. And he wanted Steve Morris to go to prison for it."

Mrs. Allen stared at me, the color draining out of her face, and then moved her stricken gaze to him.

Enoch showed teeth, like a feral wolf. "Shut up, you stupid bitch!"

"I don't know why he did it," I added. "Maybe just because he could. Maybe he saw her, and he couldn't help himself. Or maybe she was friendly to him, and he thought it meant more than it did, and when she told him no, he couldn't handle it..."

Shades of Lila Vaughn, my friend who had died at the hands of another man who couldn't handle being refused.

Enoch's eyes narrowed. "I said shut up!" He pulled the gun up in a more businesslike manner. The barrel pointed straight at my forehead. I shut up.

"You..." Mrs. Allen had to clear her throat. "You killed Natalie?"

"And Steve Morris," I said. "And Ida Burns, when she started reconsidering who she'd heard arguing. I guess he was afraid she'd go back on her testimony in the second trial, and Morris would get off."

"But he got off anyway." Mrs. Allen's voice was faint. "Even without... you killed poor Mrs. Burns?"

"And Mrs. Oberlin," I said. "He saw me talking to her. He was probably afraid she'd seen something, or heard something, or realized something, or that I'd said something that might make her realize something." Or something. "Or maybe he'd just started liking killing people by then."

"The old bat was your fault," Enoch told me, callously. "You should have just left things alone. Jarvis would have arrested someone for Morris's murder—"

"The two main suspects were my friend Charlotte and Mr. Allen!" How was I supposed to leave that alone?

Enoch shrugged, looking unrepentant, like that wasn't his problem.

Meanwhile, Mrs. Allen was still trying to process things. "You killed my daughter? And Steve? And you tried to frame my husband for it?"

"For Morris," I said. "He framed Morris for Natalie's murder."

She gave me a look. I ignored it in favor of getting information from Enoch. "There's something I don't understand."

I didn't wait for him to nod, or give me any other kind of indication that I should go on, because I wasn't sure he would. "You aren't even from Alabama. How did you know about Morris's past?"

"I didn't," Enoch said, scowling. "I had no plans to frame anyone for anything. Natalie was walking home. I offered her a ride. She said no. I put her in the car, because I didn't think she should be walking home so late on her own. It wasn't safe."

He said it with a matter-of-factness that was chilling. Like it was his responsibility and his right to dictate what someone else could or should do. Like Natalie didn't have the right to walk home from work if she wanted to. And the picture of him 'putting her' in the car... I fought back a shiver, and I'm sure Mrs. Allen did the same thing.

"But then she started fighting me, and I had to keep her quiet, and one thing led to another..."

He trailed off. I didn't pursue that particular train, because Natalie's mother was sitting next to me, as brittle as a dry twig, and she didn't need to hear the details.

"And you left her in the field," I said.

Enoch's eyes came back into focus. For a second he looked at me like he didn't know who I was, and then he nodded. "And the next morning I went jogging, and I ran by and 'found' her, just in case some of my DNA was still around."

A habit he'd kept up with Ida Burns, and Steve Morris, and Mrs. Oberlin, it seemed. "And Jarvis was assigned to the case."

Enoch smirked. "Paul Jarvis wouldn't know his you-know-what from a hole in the ground." He didn't say you-know-what; I did. "He kept coming to me, asking questions about the neighbors and who might have looked a little too much at Natalie..."

"And you pointed him in Steve Morris's direction."

"Chief Carter did that," Enoch said. "Jarvis went to him, because Natalie's parents—" he shot a look at Mrs. Allen, sitting like a statue next to me, "said that sometimes I'd yell at Natalie about her and Rodney fogging up the windows in the car in front of the house. And Jarvis thought it was interesting—" he made quotation marks in the air around the word, "that I'd been the one to find the body..."

Sounded to me like Jarvis could find a whole lot more than

the proverbial hole in the ground, but I didn't say so, because Enoch was on something of a roll, and I didn't want to derail him.

"And Carter called me in to his office and asked me about it, and I said that Jarvis was spinning his wheels because he didn't have any good suspects, and Carter told Jarvis to stop wasting time on fellow law enforcement, and to do his job and focus on Morris, because Morris had been accused of statutory rape in Alabama. And Jarvis ran with it and I got Ida Burns to say that she thought it was Morris she'd heard arguing with Natalie, and then Jarvis arrested Morris."

He'd got going so fast at the end that he had to stop and take a breath.

"And you were off the hook," I said.

He nodded. "But then the first jury didn't convict him. And that bitch Renee Oberlin convinced Ida Burns that maybe she hadn't heard Morris after all…"

"And you thought that if she was alive to say that in the second trial, they wouldn't convict him then either. So you killed her."

"It was easy," Enoch said. "All I had to do was get into her house in the middle of the night, while she was sleeping. A little potassium chloride in a syringe, and it was goodnight, Ida."

He giggled. The sound made the little hairs on my arms stand up.

I tried not to let it show in my voice. "And you did the same with Mrs. Oberlin, I assume?"

Enoch nodded.

"Just out of curiosity, where did you get the drug? Potassium chloride isn't something you can buy at the store, is it?"

"It is if you know where to go." He winked at me. "You'll

appreciate this. You want to know who my source was?"

"Sure," I said, while I wondered why I, particularly, would appreciate it.

"Remember Billy Scruggs?"

How could I forget? Rafe had gone to prison thirteen years ago for beating up Billy Scruggs. And going on a year ago, Billy Scruggs had ended up dead in the Colliers' trailer in the Bog, making the sheriff think Rafe might have had something to do with it.

Both of those were old pieces of news by now, but I could see why Enoch thought I might appreciate the irony.

"Billy's been dead eight or nine months," I said.

"Ida died before that," Mrs. Allen murmured.

And Enoch must have had enough of the drug left to take care of Mrs. Oberlin this week. I guess the one positive thing about all of it, was that they hadn't suffered. Potassium chloride is the same stuff the authorities use in lethal injections, and it works quickly and painlessly.

"So now what?" I asked.

Might as well. I mean, here we were. Two women and a baby. Surely he didn't plan to shoot all three of us?

Surely he had to realize that he couldn't get away with this forever? There'd been an extraordinary number of deaths on Fulton Street already. Three more—especially mine and Carrie's—would bring the wrath of Rafe down on this street. The wrath of Grimaldi, too. And throw in the wrath of Sheriff Satterfield once Mother got onto him. Neither of them would rest until they'd figured out what was going on. And Grimaldi was no Chief Carter. She wouldn't let the fact that Enoch was a cop stop her from arresting and prosecuting him. Todd would nail Enoch's hide to the wall in court. And Rafe wouldn't let any of the others stop him from tearing Enoch limb from limb.

Since that would only happen after I was dead, though, I

couldn't find much comfort in it. "You won't get away with this, you know. Jarvis isn't stupid. He'll figure it out. And even if he doesn't, Rafe and Grimaldi will. You have no idea what you're dealing with in the two of them."

Enoch smirked. "Don't worry. When I'm done setting the scene, it'll all make perfect sense."

"How do you figure that?"

"I heard screaming," Enoch said, "when I came home from work. Being a good cop—"

My mouth turned down at the corners, and he giggled that breathy giggle again. Like last time, it made the hair stand up on my arms.

"I ran across the street to see what was going on. Imagine my shock when I saw, through the window—"

He nodded to it: a big plate glass window looking out over the street, "Mr. Allen holding the two of you hostage."

"Gary?" Mrs. Allen said. Her eyes drifted past Enoch to the kitchen door, sort of wistfully. "Gary isn't home."

"We can wait," Enoch said genially.

There was a pause while we all thought about that.

"So let me guess," I said. "In this scenario, you came home and heard screaming. And you ran across the street—to this house—and saw Mr. Allen—who isn't home yet—holding his wife and me at gunpoint. I assume you've figured out a reason he might be doing that?"

"He killed Steve Morris," Enoch said. "You figured it out. And he had to kill you, so you wouldn't go to the police and tell them. But Nancy—"

He glanced at her, "—didn't want him to shoot you, too. She thought it was OK that he'd killed Morris—after all, Morris killed their daughter—but she didn't think he should kill anybody else. She thought he could maybe plead diminished capacity on Morris, and maybe that way, he wouldn't have to go to prison. So they were arguing about that. But Mr. Allen said it had to be done, and when he tried to shoot you, Mrs. Allen threw herself in front of you—"

He turned the gun on her. Mrs. Allen closed her eyes, and my heart stopped for a second. I made an abortive movement, but it didn't turn out to be necessary. Enoch just grinned at our reactions and turned the gun back on me.

"And when he realized he'd killed his wife," he continued, "he turned the gun on you, and before I could stop him, he shot you, too. And then I had to shoot him, of course, because it was him or me, and he'd already killed two people. Three if you count Morris."

"Gary would never kill anyone," Mrs. Allen said faintly.

Enoch shrugged. "I could make it stick. There wouldn't be anybody left to say differently. The baby would survive, but it's too small to talk."

"She," I said.

But yes, the baby would survive, and at least that was one thing to be grateful for.

The thing was, though, that while he probably could make all this sound reasonable, and like it could have happened this way, I didn't think he'd be able to make it stick. Both Rafe and Grimaldi are too smart and too seasoned for that. They'd insist on a ballistics match, if nothing else, to make sure the bullets hadn't all come from the same gun.

Besides, I had no plans of letting him get away with it. I had no idea how I would stop him, but if I could keep him talking, maybe something would occur to me. "So in this scenario, Mr. Allen killed Steve Morris because Morris killed Natalie. Is that right? Who killed Mrs. Burns and Mrs. Oberlin?"

"Nobody," Enoch said, sounding surprised that I'd ask. "Mrs. Burns's death was never investigated as anything other than a heart attack. There's no reason why anyone would look at it again now."

There was every reason why someone would. I had talked about it to Rafe, and he'd remember. Especially if something happened to me.

No reason to point that out to Enoch, though. "What about Mrs. Oberlin? That case is still open. And for it to happen so quickly after Steve Morris's murder is suspicious, to say the least."

"I'm a cop," Enoch said with a shrug. "Nobody has any reason to suspect me. Cops never suspect other cops of committing crimes."

These cops will.

But there was no sense in saying that, either. "I guess we just wait for Mr. Allen to get home from work." I glanced at Mrs. Allen, sitting pale as a statue next to me. "When does your husband get off work?"

She glanced past Enoch, at the clock just visible through the door into the kitchen. And inexplicably, her lips curved.

Enoch's eyes narrowed, and he whipped around, but it was too late. Mr. Allen—or I had to assume it was Mr. Allen; I'd never seen him before—launched himself through the air and at Enoch. The gun went flying, and hit the carpeted floor with a thud, but didn't discharge. The two of them landed in a tangle on the coffee table, which broke under the strain. I managed, just barely, to snatch Carrie and the seat out of the way in time to avoid being crushed.

"Gary!" Mrs. Allen shrieked.

"The gun," I yelled as I swung the seat out of the way of the heaving bodies. "Get the gun!"

Carrie was screaming, too, of course, her shrill sounds mingling with the sounds of fists thudding into flesh and male grunts. I scrambled toward the door. Mrs. Allen scrambled toward the wall, and the gun. Mr. Allen was on top of Enoch, and was holding his own pretty well, I thought, in spite of being fifteen years or more older than Enoch, and not in as good condition. It was rage, no doubt. Rage for his dead daughter, and rage that Enoch had held his wife at gunpoint. Rage—depending on how much of the conversation he'd overheard—that Enoch had planned to slaughter us all and pin Steve Morris's murder on him.

Enoch was shaking off the surprise, though, and as I stood there, he recovered enough to flip Mr. Allen off him. And suddenly he was on top, raising his fist to pound it into Mr. Allen's face.

Nancy Allen scrambled to her feet, gun in hand, and took in the scene. Her face contorted in fury, and before I could call out anything whatsoever, she switched her grip on the gun, and slammed the handle into the top of Enoch's head with all the strength she could muster.

Twenty-Three

"It's been a hell of a day," Charlotte said thirty minutes later.

After Mrs. Allen hit Enoch, I put the baby down away from the carnage, and walked over and took the gun out of her hand. "I'll take this. I don't trust you not to shoot him."

She gave me a look, but didn't say anything. Down on the floor, Enoch had collapsed on top of Mr. Allen, who was wheezing under the weight of Enoch's larger body.

"Gary!" Mrs. Allen bent to grab Enoch and haul him off her husband, but I stopped her.

"Get the handcuffs off his belt first. If he wakes up when we start to move him around, it's better if we cuff him first."

She managed to unhook the cuffs, but it took both of us to get them around Enoch's wrists, and secure. Her hands were shaking, and I'm sure mine were, too.

That done, we grabbed Enoch by the shoulders and rolled him off Mr. Allen, who drew in a deep, shuddering breath. He was looking florid, and Mrs. Allen dropped to her knees beside him with a cry. "Gary! Are you all right?"

He clearly wasn't all right, but I've asked stupid questions under duress, too, in the past, so I didn't say anything about it. "I'm going to call for help," I said instead. "Anything in particular you need me to tell them? Heart attack? Broken bones?"

He shook his head. "I'm just out of breath."

His voice wheezed, and his chest was still rattling a little, but he was starting to sound better. And having Mrs. Allen on her knees next to him, holding his hand and dripping tears on his shirt, probably helped as much as having the weight of Enoch removed.

I stepped behind the sofa, to where I could see Carrie and Enoch at the same time, and pulled out my phone.

Rafe was in the middle of a SWAT maneuver, so I figured it was no point in calling him. I tried Grimaldi, but she didn't answer, so in desperation, I dialed Paul Jarvis's number.

"I need some help," I told him when he picked up.

"Mrs. Collier?" He sounded wary.

"I'm over at the Allens' house on Fulton Street. Natalie Allen's parents' house. I need you to come here and arrest Carl Enoch for murder."

There was a pause. Not a very long one, I have to say. Points to Jarvis for recovering quickly.

"I knew it!" he said, his voice laced with quiet triumph.

"I tried to call Gri… um… Chief Grimaldi, but I couldn't get her on the phone. And Rafe's at some sort of SWAT practice, so there's no use trying to get in touch with him. But if you could try to let both of them know what's going on, I'd appreciate it."

"Everyone all right?" Jarvis wanted to know.

I glanced over the back of the sofa down on the mess on the floor. Bodies everywhere. "Everyone except Enoch. He's out cold. But we put his own handcuffs on him, so he isn't going anywhere. He'll probably have a headache when he wakes up."

"Maybe a concussion," Jarvis said, sounding hopeful.

I agreed that it might very well turn out to be a concussion. "Mr. Allen had the wind knocked out of him, but he says he's all right. No broken bones, no heart trouble. It probably wouldn't hurt to send an ambulance, though, just to make sure everyone's going to live."

"Is there any doubt of that?"

None at all, and I said so. "So you'll come?"

"I'm on my way," Jarvis said. "Half an hour."

Half an hour?

That was a lot longer than I would expect it to take from the Columbia PD to Fulton Street, but maybe he was overestimating. Or maybe he'd gone home for the day—it was after five—and had his feet kicked up on the coffee table and a beer in his hand while he was watching *Jeopardy.*

And anyway, I couldn't get hold of Rafe or Grimaldi, so it wasn't like we could do anything but wait.

"We'll be here," I told him, and dropped my phone in my pocket so I could pick up Carrie and soothe her now that everything else was settled, at least for now.

The sofa was still intact, so I dropped down there. And although it wasn't quite mealtime, I opened my blouse for Carrie anyway, since the skin-to-skin contact would be calming for both of us, and since we could both use some calm.

No sooner had I got her situated, than the phone in my pocket rang, and I had to fish it out with one hand while holding Carrie in place with the other. I knew before I put it to my ear who was on the other end. "Yes?"

"What the hell, Savannah?" my husband said.

"I didn't do anything," I protested. "None of this was my fault. I was over at the house on Fulton looking at my grout when I saw Mrs. Allen get home. So I walked across the street and knocked on her door. We were just having a nice conversation when Enoch showed up and held us both at gunpoint."

"Jarvis told me. Any reason I had to hear it from him?"

"I thought you were busy," I said. "Aren't you at that

SWAT thing?"

"Not anymore." I could hear faint honking in the background, and deduced he was on his way over here as fast as the Chevy could carry him, to the detriment of the other drivers on the road.

There was also the murmur of another voice in the background, and I narrowed my eyes. "Is someone there with you?"

"Tammy," Rafe said. "We're five minutes away."

In the background, that same voice said something else. If I knew her, it was a probably a strongly worded request not to refer to her as Tammy.

At any rate, they were a lot closer to us than Jarvis was. "It's the yellow house," I said. "Just come to the front door. But I promised Jarvis that he could arrest Enoch, so you're going to have to leave that for him."

"I wouldn't dream of taking it away from him," Rafe said. "Carrie all right?"

I glanced down at her curly little head. "Fine. Having a bracing little snack right now. She was pretty upset by all the noise, and I thought it would settle her down." And me too.

From the phone came a squeal of brakes and the irritated toot of a horn, along with a curse from Rafe.

"I'll let you go," I added. "I'll see you when you get here."

"Three minutes."

It hadn't been two minutes since he'd said he was five minutes away, but he hung up before I could answer, and it didn't really matter anyway. He was close, and that was the important thing.

By the time Rafe's loaner Chevy pulled up in front of the house—leaving the driveway open for the ambulance that came up the street behind them—Mr. Allen was sitting up and Enoch was starting to twitch.

Nancy Allen, who had kept all her attention on her husband, and hadn't seen them come across the grass, jumped and paled when two cops in full SWAT gear—minus the Kevlar they had probably removed before getting in the car—burst through the door.

Yes, Grimaldi was in SWAT black, too. Somehow I managed to contain my surprise. I mean, I should have expected it. It explained why I hadn't been able to raise her on the phone, and it was totally something she'd want to be part of.

So she stood there, inside the door, hands on the hips of black cargo pants, and surveyed the room with flat cop eyes while Rafe came straight to me. And pulled me into his arms, baby and all. "You OK, darlin'?"

"Fine," I said against his chest. "I'm getting used to this by now."

"I'm not."

Bull… um… crap. "I've seen you face down guns and knives and crazed killers before," I told his shirt. It smelled good, like spring and healthy male. "It's never bothered you."

"It bothers me to think of you facing'em."

Well, yes. It bothered me to think of him facing them, too. Even though I knew he was perfectly capable, more capable than most, of handling himself. "Welcome to my world."

He didn't say anything to that, but his arms tightened for a second before he let me go, with a soft brush of lips on my forehead. "Later," he told me.

I nodded. Definitely later.

He dropped another kiss on top of the baby's head, and turned to take in the battleground.

By now, Gary Allen had made it into a wingback chair, and looked mostly back to normal, except for the blood pressure cuff one of the paramedics was unwrapping from his arm. The florid color had receded from his face, and he was breathing normally. Nancy Allen was sitting on the arm of the chair on the other side, holding his other hand, while Grimaldi had taken the chair opposite and was asking questions. Enoch was still on the floor, handcuffed, but groaning now. A second paramedic had peeled up one of his eyelids and was shining a light into his eye, checking for concussion. I'm sure I would be groaning, too, under the circumstances.

"Quite a day for you," one of the paramedics told me, and that's when I realized that it was the same pair that had been tending to Mrs. Albertson when Charlotte and I and the kids got back to Green Street this morning.

That was the situation when another car pulled up outside, and another set of shoes slapped against the walkway outside. Or two. The door opened, and Jarvis burst in, trench coat flapping, followed by—

I blinked. "Charlotte?"

Well, that explained why it had taken him thirty minutes to get here, anyway. He'd been all the way in downtown Sweetwater, halfway across the county.

"Detective Jarvis was picking up Chester when you called," Charlotte said, and stopped in front of me while Jarvis continued into the fray. "Are you OK, Savannah?"

"I'm fine," I said. "All I did was sit there on the sofa."

With a gun pointed at me, but given Charlotte's ordeal this morning, it was probably better if I didn't mention that. "Mr. Allen got the brunt of it. He attacked Enoch."

Charlotte lowered her voice. "Is he OK?"

I wasn't sure whether she meant Gary Allen or Enoch, but I nodded. "Fine." And if it was Enoch and he wasn't fine, I didn't care. But the paramedic with the flashlight had sat back on his heels and was checking Enoch's pulse now, so chances were

Enoch was going to survive the encounter without much damage. And hopefully live a long and unhappy life behind bars. If he got real unlucky, maybe he'd end up sharing a cell with Big Ned.

"He killed Steve Morris," I told Charlotte. "And Mrs. Oberlin. And Mrs. Burns, before we even knew this house existed. And Natalie Allen."

She stared at him, wide-eyed. "So he's a serial killer."

I guess he was. Not in the sense that he only killed women with brown, shoulder length hair who wore red shirts, but he'd certainly managed to commit a series of murders. Right under everyone's noses, too.

"We got him now," Rafe said, and put an arm around my shoulders. "And he ain't going nowhere. Charlotte." He nodded to her.

She nodded back. On the other side of the sofa, Jarvis concluded a low-voiced conversation with the male paramedic and glanced at Grimaldi. She nodded.

Jarvis cleared his throat. "Carl Enoch," he intoned, "you're under arrest for the murder of Natalie Allen, the murder of Steven Morris, the murder of Ida Burns, and the murder of Renee Oberlin, as well as the forced imprisonment of Nancy Allen, Savannah Martin Collier, and minor child Caroline Collier. Further, you are charged with obstruction of justice in the case of Natalie Allen, reporting of false evidence in the case of Natalie Allen, perjury in the case of Natalie Allen—"

Down on the floor, Enoch groaned and dropped his head to the floor with a thud.

"Come on," I told Charlotte. "This could take a while. I'll drive you home."

She nodded, and looked around the room. "It's been a hell of a day. First I was held at gunpoint, and then you were. And now you've solved four murders and discovered a serial killer."

"And the day isn't over yet." I winked at Rafe, who was listening to the conversation while standing by in case Jarvis needed help manhandling Enoch to the car.

His lips curled up.

"I'll see you at home," I told him.

"I'm looking forward to it." His voice packed enough heat that even Charlotte blushed.

"Don't get any ideas," I told her, as I nudged her out the door with the baby carrier.

"I wouldn't dream of it." Although she did turn around for a last look into the living room as we passed through the door and out onto the porch. But I don't think it was Rafe she was looking at.

"Come across the street and look at the kitchen tile before we leave," I said, as we skirted the ambulance in the Allens' driveway and headed toward the Volvo parked in front of our house down the street. "It turned out pretty good, if I do say so myself. Tomorrow, we can start tiling the tub surround, now that I know what I'm doing."

Charlotte nodded. "The sooner we can get this house done and on the market, the happier I'll be. Richard will probably spend all the money in our accounts on his legal fees, and by the time it's all said and done, he'll be in prison and there'll be no money left for the kids. I need an income."

"You've come to the right place," I told her, as I led the way across the grass toward our first flip.

About the Author

Jenna Bennett is the New York Times and USA Today bestselling author of more than forty books, most of them in the mystery and suspense genres. She lives in Nashville with a husband and two boys.

For more information, please visit her website,

www.jennabennett.com